CLOSER

Rock
& ROMANCE
Stars

A.K. EVANS

ISBN: 978-1-951441-23-4

Cover Artist
cover artwork © Sarah Hansen, Okay Creations
www.okaycreations.com

Editing & Proofreading
Ellie McLove, My Brother's Editor
www.mybrotherseditor.net

Formatting
Stacey Blake at Champagne Book Design
www.champagnebookdesign.com

CLOSER

PROLOGUE

Walker

THIS WAS SUPPOSED TO BE A HAPPY OCCASION.

I guess for everyone else it was. For me, it was anything but happy. I was miserable, a feeling I hadn't been a stranger to over the last few months and had only gotten worse over the last two days.

"So, are you going to be going on tour, too?"

I tried not to react to that question. The likelihood was that I was overthinking things, though. Considering that question came from Demi and was aimed at Chasey, the truth was that nobody would have been paying attention to me anyway.

Demi was Cash's girl, and Chasey was Beck's fiancée.

It was New Year's Eve, it was late, and we were all at Beck's house.

As it turned out, once Beck and Chasey got serious—or more serious than they already had been—he wanted her to meet the rest of the band.

So, we were all here now.

In fact, it was more than just the band. Not only were the remaining members of the band—Holland, Killian, Roscoe, and myself—here, but so were quite a few others. My brother

Raiden, who was our road and tour manager, had arrived along with a few other roadies. Beck's sister Sadie and some of our security staff were also here. And Killian and Roscoe had each brought a woman with them.

There was a full house, but it wasn't rowdy. Several smaller groups of individuals had huddled together to talk, drink, eat, and have a good time. We'd been here for a couple hours now, and it had been nice.

Well, nice for everyone else. On the surface, I was sure I looked like I always did. Not overly enthusiastic, not exactly sulking either. That was the beauty of how I'd lived for a long time. I'd learned to control my reactions.

It seemed most of the band had congregated in one area.

And now, the subject of touring had come up.

Chasey, sitting beside Beck on one of the oversized chairs, perked up beside him and said, "I didn't know the tour had been scheduled."

"It hasn't been," Beck assured her.

That's when Demi clarified, "Sorry, I worded that wrong. If the band decides to do another tour, do you think you'll go?"

"It's not a matter of if," Cash interjected. "It's a matter of figuring out how soon we want to do it."

"Well, you did just finish one up not that long ago," Sadie chimed in.

That was the truth.

We'd just finished up a tour at the beginning of November. Technically, it was finished at the end of October, but Cash had asked us if we'd play one more show back in Demi's hometown in New Hampshire.

We all agreed. What was one more show?

But now we were back, and there had been talks of planning another tour. Not only that, but the discussion had been leaning toward that tour starting soon.

Unfazed by that fact, Roscoe noted, "Yeah, but life on the road is nice. New places, new people. It's a pretty sweet life."

That was Roscoe. He loved this life.

Truthfully, we all did.

But where I believed we'd all get to a point when we'd want to settle down—something I didn't expect to have happen any-time soon—Roscoe could probably make music and go on tours until the day he died.

"So, what do you think, Chasey? Would you come on tour?" Demi pressed, returning the conversation to where it had started.

I was mildly curious about what her reaction would be. Chasey had a daughter named Luna who wasn't even a year old yet. It was one thing to have her sleeping soundly in the room Beck had set up all for her in this house while a party was hap-pening downstairs, and it was something else entirely to take a baby on tour.

That's not to say that it couldn't be done or that nobody in the industry hadn't ever done it. It was just that I couldn't imag-ine it would be easy.

"As I told Beck already, I don't think I'll go on the tour," Chasey started. "Of course, that doesn't mean I won't ever go to any show that's close or that I won't consider flying to a lo-cation when there's a longer break, but I'm planning to spend my time here with Luna. She's still very young, and I want to be with her and keep her where she's most comfortable."

"That's really amazing that you're so supportive of his ca-reer," Demi declared.

Chasey shrugged. "I don't think so," she replied. "I'm con-tent to see Beck do his thing while I do mine. Obviously, I'll miss him terribly, but I'd never want him to give up his passion."

That was nice to hear. I was glad that Beck had found some-one who supported his career like that. I knew there had been a point in time, only a few weeks ago, where the topic of touring had come up, and everyone had been wondering how things would play out with Beck considering he'd gotten involved with a single mom.

"So, if we know that Chasey and Beck aren't a problem, I think we should just get on scheduling something to start up again," Roscoe put in. "I'm ready."

"Me too," Killian added.

Those responses had been expected. If they could have their way, I had no doubt Killian and Roscoe would have had us out performing next week.

"That's cool with me," Cash said. "I've got my girl, so I'm good to go whenever, wherever."

That was the truth because after discussing it with the rest of us first, Cash had offered to have Demi come on board as an official employee for My Violent Heart. Her best friend from when she lived in New Hampshire designed T-shirts had worked on creating some designs for the band, and Demi was going to now be the official swag and merchandise manager.

Demi leaned her torso into Cash's body. He effortlessly took her weight and curled his hand around her shoulder.

Just then, Holland walked up and joined the conversation. She sat down between Sadie and Demi as Killian asked, "What about you, Holland?"

"What about what?" she said.

"You up for another tour?" he clarified.

"Totally," she answered.

I had to speak up. Instantly, I chimed in for the first time since the conversation had started. "I'm thinking we should take a break for a little while."

"What's a little while?" Roscoe wondered.

I shrugged. "I don't know. Maybe a year?" I threw out.

I hadn't really considered a time frame. I just knew I wanted time. Actually, I needed it so I could sort things out.

"A year?" Cash repeated.

4

"Yeah."

"Walker?" Beck called.

I brought my attention to him. "Yeah?" I returned.

"We all know."

My body went solid. There was no way they knew. Not wanting to jump to conclusions about it, I asked, "What?"

"We get it," Beck replied, his voice oddly reassuring. "You guys took a chance, kept it quiet, and it didn't work out. If she can move on from it, I know you can, too."

My eyes narrowed on him. He wasn't making any sense. "What exactly are you talking about?"

Beck shot me an incredulous look, and I could feel everyone else's eyes had been darting back and forth between us.

"You and Holland," he blurted.

Holland gasped.

I cocked an eyebrow as my gaze shot to the side where Holland was sitting. My focus moved through the entire group, and I was suddenly very angry.

"Are you shitting me?" I clipped.

I didn't get angry. Not ever. Never with the band. And yet, right now, I was fuming. Because of that, I lost my temper. "You think I've been fucking Holland? You think I'm in some secret relationship with her?"

The look on Beck's face indicated that that was exactly what he thought.

"You aren't?" Cash asked.

"Fuck no," I fumed. "She's like a sister to me."

"So, what's going on with you?" Roscoe asked.

What was going on with me?

This was bullshit. All of them, all of these people that were my family, had made some assumption about me and had discussed this all at some point behind my back.

Shaking my head in disgust, I barked, "Fuck this. I'm out of here."

"Walker, man, don't leave," Killian jumped in, yanking his arm free from the woman who'd been hanging on him since the moment they arrived.

I didn't listen. I took off toward the front door.

I'd been dealing with enough over the last several months, even while we were still on tour. The last two days had been the worst of all. I didn't need to add this to it.

Though, that was the problem.

I'd been keeping a secret from them for years now. If it got out, it was likely that I'd have to make an impossible choice.

Either the band and my passion or the woman I loved.

CHAPTER 1

Walker
Seventeen Years Earlier

"**M**AN, THAT WAS SO SICK!"

That came from the guy who'd been singing when I walked up.

I was trying to play it cool, so I simply replied, "Thanks."

"Seriously, where did you learn to play like that?"

That question came from the guy who'd been playing the keyboard before I interrupted their jam session.

"My mom," I answered honestly.

Three sets of eyes came my way.

"Your mom?"

That came from the guy who'd given me a hard time since I strolled up to the open garage door not more than ten minutes ago. He was the guitarist, and from the little I'd seen, he was really good at it. In fact, he wasn't just good; he was phenomenal.

It was summertime, and I'd been out walking my dog through our new neighborhood. My parents had moved us here after my brother, Raiden, and I finished school for the year just a few weeks ago. We hadn't moved far, but we were in a new town. Steel Ridge, Pennsylvania was about an hour east and north of where we used to live.

At sixteen years old, I really wasn't too worried about the move. It was what it was, and I'd be getting my license any day now. I could always go visit my friends if I really wanted to.

Raid was thirteen, though, so he wasn't exactly thrilled about our new home. He'd been worried about leaving his friends behind and having to start over again at a new school. I felt for him, but he was one of the best people I knew, so there was no doubt he'd make friends right away when school started at the end of the summer.

When I left my house to take Titan, my German shepherd, out for a walk, I hadn't expected I'd stumble upon a group of teenagers who looked to be about my age making music in a garage.

But I did.

And not only were they not bad, they were really good.

Unfortunately, they lacked a drummer, and I let that be known. I also told them that I played. Without any formal introductions, I walked in and showed them what I could do.

Now I was here with them singing my praises and perhaps feeling a bit of shock that it was my mom who had taught me everything I knew about music.

I stood up and walked from behind the drum set to stand next to them. Once there, I confirmed, "My mom."

"What? Is she, like, in a band or something?" the tough guy guitarist asked.

I shook my head. "She's a music teacher," I answered.

"What's your name?" the singer asked.

"Walker."

He smiled and said, "I'm Cash."

Before I could respond, the kid who'd been playing piano introduced himself. "I'm Beck."

Assuming he'd be next, I slid my eyes to the guitarist. He hesitated a moment, clearly assessing me, but eventually said, "Killian. And I think we've just got ourselves a drummer."

Initially, I thought Killian was a dick. Then again, when I'd walked up and seen him playing, I realized he had a right to be. He wasn't simply a dick for the sake of being one. He was the way he was because he was just that good. Settling for someone who didn't meet that standard would have been foolish.

"Seriously?" I asked, still trying not to seem too eager.

"Definitely," Beck replied. "Are you from around here?"

Nodding, I shared, "I live in the cul-de-sac on the other side of the development. We just moved here."

"You and your mom?" Beck asked.

"And my dad and my younger brother," I told him.

Something strange washed over his face, but I couldn't read it.

"Cool," Cash declared, pulling my attention away from Beck. "This is my house, and my parents don't mind letting us practice here all the time. And when I say all the time, I mean all the time. After school when school's in session and nearly all day in the summer. Killian also lives in the development, but he's on the opposite end from you."

What were the chances of that?

"What about you?" I asked Beck.

"I go to the same school, but my younger sister and I live with our mom in a different neighborhood," he responded.

"That's cool," I returned.

"So, what do you think?" Killian asked.

"About what?"

"Playing with us," he answered. "Like Cash said, we practice all the time. Can you meet us here every morning?"

This was a good opportunity. Even if being part of this

band didn't amount to anything, I'd at least have my first chance to make some friends in a new town.

"I can be here every morning," I assured him.

For the first time since I'd walked up, a proud look washed over Killian's face.

Yeah, I was definitely going to have some new friends.

"We start playing at ten, but you can get here as early as nine," Cash shared.

"Cool," I replied. "I'll see you tomorrow then."

I started to walk toward the opening of the garage where Titan was still patiently waiting. As I made my approach, he stood.

"Hey, Walker," Beck called.

I stopped moving, turned, and looked back. "Yeah?"

"You said you have a brother. Does he play?"

I shook my head. If all of my hopes and dreams came true, I knew Raid would be right there by my side, supporting me. But he was no musician.

"No. He loves music but doesn't play."

Beck dipped his chin in understanding.

"Being new in town, it might be hard to find friends. He's welcome to come and hang while we play if he wants," Cash offered.

Raid would love this.

"That's really cool of you," I replied. "Thanks."

"No problem. See you tomorrow."

"Later," I said. Looking down at my dog, I grabbed his leash and commanded, "Let's go, Titan."

Titan fell into step beside me as we walked away.

It wasn't until I'd gotten several hundred feet away that I let out a huge sigh of relief. I was part of a band.

I couldn't wait to go home and tell my mom and my brother. When my dad got home from work, I'd tell him, too.

They'd all be ecstatic for me, especially my mom since she loved music so much and had made a career out of it.

That's why, when I finally reached the end of the block with Titan and needed to make the turn to head down into the cul-de-sac, I broke out into a jog. I wanted to get back and share the news with my family.

Because even if they thought deep down that this would never amount to anything, they'd never make me believe anything but the best-case scenario was possible.

"Take this with you."

"What?"

"I made breakfast for you and the boys," my mom said as she held out a brown paper bag to me.

My eyes shifted between her face and the bag in her hand.

"Take the bag," she urged.

"Um, I'm not sure—"

"Walker Rhodes, you take this bag filled with breakfast sandwiches and you give them to your friends," she demanded. "From what you've been telling me, Cash's mom has been feeding you, Beck, Killian, Cash, and Raiden when he tags along, lunch and snacks for the last three days. Something tells me she was doing that long before you joined the group. I'm doing my part to thank her for that by feeding her son breakfast."

I couldn't say no and hurt my mom's feelings.

But I didn't know how the guys would react to me bringing breakfast.

I sighed and took the bag from her. "Thanks, Mom."

"I'm proud of you, Walker," she said.

"It's only been a few days," I pointed out.

Shaking her head with a smile on her face, she insisted, "That doesn't matter. I'm still proud of you. I know how much you love playing, and I'm so happy you found some kids who are just as talented. I can't wait to meet them. Maybe you can bring them by here one day for dinner."

I didn't know if the guys would want to leave Cash's place to have dinner at mine, but I refused to be negative about it.

"Yeah, I'll talk to them about it," I promised.

"Okay. Have fun today," she said.

"I will. Later, Mom."

With that, I walked out the door and to Cash's house. As I approached the driveway, I saw Killian coming down from the opposite end. I lifted a hand and waved before turning toward the open garage door.

Beck and Cash were already there.

"Hey, guys," I greeted them as I stepped inside the garage.

"Hi, Walker," Cash replied.

Beck's eyes dipped to the bag in my hand. "What's that?" he asked.

I held it up as Killian walked up to us and mumbled, "My mom insisted on making everyone breakfast."

"Sweet," Killian declared. "What did she make?"

"Bacon, egg, and cheese on toasted and buttered English muffins," I answered as I pulled the foil-wrapped sandwiches out of the bag and handed them out.

Barely a single bite in and Beck said, "This is awesome. Tell your mom we said thanks."

Gratitude for my mom swept through me at that moment. Ever since I'd met Cash, Beck, and Killian a few days ago, they'd been great. But since I knew that it had just been the three of them for a long time, I did have my concerns about whether I'd really become part of the group. In that moment, I knew I had.

"You can tell her yourself if you want," I replied. When they looked up at me, I added, "She wanted me to invite you all over for dinner one night so she could meet you."

"I'm down for that," Beck said.

"My mom will love not having to cook," Cash added.

"You tell us when, and we'll be there," Killian assured me.

I fought breaking out into a full-blown grin and returned, "Definitely. I'll talk to her and let you know."

Minutes later, after we all finished breakfast, we got to work. And we spent the entire day working on our music, only stopping when Cash's mom told us lunch and dinner were ready.

If it was always going to be this easy, I had a feeling we were destined for something big. I couldn't wait for it to happen.

Eight years later

We made it.

We'd actually made it happen.

It didn't happen overnight, but with all the hard work we put in, we'd done what we set out to do. We simply needed the two missing pieces to make it happen.

Roscoe joined the band three years after I did as our bassist. We'd had some success with the two albums we released, but it was just a year ago that things really took off. We'd added Holland to the mix. She was the only female in the group. She had a hell of a voice and an incredible talent for writing songs. We rerecorded a couple of songs, recorded a few new ones, released an album and went on tour.

Things exploded once Holland became part of My Violent Heart.

And I couldn't have been happier that it happened.

All of us felt the same.

It was beyond incredible to know that all the hard work we'd put in in the beginning wasn't simply about a group of kids just finding something to do with themselves in their free time. In a way, I guess it was. But it was still much more than that for all of us.

And what we all had between us was so much more than just music.

Obviously, music was the thing that brought us together, but there was something else that lingered there. Over the years, it became about love and respect and family.

Cash, Beck, Killian, Roscoe, and Holland had become like my second family. They became like that for Raid, too. Because while he didn't play any instruments in the official capacity—I'd seen him dabbling—nor did he sing, he'd been there from the time they brought me into the fold, and he went on tour with us. He was essentially our road manager. I just hoped all the good fortune would continue, and we'd be able to hire him an entire crew to manage.

For now, for tonight, we were all going to be celebrating because we'd just returned home from our first real tour after making it big.

It wasn't a huge tour, nor was it a global one. But it was ours, and for the first time, we all felt the efforts of our hard work pay off.

Every night, after finishing a show, we'd all go back to our dressing room and try to let it sink in that we'd made it as far as we did.

I didn't think it was a feeling we'd ever get used to, and

damn, if that didn't feel good. I could easily get used to this life. Music, women, drinks, and having a good time.

Even better than that was knowing that my family was so proud. And it wasn't just my family.

Apparently, the fact that my mom, Cash's mom, and Killian's mom all lived in the same neighborhood had worked to their advantage. The three of them had gotten together and decided they wanted to have a huge celebration once My Violent Heart returned from tour. They'd planned the whole thing, inviting extended family members and friends.

Part of me thought I'd come home from the tour and just be able to relax, but I felt like I'd barely gotten through the front door of my place when I needed to get myself ready to head right back out.

Now, I was here at the venue. And even if I was ready for a bit of a break, I was also excited about this. It was going to be nice to finally be able to see everyone while meeting more of the family and friends of my bandmates.

I'd be able to kick back tomorrow. And truthfully, this wasn't like being on tour any longer. This was about finally being home and being with the people we loved and cared about.

For the first two hours of the party, I'd spent the majority of my time making my rounds through my family and family friends. Everyone had also sat down to have dinner, too.

Following dinner, I'd met more of Killian's extended family. I'd even met his cousin, Royce, who owned a private investigation and security firm here in our hometown of Steel Ridge. He let me know that he'd already shared with Killian that whenever we were ready, he'd be more than happy to provide us with security.

I couldn't say that would be a bad idea. Seeing how things sort of took off for us and how it had been when we went on this tour, it would actually be a really smart move. We were all getting noticed more, and I had no doubt that by the time we recorded another album—something we were planning to get started on almost immediately—and went on another tour, we'd see even more of a need for private security.

After talking with both of them for a bit, Beck walked by and interrupted us. "Hey, Walker, I don't think I introduced you to my sister yet."

I shook my head. "No," I confirmed. Then I looked back to Killian and Royce and said, "It was nice meeting you. I'm sure we'll have more time soon enough to catch up again."

"Sounds great. Nice meeting you as well," Royce returned.

I turned my attention toward Beck, who said, "She's over here. Come on."

It was strange. I knew certain relatives of each of my bandmates rather well. Cash's parents were like my second set considering how much time we'd spent at his house when we were first starting out. And while I'd met Beck's mom before when we'd stopped at her place a couple of times over the years, I hadn't ever met his younger sister.

But that didn't mean I didn't know anything about her. I wasn't sure there were two people more important to Beck than his mom and his sister. He was very protective over both of them, which was partly due to the fact that he took on the role of being man of the house at just six years old.

"Sorry to interrupt you there with Killian and Royce," Beck began. "But Sadie's going to kill me if I don't introduce her to everyone. She's been angry at me."

"Angry?" I repeated, turning my gaze to him as he continued to walk across the room.

"Angry," he confirmed. "She's pissed that we've all been together for so many years and she's not been able to meet anyone besides Cash and Killian yet. She acts like it's my fault that all of the shows we played locally were in locations she couldn't get into."

That made sense. From what I could recall, Beck's sister was four years younger than him, which meant she was still just nineteen years old.

"Well, then I guess it's a good thing we had this tonight, isn't it?" I countered.

A moment later, I looked straight ahead in the direction we were heading and saw Holland facing me talking to a woman who had her back turned to me.

Coming to a stop behind that woman, Beck put a hand to her shoulder and called, "Sadie?"

She twisted her neck in his direction, and I watched as his face softened when she answered, "Yeah?"

His eyes went over her shoulder toward me, and he said, "I wanted to introduce you to Walker. I think he's the only one you haven't met."

I thought I saw something, perhaps her body going tense, but I couldn't take the time to assess that because she turned around and looked at me.

Shit.

Shit. Shit. Shit.

This could not be Beck's sister.

Gorgeous hazel eyes with long, dark brown hair, and a pair of perfectly shaped pink lips. She was wearing a short dress that fit tight to her torso but flared out at her waist. Her legs were long and toned and her breasts could only be described as perfect. Not too big and not too small.

She was... fuck, she was my best friend's little sister. I couldn't even think about going there.

No way.

No way I could do it.

But then... she smiled at me—a smile that nearly

knocked me on my ass—opened her arms, and pressed her body to mine. "It's so nice to finally meet you, Walker."

That's all it took.

That smile, her voice, and her body pressed close.

Holland was like a sister to me. And Beck, Cash, Killian, and Roscoe were like brothers to me. Their families had become like mine. Hell, Cash's parents were like a second set of parents to me.

But in this scenario, there was not one single thing that made Sadie Emerson feel anything like a sister to me.

I didn't know how I'd ever be able to forget that this woman existed.

Unfortunately, I didn't have to figure it out. Because three weeks after I met her, my life imploded.

CHAPTER 2

Sadie

THIS WAS IT.

It was time to take matters into my own hands.

I'd waited long enough for something to happen, and I couldn't hold myself back any longer.

Especially not now. Not after I'd *finally* met him.

For the better part of the last four years, I had followed My Violent Heart much like a crazed fan. But where it might have been considered an obsession for some, it didn't exactly appear that way in my situation. I mean, my brother was one of the members, and it was only natural that I'd want to support him.

Beck and I were close; we always had been. For as long as I could remember, he was my very best friend. He had also been my protector. Of course, I'd never really found myself in any situations that I thought warranted any sort of real protection, but the bottom line was that I knew I could always depend on him to be there for me if I ever needed him.

I kind of felt like I needed him now. Unfortunately, what I needed him for wasn't something I believed he'd want any part of.

Because I had a massive crush on one of his bandmates, a man who was like a brother to Beck.

In Beck's world, I wasn't sure he thought there'd ever be a man good enough for me, even someone he knew well.

Someone like Walker Rhodes.

I sighed just at the mere thought of the man.

For four years, I'd admired him from afar, never finding myself anywhere that he was. Then again, at my age, it wasn't like there was a whole lot of opportunity. My brother adored me, but it wasn't like he could invite me to go out with him and the band when they went to grab drinks together.

And although I'd been following the band and was incredibly proud of Beck for everything he'd accomplished, I had to admit that I'd spent most of my time having a major crush on Walker.

I was nineteen now, but I was only a few months away from turning twenty. Regardless, I was an adult. Walker might have been five years older than me, but I saw that as a good thing. Didn't they say that men matured slower than women anyway? I figured our age gap was perfect and would put us on a level playing field.

So, I was done waiting.

Meeting him three weeks ago sort of sealed the deal for me. That crush I had was long gone. I was now dealing with a full-fledged attraction.

I mean, the man was utter perfection. Physically speaking, he'd gotten his darker skin tone from his mother, who I'd learned after researching online was Polynesian. He had dark brown eyes, beautiful lips that were surrounded by a neatly groomed full beard, and a gorgeous smile that did things to my body I didn't know were possible.

He was built. Solid. It was clear he took care of his body and exercised on a regular basis. His right arm was covered in tattoos from shoulder to wrist, and as lovely as that was to look at, I was just as drawn to the bare skin of his left arm. The veins that stood out on his biceps and forearms also did things to my body that I didn't know were possible.

I couldn't stop thinking about him.

About the way he looked.

About the way he smelled.

About the way his body felt pressed against mine.

During the night of the welcome home party for the band, I'd gone out of my way to purposely hug every member of the band when Beck introduced me to them. I wanted my arms around Walker, and I knew if he had been the only one I'd hugged, my brother would have taken notice.

But if I was being completely honest, I definitely held on to Walker just a little bit longer than the rest.

I smiled recalling our interaction that night.

"It's so nice to finally meet you, Walker," I said as I plastered my body to his.

I relished in the feel of his strong arms wrapping around me as he hugged me back, silently telling myself this wouldn't be a one-time thing.

"It's great to meet you, too," he returned.

I loosened my hold on him and stepped back just as my mom walked up and said, "Beck, your grandmother just informed me she hasn't seen you all night."

"Ah, alright," he replied. "I'm coming."

Without wasting another second, my brother took off, and when I glanced to my side, I saw that Holland had been whisked away by Cash's family.

It was just the two of us.

Walker and me.

Walker and me.

I never thought I'd ever see the day.

Without anyone else around to help take any of the pressure off, I needed to make sure I didn't make a fool of myself.

Well, that and make sure that Walker knew, even if just a little bit, that I was into him.

"I can't believe it's taken so long for me to meet everyone," I declared.

Nodding his agreement, he returned, "Yeah, it's kind of crazy that I met Beck eight years ago, and this is the first I'm meeting you."

"Kind of crazy and definitely disappointing," I noted.

Something flashed in his face as his eyes widened. I offered a smile but kept it friendly. I didn't want to send the guy running in the opposite direction right off the bat.

"So, are you happy the tour is over?" I asked when he made no move to respond.

"I guess," he answered. "Part of me is glad to be back. It'll be nice to have some downtime, but I'd be lying if I said I wasn't going to miss it."

"I can't imagine what it must be like to have so many screaming fans," I said.

He let out a laugh. "I'm not sure it's something I'll ever get used to," he shared. "It's a bit surreal."

"Well, you all definitely deserve it. I know how hard you've worked to get here, so I'm very happy for you."

Walker assessed me a moment before his voice dipped a bit lower, and he said, "Thanks, Sadie. That's really sweet of you."

Something happened inside my body when I heard him say my name.

God, I wanted this man so bad, and I didn't have the slightest clue what I was doing.

Smiling at him, I kept my voice just a touch over a whisper and replied, "You're welcome, Walker."

I couldn't say for sure what it was, but I saw his eyes flash with something. I wanted to believe that him hearing me say his name made him feel the same way I felt hearing him say my name. Since he didn't offer any indication to the contrary, I convinced myself that's what it was.

For the next few moments, there was a bit of an awkward silence. I didn't know what to say, and I was incredibly nervous.

It turned out to be much harder than I thought it would be.

And I was completely disappointed with myself. After all these years, I should have taken the time to come up with a plan. I was a relatively outgoing person, even if I preferred a much quieter life in comparison to my brother, and I had just assumed I would be able to wing it.

Or maybe it was something else.

Maybe there was some small part of me that had hoped Walker would take one look at me and find himself very interested. Maybe I wanted—no, maybe I needed—him to be the one to take the lead.

I had no clue what I was doing, and there was no question in my mind that he had far more experience in this situation than I did.

Sadly, he wasn't making any moves, and I needed to do something.

"Walker, I wanted to—"

"Hey, guys, sorry to interrupt, but Walker, I need to talk to you."

Walker seemed slightly frustrated by the interruption and begrudgingly tore his gaze from mine to look to his left.

He narrowed his eyes on the man standing there before he let out a sigh and asked, "Raid, have you met Sadie?"

Raid shifted his attention to me. "No, it's nice to meet you, though. You're Beck's sister, right?"

I nodded. "That's me," I confirmed.

"Sadie, this is my brother, Raid, who clearly has impeccable timing," Walker said, the sarcasm dripping from his words.

I smiled, feeling awkward. "It's totally okay. I should pro'ably go mingle anyway. It was lovely to meet you, Raid."

my gaze to Walker and rasped, "I'm really glad I got to meet you, Walker. Maybe we can catch up with each other later."

Surprise washed over him, and I was curious what he'd say, but I was too afraid he'd shoot me down. So, I turned and walked away before he could respond at all.

And sadly, we never had the chance to catch up later. But that didn't mean I didn't notice Walker looking in my direction several times throughout the remainder of the night.

Now that it had been three weeks since that night and my fondness and attraction for Walker had only seemed to intensify, I had to take matters into my own hands.

I was going to crash the band's recording session today.

Actually, I wasn't completely crashing the session. I had begged Beck to bring me to the studio with him.

Gone were the days of playing in Cash's parents' garage. My Violent Heart had rented studio time a few years ago to record their albums. And now that they were doing as well as they were, they invested in their very own recording studio.

I hadn't been there to see it yet, and I thought it was the perfect excuse to get myself there. That and the fact that I'd never actually witnessed them recording an album.

So, with my promise to not get in the way or intrude but to simply be there to observe, Beck agreed. Truthfully, it didn't require much convincing.

And now that I was here, sitting on the couch while Beck, Cash, and Killian talked waiting for the rest of the band members to arrive, I started to panic just a little bit.

I thought I'd made it clear to Walker that I had at least some interest in him. And I wouldn't have left the door open by telling him we could catch up later in the evening three weeks ago if I wasn't interested in seeing that happen.

Maybe I wanted something that he did not want in return.

My body tensed when I heard a chime indicating that someone had walked into the studio. I sat there nervously biting my lip watching and waiting to see who would walk down the hall and into this room.

Some of my nerves vanished when both Roscoe and Holland stepped inside.

"Sadie!" Holland bubbled. "What are you doing here?"

I smiled at her and answered, "I just thought I'd come and check this out. I guess I figured since I met all of you that it wouldn't be so awkward for me to show up and watch now."

"That's awesome. I'm glad you came. I meant to grab your number the night of the party, but I completely forgot to do it before I left. It'd be cool to hang out every now and then," she said.

I perked up. "Really?"

"Totally."

I pulled out my phone and asked, "What's your number?" Holland rattled off her number, and I saved it into my phone. "I'll shoot you a text so you have my number."

"Awesome."

It was awesome. I wouldn't mind forging a friendship with Holland. I liked her, and I thought we'd get along great. She was the youngest of the group being only twenty-one, and being the only woman in the band, I had to imagine she'd like having some female energy around her every now and again.

"Hey, Sadie," Roscoe greeted me after Holland moved off to the side.

"Hey, Roscoe."

No sooner had I returned that greeting when the door chimed again.

Everyone else was here, so I knew it had to be him.

My belly dipped at the thought of seeing him again. I couldn't wait.

Only, the moment he stepped into the room, I could see that something was very, very wrong. His tortured eyes slid through each member of the band before they got to me. For several long seconds, he stared at me.

My body was itching to squirm under the intensity of his gaze, but I didn't dare move. I tried to keep my focus on him and the fact that I knew something wasn't right.

"Walker?" Beck called.

Walker closed his eyes, dropped his head, and let out a deep sigh. Seconds later, he lifted his head, and when he opened his eyes, I could see the tears forming in them.

My God, what had happened?

I barely knew the man, but in that moment, I wanted to fix whatever was wrong.

"Walker, are you okay?" Holland asked.

He looked at her, bit his bottom lip, and shook his head.

"Man, what's wrong?" Killian pressed.

Letting his lip go, Walker clenched his jaw tightly.

He looked so broken. So tormented.

He looked numb.

The seconds that passed were long and tense. Walker didn't speak. He didn't move.

Nobody did.

They waited.

I waited.

Finally, his lips parted. His ragged voice shared, "Last night, I found out my mom was just diagnosed with cancer."

Unable to stop myself, I gasped in horror. I didn't have to worry about drawing anyone's attention, though, because they all had similar reactions.

"Shit," Roscoe hissed.

"Fuck," Beck clipped.

"Damn it," Cash snapped.

Killian stepped forward, put a hand to Walker's shoulder, and squeezed. "I'm so sorry to hear that," he lamented.

Walker nodded and dropped his gaze to the ground. "Stage

four, cervical," he added, his voice sounding so broken and beat down.

God, I wanted to comfort him.

But Holland beat me to it.

She stepped forward, wrapped her arms around him, and held on tight. "I'm sorry, Walker," she said softly.

Walker hugged Holland back and replied, "Yeah. Me too."

When she stepped back, she asked, "What's the prognosis?"

"One to two years at best," he shared.

"You should be with her now," Cash urged him.

Walker shook his head. "I can't," he told him. "Not only would she not have an ounce of that, but I need the distraction."

"Are you sure you can handle this right now?" Beck pressed.

"No," he answered honestly. "But I'm not sure I can handle much of anything right now. If this can give me a few hours to focus on something other than cancer and radiation and treatments and doctors, I'll take it."

"Treatment?" Killian repeated. "Is there a chance for her to beat this?"

Walker shook his head again. "No. It's spread too far."

"What can we do?" Roscoe asked.

"Make music with me," he answered. "If I can give her another album before…"

He trailed off. I couldn't even begin to imagine how he must have felt. If I were in his shoes, I wasn't sure I would have been able to say the words either.

"We can do that," Beck promised.

"Absolutely," Holland agreed. "Anything you need. We've got you."

"Thanks."

With that, they all started to shuffle toward the door that led into the next room. I still hadn't gotten up off the couch.

What kind of person was I? I had to say something.

Walker was at the back of the pack, so I jumped up from

the couch—probably a little too eagerly—and called softly, "Walker?"

He twisted his neck in my direction. "Yeah, Sadie, I'm sorry," he apologized.

Why was he apologizing to me?

Shaking my head, I insisted, "There's nothing to apologize to me for. I just… well, I'm really sorry to hear about your mom."

"I appreciate that."

I shifted back and forth on my feet, unsure of what to say. Damn.

The first time I met him, I hadn't prepared anything to say. This time I had had it all worked out.

But I couldn't very well say any of the stuff I wanted to say that would indicate to him that I wanted to get to know him better. This *was not* the time for that.

So, I simply offered, "If there's anything I can do, please don't hesitate to ask."

His beautiful brown eyes, still looking as tortured and haunted as ever, stared at me. "Thank you, Sadie."

"I mean it. Anything at all, and I'm your girl."

Something washed over his face, but he didn't respond. He simply gave me a nod, turned, and followed the rest of the band into the next room.

I stood there feeling awkward for a few moments before I sat back down and watched the band through the glass.

Truthfully, my gaze never left Walker.

And watching him that afternoon, all I could do was feel my heart break for the loss I knew he'd soon be facing.

CHAPTER 3

Sadie
Four months later

I DIDN'T TAKE MUCH NOTICE OF WHAT WAS HAPPENING AROUND me.

My head was down and my nose was buried in my books. Textbooks and notebooks alike. I didn't know why I was torturing myself with all of this. I already knew what I wanted to do. Heck, I was already doing it.

But I felt obligated.

If it hadn't been for Beck, I wouldn't have had this opportunity. Okay, maybe I would have had the opportunity, but it certainly wouldn't have been this easy.

I was in my junior year at a local college—early because I'd graduated high school early—and I was currently studying for my final exams. I was an art major.

It was Tuesday morning, and I was trying to squeeze in all the last-minute studying I could before my final exam of the semester tomorrow morning.

With my attention on the books in front of me, I was oblivious to everything else around me. But when, out of the corner of my eye, I saw a pair of jean-clad thighs, my concentration on all things art and final exams flew out the window.

It was him. Without a word exchanged between us, without even seeing his face, I knew it was him.

I turned my head fully to the side, took in the legs standing beside the table I was sitting at, and allowed my gaze to slowly drift up. Suffice it to say, my eyes lingered in the area of his groin before continuing their ascent toward his face.

I'd felt a bit of nervousness creeping in, as I wondered what I'd find when my eyes connected with his. But I was surprised to see that there was no longer the pain and anguish in them I'd seen months ago. There was some sadness that remained, but it wasn't as overpowering as it had been before.

Something came over me, and I jumped out of my seat to throw my arms around him. "Oh my gosh, Walker, what are you doing here?"

"How are you, Sadie?" he replied as his arms came around me, and he hugged me back.

This time, it wasn't me who held on longer. It was him.

I loved the way it felt.

When he finally loosened his hold, I took a step back and apologized, "I'm sorry. I didn't mean to attack you. It's just…"

I trailed off because I wasn't sure what to say. Could I tell him that I'd thought about him every day? Should I tell him that I'd been so worried about him? Did he deserve to know that I tried to find out how he was doing by bringing up conversations about the band casually with my brother?

"It's okay. It's really good to see you," he insisted.

That was very nice to hear, so I smiled again and returned, "You too. What are you doing here?"

He looked back toward the deli counter before he brought his attention to me again and said, "Just came in to grab some lunch."

My eyes widened.

"What?" he asked. "What's that look about?"

I lifted my phone off the table and lit up the display. "It's already lunchtime," I murmured.

"You haven't eaten anything yet?" he questioned me.

I shook my head. "I've been studying. I didn't realize how late it was."

He dropped his gaze to the table, saw my notes and textbooks all spread out. "I'm sorry. I didn't mean to interrupt you," he said. "I just… well, I walked in and saw you here, so I wanted to come and say hello. I can let you get back to it."

"No!" I practically shouted at him. He jerked back at my reaction. I panicked. I hadn't seen him in so long. I wanted more than just a mere two minutes with him. "Sorry. Um, you don't have to go. I should probably take a break and eat something anyway. If you want to join me, I'd be happy for a distraction for a bit."

Walker looked a little unsure, but ultimately asked, "Are you sure?"

Nodding, I confirmed, "Definitely." Then, gesturing toward the table, I urged, "Let me just clean this up"

He dipped his chin and said, "Okay. While you do that, how about I order the food? Do you know what you want?"

I did.

I got the same thing every time I came here.

"The veggie and hummus sandwich," I answered. "No cheese."

Walker made a face that looked like he was repulsed, and I stifled a laugh.

"What's that look about?" I countered, using his own words against him.

"Veggies and hummus," he declared.

I let out a laugh. "It's my favorite sandwich," I told him.

Something flashed in his face. "Okay. I'll be right back."

"Wait," I called out as I started to reach for my bag.

"What's up?"

"Let me give you some money," I replied.

"Sadie, I've got it," he insisted.

"Are you sure?"

Walker cocked his eyebrow and shot me a look of disbelief. What he didn't do was answer what he clearly deemed to be a stupid question.

With that, he turned and walked toward the counter. I allowed my eyes to drift down over his backside while simultaneously biting my lip. I hadn't noticed I was doing that until he stopped moving. When I took my eyes from his ass, I realized he had not only stopped but that he also turned back to look in my direction.

His lips twitched when my eyes met his.

"Something to drink?" he asked.

"Wa…" I stopped to clear my throat. "Water," I rasped.

He held my gaze a bit longer than I would have expected or liked in that moment before he continued his journey to the counter. When he did that, I did not allow myself to get distracted by his ass.

Instead, I began shuffling all of my papers together, shoving them inside my notebook. They were an utter mess, and it was completely disorganized.

I didn't care, though.

I had to figure out how to pull myself together before Walker returned.

If I thought I hadn't been prepared the first time I met him, I definitely wasn't prepared now. I hadn't believed I'd get this opportunity again.

Or, at least, I didn't think it'd happen this soon.

The truth was, after Walker revealed that his mom had been diagnosed with stage four cervical cancer, I sort of gave up on my pursuit of him. It felt wrong. It felt icky.

Judging by how tormented he was that day, I didn't think it

was a far stretch to assume that he'd be distracted by what was going on with her. His focus needed to be on her and what he was doing for her before her time was up.

So, I sucked it up and pulled back.

I put all of my effort and attention into school.

But that didn't mean I didn't think about him.

I thought about Walker often, I hoped for the best for him, and I prayed for peace for him and his family as they navigated through something so incredibly difficult.

And I held out hope that one day soon I'd see him again when he was in a better headspace. I would try again then.

Of course, even if he hadn't gotten into a better headspace, I would have been more than happy to be there for him if he wanted or needed that from me.

What I hadn't expected was that that day would come so soon. Sure, it had been four months. Four months of continuing to be plagued by my attraction to him. But it was certainly not nearly as long as I had anticipated.

By the time I'd gathered up all of my things, put them into my bag, and given myself a full two minutes to calm myself down, Walker returned.

"Okay, so I owe you an apology," he began as he placed the food down on the table in front of me. He'd gotten himself the Hawaiian BBQ pulled chicken sandwich.

"An apology for what?" I asked.

"I can't deny that your sandwich looks good," he shared as he sat down.

Lifting one half of it up, I held it out to him. "Would you like to try it?"

He held up a hand and said, "I'll just observe and compliment how it looks for now. It's all yours."

"Your loss," I goaded him. "Thank you, by the way."

"It's just lunch, Sadie," he said softly.

Maybe to him it was. To me, it was more.

"Right. So, how are you doing?" I asked.

"I'm okay. Just trying to keep myself busy," he answered.

"And your mom?" I pressed. "How is she doing?"

He took in a deep breath, and I could instantly see how his mind went somewhere else. I immediately regretted asking him. The last thing I wanted to do was to upset him, but I also didn't want him to think I was some heartless bitch who didn't have a care about what he and his family were facing.

"She's alright," he finally replied. "She's taking it one day at a time. Somehow, though, she seems to be the strongest one of all of us."

"I think that's a mom thing," I said. "They seem so much more capable of enduring things for the sake of their family."

"Yeah. I'm really proud of her."

"I'm sure she's just as proud of you," I countered. "I've heard the album is going well."

Though we talked regularly, I always made it a point to talk to Beck about how things were going with the band and the album. From his point of view, it was simply me being the supportive and curious sister.

And while that was a big part of it, there was something else I was much more interested in learning about.

I wanted to know how Walker was doing.

So, I found ways to casually bring it up, and I often learned that Walker was doing okay and getting lost in the music when he was in the studio.

Walker nodded. "Yeah, we're about half through it at this point," he confirmed. "I hope the second half goes at least as well as the first half."

"You guys are all so talented, so I don't see why you'd have any trouble making it happen," I told him.

"I hope so. And I appreciate the compliment."

I bit into my sandwich, which I could just barely fit my mouth around for how high the veggies were piled, and watched

Walker's face light up with amusement. I was surprised at how good it felt to put that look on his face.

For the next few minutes, we both ate a bit of our food. It wasn't an awkward or uncomfortable silence. It was simply about two hungry people filling their bellies.

But after he'd gotten about halfway through his sandwich, Walker asked, "So, you're studying?"

"Yep."

"Anything interesting?"

I grinned. "I guess that depends on who you talk to," I began. "It's history of art of the twentieth century."

With his sandwich lifted halfway to his mouth, Walker stopped moving and stared at me. "You find that interesting?"

I shook my head. "Well, some of it is interesting," I answered. "But it was a requirement for my art degree, so I kind of didn't have a choice. If I did, I definitely wouldn't be sitting here studying for this final exam right now."

"Are you done for good after the finals?" he asked.

"No. I have one more year."

Nodding his head in understanding, he asked, "And what are you going to do when you graduate?"

I smiled at him and shared, "I'm already doing it."

Confusion washed over him. "What?"

"I paint," I revealed. "I've always been very artsy, even as a kid. I guess Beck and I both have a thing for the arts. But where he gravitated toward the music, I went with something much quieter."

"I never knew you were into painting," he said. "I mean, Beck has talked about you before, but he's never really gotten into any details. Although, I'm not sure if I paid that close of attention beforehand anyway."

I wanted to ask him if he paid attention now that he'd met me, but I was too much of a chicken.

"As long as he's saying good things, I guess that's cool of

him," I joked. "And yeah, I've really found my love for painting in the last couple of years. In fact, it wasn't long after I started school that I figured out what I wanted to do and started making it happen."

"What exactly is that?" he wondered.

I let out a laugh. "I'm not sure I could fit it into one little box because it's a bit of everything. Mostly, I paint canvases and sell them. I like doing landscapes, but I'll dabble in other things occasionally. But I also recently started working a lot with watercolors and creating lots of custom things like stationery or holiday cards."

"That's cool. I've never been much of an artist in that sense, but I have a huge appreciation for it."

He got those words out and glanced down at his tattooed arm. What I would have given to inspect them closer. To touch them. To allow my fingers to trace over them.

Stop it, Sadie.

"We all have our talents, I guess," I returned.

"Yeah," he agreed. "I'm a little confused still, though."

"About what?"

He took a sip of his drink and set it down before he said, "Well, if you already know what you want to do and have been doing it, why are you in school and studying for a final exam for a class that you aren't really thrilled about?"

"Beck."

"Beck?" he repeated. "Beck didn't go to college. What does he have to do with it?"

I was silent a moment while I figured out how to respond to that question. Walker gave me the time I needed to do that. Then I explained, "I'm sure you already know that Beck and I were really young when our father left our mother. Beck actually witnessed it the night it happened. I was honestly too young to really remember any of it, but from that day on, Beck apparently took a new role on his young shoulders. He became the man of the house."

Smiling at me, Walker replied, "I can see that being the case. Even if I haven't always listened to every detail of everything he's ever said, I do know that he's very protective over you and your mom."

"Yes, he is. But he also did something I didn't know about," I began again. "Before I even graduated from high school, Beck started asking me what my plans were. I didn't realize it at the time, but he was trying to figure out how much he would need."

"How much what?"

"Money," I answered. "By the time I decided to go to school and started preparing to complete financial aid applications, Beck had walked up to me one day and tore them up. Little did I know, he'd been setting money aside for me to go to school for years. It's all paid for, and I wouldn't have had this opportunity if it weren't for him. Or, maybe I would have had it, but I would have had it with the financial burden. So, the least I can do at this point is finish up my last year."

"That's very admirable," Walker said, a look of respect on his face.

"Thanks."

For the next few minutes, Walker and I didn't speak. We finished up our food and exchanged happy looks, which came from him, and tentative smiles, which came from me.

"Well, I should probably let you get back to your studying," Walker started as he sat back in his chair. "This was really nice, Sadie. I enjoyed talking with you."

"Yeah, me too, Walker," I replied.

"It was nice to get my mind off of everything else going on in my life right now," he added.

This was my chance.

I didn't want to waste it.

"It doesn't have to be a once and done thing, you know?"

He grew alarmed. "What? What do you mean?" he asked.

I shrugged. "If you need someone to talk to, I'm happy to lend a listening ear," I told him. "And if you don't want to talk, but you need a distraction, I'm happy to do the talking."

He stared at me for a long time without saying a word. I started to wonder if perhaps I'd gone too far. I mean, I was merely trying to be nice.

Okay, I was also hoping that one day down the road we could possibly be something more. But right now, at this very moment, I really was just trying to be nice.

"Sadie, that's really kind of you, but I'm not sure—"

"I'm offering my friendship, Walker," I said, cutting him off. I panicked again because I didn't want to risk having another four months go by without being able to talk to him. "We can exchange numbers if you want. If you never call, fine. But if you need me, at least you'll have a way to reach me."

I might have said those words and looked the picture perfect image of calm and collected, but inside, I really didn't know how I'd feel if he never called.

Walker took a few more seconds to consider his options. Eventually, and much to my relief, he pulled out his phone, unlocked it, and held it out to me. "Put your number in," he urged.

I put my phone number in and handed it back to him. Walker looked down at the screen, saved the number, and put his phone away.

"Thank you for offering this to me," he said. "I appreciate it."

I smiled and replied, "You're welcome."

He stood from his chair, looked down at me, and gathered up the empty trays for the food. After putting them in the trash, he came back and said, "It was really good to see you, Sadie."

Not knowing when I'd have the chance again, I wanted to get up and hug him.

So, I did.

I stood, moved close, and lifted my arms over his shoulders to give him a hug. "It was really nice to see you too, Walker. Thank you, again, for lunch."

When I pulled back, he looked like he wanted to say something, but he didn't. Instead, he simply replied, "You're welcome. Take care, Sadie."

"You too."

Following a moment of brief hesitation, Walker turned and walked out of the café.

I sat back down and couldn't stop myself from smiling. That had been the best surprise I'd had in a really long time.

But if I had been worried it would be another four months until I felt that good again, I would have been wrong. Because not long after I woke up the next morning I received a text message from Walker.

He wished me luck on my final exam while also telling me that if I ever needed him, I could always give him a call.

Suffice it to say, I breezed right through my exam.

CHAPTER 4

Sadie

I WAS ELBOWS DEEP IN MY WORK, SOMETHING THAT I'D STARTED putting a lot more of my focus into once my summer break before my final semester at school began, when my phone rang.

Glancing over, I was shocked to see Walker's picture on the display.

Yes, the morning after we'd had lunch together and he texted to wish me luck on my last exam, I didn't just save his number. I also found one of my favorites of him online and added it to his contact.

Other than when I put that picture on my phone a month ago, I hadn't ever seen it come up on the display. Until now.

Walker was calling me.

Finally, he was calling.

As much as I had wanted to talk to him well before now, I couldn't bring myself to be the one to reach out to him first. I guess there was a small part of me that was simply old fashioned. That said, it seemed once I was around him, that dated mindset went out the window. It just wasn't nearly as easy to hold myself back when I had that man in front of me.

Seeing his call coming through now, I had to admit that I was excited about it, even if I wasn't prepared for it. Then again, that seemed to be the case every time I'd been around him. I was never prepared for what came from it. Even still, it always seemed to go okay.

So, I set my brushes down and picked up the phone.

"Hello?" I answered.

"Sadie?"

My body instantly tensed up. He sounded tortured. His voice was ragged.

Oh God. Oh no.

"Walker?" I returned. "Are you okay?"

The silence stretched briefly before he lamented, "I'm really sorry to bother you, but I was wondering if your offer still stood? I could really use a distraction right now."

I didn't hesitate.

Without even taking a moment to think, I sprang to my feet and replied, "Absolutely. Where are you?"

"I'm home, but you don't have to—"

"I know I don't," I insisted, cutting him off. Then, I ordered, "Let me give you what you need right now. Text me your address, and I'll be there as soon as I can. Okay?"

He didn't respond.

"Walker?" I called after too much time had passed.

"Okay. I'll text you," he confirmed.

"Good. I'm going to go now, but I promise I'll be there soon."

"Thanks, Sadie," he rasped.

"Anytime," I assured him.

With that, we said goodbye and disconnected the call. I dropped my phone, ran to my bedroom, and changed my clothes. I had been wearing clothes for painting, and I was not going to go meet Walker in them. As quickly as I could, I got myself dressed, confirmed I looked presentable, and dashed back out to grab my phone, my keys, and my purse.

Five minutes after I ended the call with Walker, I was in my car and on my way to him. Surprisingly, I didn't give myself the chance to think about the fact that I was heading into an encounter with Walker. I didn't give myself time to be nervous about it.

The only thought running through my mind was the tortured sound of Walker's voice. My only concern was getting to him so I could fix whatever was wrong. Or, at the very least, I wanted to give him what he needed and offer a distraction.

I made it to Walker's place and rang the doorbell.

Not even thirty seconds later, the door opened. I took one look in his eyes and saw so much pain and anguish there.

I had to fix this for him.

So, I didn't wait for him to invite me inside. I stepped forward, right into his arms, and held on to him.

Walker and I had hugged several times since I'd met him, but there was no doubt in my mind that this one was different. Completely unlike any hug we'd shared to this point.

As I tried to pour every ounce of comfort I had to offer into the hug I gave him, he held on to me like he never wanted to let me go. There were so many ways in which I hoped that would be the case, but now was not the time for me to consider any of that.

Right now, it was all about giving Walker what he needed so he could cope with whatever was in his heart and on his mind.

After sharing an extended hug, Walker loosened his hold on me and allowed me to take a step back.

I looked up at him and saw that he was still suffering, but I also noticed a bit of something else had seeped in.

Relief, maybe?

Unsure if it was the right thing to do but knowing I made a promise to him, I asked, "So, how's your golf game?"

A crease instantly formed between his brows. "Pardon?"

"Not the real golf," I clarified. "The miniature kind. Are you any good?"

The relief settled in his eyes and he let a little bit of light in, too. "I'm pretty good," he answered.

I glanced down at his bare feet—feet that I was now realizing were just as sexy as the rest of him—before I said, "Then you better get your sneakers on and see if you can beat me. I don't know if they have professional miniature golf players, but if they did, I think I could make a pretty decent living at it."

Walker chuckled.

Mission accomplished.

"You're a little nuts, you know that?" he teased.

He was teasing me.

Yep, I definitely accomplished what I came here to do.

"Maybe," I replied. "But I know you're too curious to not see if you've got what it takes to beat me."

Cocking an eyebrow, he countered, "Maybe I'm worried about showing you up and making you feel bad about your skills."

I narrowed my eyes playfully. "And yet you're the one still standing there with bare feet," I noted.

With a smile tugging at the corners of his mouth, Walker shook his head at me. "You're something else," he muttered as he turned and walked away.

I closed the door and took a few steps deeper into the house. While Walker went to get his sneakers on, I took a look around. I didn't go snooping or anything. In fact, I didn't get much beyond the foyer and into the great room. It was large, inviting, and cozy. I had to wonder if Walker's mom had a hand in helping him decorate because while the style was all Walker, he just didn't strike me as the decorating type.

I would have likely continued my perusal of the space, but my eyes landed on a picture frame on the mantle over the fireplace. I moved toward it and stared. It was a picture of Walker with his mom, dad, and brother. They were all smiling, looking happy and content. I began wondering how long ago the photo had been taken and if they'd ever all feel that happy again.

"Were you busy?"

My head flew up and to the left as my hand went to my chest. "Oh, gosh, you scared me," I said, feeling my heart pounding.

"Sorry," he returned.

I brushed it off. "It's okay."

Walker assessed me a moment before he pressed, "So, were you?"

"Busy?" I replied.

He dipped his chin.

"I mean, I was working, but it's probably a good thing I took a break," I shared. "I'm in the middle of making a hundred and fifty custom invitations."

Surprise washed over him. "What?"

I let out a laugh as I moved toward him and explained, "I don't know if you remember when we had lunch at the café a few months ago and I told you about how I made custom holiday cards."

"I do."

He did!

Unable to stop the grin from spreading across my face at his declaration, I tried to remain cool. So, I went on, "Right, well, someone had seen those and ended up reaching out to me. She wanted to know if I'd make custom wedding invitations for her. So, after we went back and forth a few times discussing what she wanted, I ended up giving her a couple of options. She chose the one she liked, and now I'm about sixty invitations into the project. Technically speaking, I guess I'm not quite in the middle just yet, but I'm close."

"That sounds like an insane amount of work," Walker declared.

One of my brows shot up, and I asked, "Wasn't it you a few minutes ago who said that I was a little nuts?"

"Fair point," he replied, letting out a chuckle. After searching my face briefly, he asked, "Are you ready to go?"

"I'm ready if you're ready."

Fifteen minutes later—following a brief showdown in Walker's driveway about who was going to drive, which I ended up winning—I pulled into the parking lot at the miniature golf course in town.

After I parked, we got out and walked up to the hut to pay for our game and get our balls and putters.

"I'm paying for this," Walker announced.

"But it was my idea," I told him.

"I don't care," he replied.

"And you bought lunch the last time we were together," I argued.

"I still don't care," he informed me. "You answered my call today, Sadie. Not only that, but you didn't waste a second in getting to my place. I'm paying for miniature golf."

I sighed. I decided to quit arguing with him. It was clear he wasn't going to budge. And since I'd managed to shift his mood to a good place and didn't want to undo any of that, I gave in.

The next thing I knew, Walker and I were halfway through the eighteen hole course, and he was totally kicking my ass.

"I cannot believe this," I muttered as we moved to the tenth hole.

"I'm waiting," Walker responded.

"For what?" I asked.

He laughed. "For the professional miniature golf player to join me."

I snarled at him. I mean, I was happy he seemed to be having a good time, but this was embarrassing. I'd gone on and on about how great I was, and this had turned out to be my worst game of golf ever.

"When was the last time you played?" I questioned him.

Still wearing a smile, he shrugged. "I don't know. Maybe two or three years ago."

My eyes widened in surprise. "You're joking."

Walker shook his head. "I am not."

I huffed as I placed my ball down at the beginning of the tenth course. "This is hopeless at this point," I grumbled.

"You still have the whole second half of the course," he pointed out.

I cocked an eyebrow. "And you think I'm just going to magically turn it around for the second half?" I retorted. "Let me guess. You think that I've just been letting you win all these rounds to make you feel good, don't you?"

"If that's the case and this is your reaction, then I've got to say that you're in the wrong business," he began. "You should be acting if this is all just about you trying to make me not feel so bad about my game because your disappointment is beyond convincing."

"I'll have to keep that in mind," I told him as I hit the ball and took my turn.

Walker and I kept it lighthearted and fun for the rest of the game, and much to my dismay, things did not improve in my game. But Walker's state of mind seemed to have improved drastically, so I was happy about that.

In the end, even if I didn't manage to show Walker just how good my miniature golfing skills were, I still had a great time with him.

Well before I was ready for it, I was pulling into Walker's driveway.

When I came to a stop, he looked over at me and said, "Thank you, Sadie."

"You're welcome, Walker."

"I mean it," he maintained. "I don't think you realize just

how much I needed this today. I appreciate you giving this to me."

"I told you I would," I reminded him. "And I won't hesitate to do it again."

"It means a lot to me, but I have to admit, you surprised me," he returned.

"How so?"

For the first time since things turned around with Walker's mood, I noticed a bit of the sadness creeping back in. "You didn't ask," he said.

My brows pulled together. "I didn't ask what?"

"You didn't ask what was going on or why I called," he clarified.

Tipping my head to the side. "That would have meant that I lied," I told him.

"Lied?" he repeated.

"Walker, I offered to be a good friend to you," I began. "I told you I was willing to listen if you wanted to talk or that I was willing to offer a distraction when you needed it. You called me today and asked me if that offer still stood because you needed a distraction. So, I did what I told you I would do and offered a distraction. Being here to support you through what you're dealing with doesn't have conditions. I'm not here to take things from you that you don't want or aren't prepared to share."

No sooner did I get that out when Walker's features softened and his expression warmed. There was a lengthy pause before he shared, "It's hitting me."

I didn't know for sure what that meant, but I had a pretty good idea of where this might be heading. "Something with your mom?" I guessed.

Walker nodded and looked away from me and out the front windshield. "I visited her last night," he started, his voice a deep rasp. "She's had good days and bad days ever since we learned of her diagnosis, and while it's always been in the back of my mind, I think it was easy to ignore what I couldn't see."

My heart broke for him, and I didn't even know what pushed him to call me just yet. I wouldn't come right out and ask Walker about his mother unless he indicated he wanted to discuss what was going on with her. Since he seemed interested in getting this off his chest, I asked, "What happened last night?"

"She was having a hard day," he began again. "And I've been there for some of those before, but this one was different. She just... there's some noticeable physical changes now, and they're making the reality of the situation a little too real."

"I'm really sorry, Walker," I lamented. "I can't imagine how hard this must be for you. I take it you two are close."

"Yeah," he confirmed. "She's the reason I got into music. She's taught me so much, and she's always supported my dreams."

"I'm sure she's incredibly proud of you and everything you've accomplished," I noted.

"She is. Lani Rhodes is beyond ecstatic about all of it. It's just really hard to imagine realizing any more success without her around to see it."

Not thinking about what I was doing, only focused on providing him some comfort, I assured him, "Something tells me she won't be missing out on any of it, Walker. She's your mom; she's always going to be around."

"Yeah," he agreed quietly. Following an extended silence, he turned his attention back to me and said, "I should probably let you go."

"Are you going to be okay?" I asked.

He nodded as he brought his free hand over and rested it on top of mine. Warmth spread through me at his touch. He squeezed and said, "I'm really grateful for what you did for me today, Sadie."

"Anytime, Walker," I rasped, trying not to freak out about his hand on mine.

He gave me one more squeeze before removing his hand and opening the door to get out. I sat there and watched as he shifted in the seat and swung his leg out the open door. Once he was standing outside it, he bent down and looked back at me. "See you later."

"Later," I returned.

With that, Walker stood and closed the door. Then he walked away from my car and toward his front door.

His whole demeanor had changed. He wasn't the carefree man that he'd been when we were out golfing. I had to believe that talking about his mom had turned his mood.

He was nearly to the walkway that led to his front door when I made a split-second decision. With my car in park, I didn't turn it off. I simply got out and shouted, "Hey, Walker!"

Walker froze in his tracks, turned, and looked back at me. I was already moving, running toward him.

The confusion grew on his face, but I didn't care. I wanted to give him one last thing.

I charged toward him and only stopped when my body collided with his, my arms going around his neck and my chest pressed tight to his. Walker brought his arms around me and hugged me back.

We held on to each other for a long time before loosening our holds on one another. When we did, Walker didn't let me go. He kept his hands settled at my lower back and asked, "What was that for?"

I smiled at him as I brought a hand to the side of his face where I cupped his cheek. Stroking my thumb gently over the apple of his cheek, I rasped, "I thought you needed a hug."

His arms tightened. "You're so incredibly sweet, Sadie."

And you're so incredibly handsome, I thought.

"Did it help?" I asked.

He grinned. "Yeah, it definitely helped."

I grinned back. "Good."

Just then, my attention was pulled away from Walker's face to the street, where a car had slowed down as it passed in front of his house. Walker's hands immediately fell away from me, and his body tensed.

The sweet moment we had between us was gone as the car suddenly took off quickly down the road.

"You should probably go," Walker urged.

Right.

That was that.

"Yeah, right, okay. Take care, Walker."

"You too, Sadie."

At that, I turned and walked away. And as I did, I did it thinking that I was the one who needed the hug now.

CHAPTER 5

Walker

ABUZZING SOUND FILLED THE AIR AROUND ME.

Except for that sound, there was no other noise in the house.

I'd woken up about an hour ago and was now doing my best to go on with my day like everything was the same.

It wasn't.

Nothing was the same, and I hated everything about that fact.

I'd tried so hard not to call her, not to reach out, but I couldn't hold myself back any longer. Ever since that day I sat with her in the café, I resisted the overwhelming urge I had to give in to the temptation to call her and ask her out on a date. I had wanted to see her again so badly.

By some miracle, I managed to focus on my music and my mom, and over time, it got easier to stay away from Sadie.

But it was still incredibly difficult.

And the minute things got tough, the moment I saw just how much my mom had been covering up precisely what she'd been dealing with, the only person that came to my mind was Sadie.

When I could no longer hold myself back and made that call, she didn't hesitate to jump into action for me. The way she did it, giving me exactly what I needed, was far more than I probably deserved.

I mean, on one hand, I genuinely needed the distraction to get my mind off things with my mom. But on the other hand, I couldn't lie to myself. She was my best friend's younger sister, and I was beyond attracted to her.

I had to stop.

I had to stop because if I didn't, there was no doubt I'd end up in a place I'd never want to come back from.

That had been my main goal when I woke up this morning. Figure out how to resist Sadie Emerson.

That wasn't going to be easy, not in any case, but especially not when I lifted my phone off the counter and saw a text from her.

Sadie: Good morning, Walker. I just wanted to check in and see how you were doing this morning.

It was so effortless for her. I admired Sadie for her incredible ability to just give so much of herself to someone she barely knew. Even if we knew each other much better now than we did months ago when we first met, we still hadn't scratched the surface. I knew there was far more to learn about her.

And I loved knowing that she was thinking about me. It made me feel a little less crazy about the fact that I couldn't stop thinking about her.

Me: Good morning, Sadie. I'm doing okay this morning. Thanks for asking.

Almost instantly, there was a response. I liked knowing she'd been holding on to her phone after she sent that text in hopes that I would reply quickly.

Sadie: I'm so glad to hear that.

A smart man would have let it go there. A smart man

wouldn't have pushed for anything else. Sadie was simply trying to be a good friend by checking in on a friend in need.

I was a friend in need alright. I just hadn't exactly communicated all the ways in which I needed her.

I wondered how she did it. How could she light up my world the way she did when everything else seemed so dark? She helped me to feel better in ways that even my music couldn't help.

And for that reason, I didn't care about being a smart man.

Me: Have you recovered?

Sadie: Recovered? From what?

Me: The devastating loss yesterday. All that talk about how great you were at mini golf, I was sure you'd kick my ass.

The corners of my mouth twitched as I thought about how much she'd talked herself up yesterday.

Sadie: Ugh. Don't remind me. I'm actually going to have to go back and practice. Then I'll be ready for a rematch.

Don't do it, Walker, I thought.

I didn't listen to the voice in my head.

Me: I could help you practice, maybe give you some pointers.

Sadie: That's the thing. I'm actually good at it! I don't know what happened yesterday.

I didn't know why we were discussing this. It was probably the most pointless conversation. It really did not matter if she was good or not at golf. I kept this going because I just wanted more of her.

Me: I believe you.

Sadie: I hope you mean that.

Me: I do. So, are you getting back on those invitations today?

Sadie: Yep. I have four days left to get them done before I have to mail them to my bride. What about you? Doing anything fun today?

Me: I'm going to head into the studio this afternoon. Might visit my mom afterward.

The moment I hit send on that text, my doorbell rang.

I set the phone down and walked to the door.

The next thing I knew, I was staring at my brother. I should have known this was coming.

"Why did you ring the bell?" I asked as I walked back into the house.

Raid had a key to my place, so it made no sense that he'd stand outside, ring the bell, and wait for me to let him in.

Then again, I knew exactly why he did, which is why I called him out on it.

I heard the front door close as my younger brother answered, "I think the better question to ask is whether or not you have lost your mind."

I made it to the kitchen, turned, and looked back at him. "I have not lost my mind," I assured him.

"Walker, man, you know the reason I didn't come barging in here now is because, despite the empty driveway, I didn't know what I might find. I figured it was best to be cautious. But I know what I saw yesterday."

I knew he knew. He was my brother. It wasn't as though I didn't know it was him the minute I saw his car slow down and eventually drive past my house.

I should have expected nothing less from him. If I thought he was doing something that was bound to land him in a bad spot, I'd wade in. Even still, I didn't like that he was trying to remind me of what I already knew was the case.

"And?" I asked as I lifted a glass of orange juice to my mouth.

"And?" he countered, leaning his hip against the island. "And imagine my surprise when I thought I'd stop by and hang for a bit and talk about what's going on with mom only to see my brother standing outside with his best friend's sister in his arms."

"It's not like that," I told him.

"Do you think I'm stupid?" he asked. "I'm not blind."

I didn't respond.

What was I supposed to do?

I had gotten myself into completely dangerous territory with Sadie, and I had no idea how to get myself out of it. Quite frankly, I wasn't sure I wanted to get out of it.

When too much time passed without a response from me, Raid said, "Walker, if I'm not mistaken, you had a woman standing outside with you yesterday. Not only was she standing there with you, but she was in your arms. She was touching your face like you were the center of her world. I swear to you, nothing would make me happier than to know you had a woman like that in your life. The problem is that I'm relatively certain the woman I saw you with was Sadie. As in Sadie Emerson, Beck Emerson's baby sister."

I wanted to tell Raid that nothing about Sadie screamed baby. She was all woman. Gorgeous. Fun. Sweet. Selfless. Creative.

Instead of telling him that, I confirmed, "Yes, it was her. But it's not what you think it is. That was only the third time I've seen her."

Raid looked at me in disbelief. "Third?" he repeated. "What do you mean it was only the third time? When were the other two?"

I nodded. "There was the day I met her at the party for the band, and there was one other time I'd gone out for lunch about a month ago and saw her already sitting at a table at the café. She had been studying all morning, and we had lunch together. It was friendly. That's it."

"And what was yesterday?" he questioned me.

I took in a deep breath. I trusted Raid with everything. Even if I wholeheartedly believed that everything I'd experienced with Sadie to this point had been completely innocent, I still wasn't sure I'd want Beck to know that she and I had hung out together. But I knew Raid would never, ever share anything like that with Beck or anyone else.

"I called her," I confessed.

"You know, it's strange," he began. "You've stood here for the last few minutes telling me that what I saw yesterday was nothing, and yet, you have her number. Something doesn't add up here. Either you're lying to me or you're lying to yourself."

"She gave it to me a month ago when I saw her at the café," I clarified. "I didn't ask for it, but we talked, it was nice, and she offered it. I wasn't going to say no."

Raid took in the space around us. When he brought his attention back to me, he asked, "Is there anything you would say no to when it comes to her?"

I swallowed hard.

Fuck, I didn't know if there was.

Sadie and I hadn't crossed that line. She was sweet and kind, and she liked to hug. God, I loved it every time she plastered her body to mine. But the bottom line was that I wasn't exactly sure if it was more than just her being who she was that pushed her to do that. It was entirely possible that Sadie was simply an affectionate woman who preferred physical touch and contact to communicate whatever was on her mind.

"I'm not going to cross that line," I assured my brother.

"I'll take that as your confirmation that this is still completely platonic between the two of you," he declared.

I dipped my chin. "It is."

"Why did you call her?" he asked.

I looked away. This was going to be tough. Because in admitting the truth about why I called her, I knew it was going to lead to a conversation about what Raid and I were both facing with regard to our mom.

"I visited Mom the night before," I told him. "She's doing worse."

"And you called Sadie to help you deal with how you feel about that?" he countered.

I nodded.

"You could have called me and not put yourself in this situation," he noted as he moved to the refrigerator and opened the door. "Walker, I don't think this is going to end well. Beck is going to lose his mind."

I could have called Raid. I knew he'd be there to listen the same way I would for him. But the truth was that the two of us would have gotten caught up in all the negative emotions. Raid would have lent a listening ear. He would have given his perspective. What he wouldn't have done is provided the distraction that Sadie had provided.

"I know," I replied. "I know he will, but I couldn't stop myself. Raid, she's… I don't know. She just makes me forget that there's anything bad happening."

He sighed, sitting down at the island after helping himself to a glass of orange juice.

"So this is like that? This is exactly what I thought it was when I saw it outside in front of your house yesterday?" he questioned me.

"No. Yes. I don't know," I answered. "It just feels good to be around her."

He took a sip of his juice, set it down, and stared at me in silence for a long time. "You need to think about this, Walker," he warned. "Before you get in too deep or do something that you're going to regret, take a step back and think about it."

It might have been too late for me to consider getting in too deep. She'd already consumed my thoughts more than I cared to admit. I'd already offered to go golfing with her whenever she wanted.

Yeah, Raid was right in his assessment of my mindset in this situation.

There might not be much of anything I'd say no to when it came to Sadie.

But even if I wanted her as badly as I did, I needed to think about what the outcome of it would be. She was my best friend's sister. Beck and I were in a band together. If it turned out that Sadie had any interest in me the same as I did for her and we took that step, it was safe to assume it could blow up in our faces.

"It's already too late," I admitted.

"Fuck," he hissed.

I couldn't say I didn't agree with his sentiment. That's how all of this felt. When it came to my mom and her cancer, I wanted to scream that word from the top of my lungs. When it came to recognizing that I was starting to like being around Sadie more than I should, I definitely wanted to curse.

Maybe Raid was right. Maybe I needed to take a step back to think about this a bit more.

But how could I?

Was it even possible to separate myself from her now? Every minute I spent around Sadie only stood to make me crave more time with her.

"I don't know what to do," I told Raid. If nothing else, I needed to stop denying what was happening and try to get some sound advice. "I don't want to create problems with Beck or the band, but walking away from her isn't an option."

"How does she feel?" Raid asked.

I shrugged. "We haven't discussed anything like this," I shared. "When I say that it's really all just been friendly, I mean it."

He nodded his understanding. "But you want more?" he pressed.

I hesitated a moment, but I wasn't quite sure why. I wanted Sadie; there was no question in my mind about it. Once I put it out there, even if I was only sharing it with my brother, it was going to become even more real than it already was.

"Yeah," I finally answered. "I do."

Raid sat there for a few seconds as he considered this. "I don't know what to tell you, Walker," he started. "I wish I had an answer that was easy, but I don't. I guess my best advice is to contemplate for a bit about what you really want. If it's her, you should talk to her. If you want her but think it's a bad idea to pursue her, then you might want to try to find a way to pull yourself back from her before this gets any harder. No matter what, I want you to be happy."

I didn't have to contemplate whether I wanted her. I did. It was now just a matter of whether I thought it was worth taking the risk and going after her like I wanted.

"And just to say," Raid started again. "If you want to talk about mom, you know I'm here for you."

Nodding, I confirmed, "I do. I just... I already know how hard it is, and I don't want to put that burden on you."

"Would you want me to keep what I was feeling to myself?" he asked.

I shook my head. "Of course not."

"Then understand that I feel the same."

"I'll try to keep that in mind," I assured him.

Raid assessed me a moment. The silence stretched between us, and I had an inkling that he still wasn't done. He confirmed I was accurate in that assumption when he said, "She's beautiful, Walker. I get it. Just make sure you really think about this. Before you get any closer to her, think about what it could do to you and to her if you tried this out and things went south."

I wanted to avoid thinking about that because the outcome would be disastrous. She could wind up with a broken heart, Beck might hate me, and I might lose both her and the band. None of it would be good.

So, I knew that Raid was right. I had to really think about what I was doing here. Maybe I needed to try to pull back before I brought us both a world of hurt.

Not wanting to allow myself to commit to the idea in front of Raid, knowing I wasn't going to like the way it felt, I decided to go for a change of topic.

"So, you wanted to stop over last night to talk about mom?" I asked.

He nodded.

"How are you holding up?"

He sighed.

And just like that, even though it wasn't an easy discussion, it was better that Raid and I moved on from Sadie. He said all there was to say. I was the one who had to make a choice.

When Raid left just over an hour later, I found my phone. In reading the text, I realized just how difficult this was going to be.

There was a text waiting there from Sadie.

Sadie: I hope it goes well at the studio and your visit with your mom brings you some peace. You know I'm here if you need to talk or want a distraction afterward.

She was the sweetest, most selfless woman I'd ever met.

I wasn't sure I deserved to have a woman like her in my life, especially when I knew that we'd both be taking a huge risk if we crossed that line.

So, as difficult as it was not to, I didn't respond to Sadie's text.

Instead, I got myself ready and made my way to the studio. But that didn't mean I could stop the visions of her from dancing in my mind.

CHAPTER 6

Sadie

"WE JUST NEED ANOTHER HOUR."

"Okay, Beck," I replied. "I'll see you then."

I disconnected the call and got up to get myself ready.

Today was my birthday, and my brother was doing what he did every year. He was taking me out for dinner to celebrate.

I loved spending that time with him, although, I had a feeling that once My Violent Heart really started to tour regularly that he might miss one or two of them. Knowing Beck, he'd be certain to make it up to me.

It had already been a wonderful day today. My mom and I spent the better part of the day together. She treated me to a spa day complete with manicures, pedicures, and massages after she'd taken me out for lunch.

My mom knew Beck and I had sort of had this tradition of going out to dinner together, so she always planned something special for the two of us to do together earlier in the day. Now that I was home, I had been waiting for Beck's call.

He was at the studio today with the band working on their new album. When we made plans, I told him I'd just get myself ready and meet him there because after dinner with him, I was going to be meeting up with Holland.

Holland and I talked regularly ever since we met each other, and we often got together to do something fun. Since her place was closer to the studio than to my apartment, it only made sense for me to meet Beck there. I'd go out with him, he could bring me back afterward, and then I'd head over to meet up with Holland.

It was a great plan, and I was excited for the evening.

There was only one small problem.

I had a feeling I was going to run into Walker.

Normally, that would have been a good thing. I would have looked forward to seeing him in any other case.

But it was different now.

Sometime over the last two months, things had changed. Ever since Walker and I went miniature golfing and I ran into his arms outside of his house, he changed. Initially, I didn't realize it happened. In fact, after texting him the next morning, I had assumed everything was okay between us. The conversation had been lighthearted and fun, so I didn't think twice about it.

Sadly, I hadn't seen Walker since that golf outing.

We remained in touch over the last several weeks; however, nothing about our communication was what I had expected. With the exception of the playful conversation the morning after we went golfing, things felt strained between us… forced.

I hated it.

And I couldn't begin to understand what happened.

Walker was never downright rude or cruel to me, but he definitely wasn't coming across the way he had in the moments I'd been around him. Initially, I had suspected that perhaps it was because we were only texting and I couldn't exactly know for sure what his tone was, but as time went on, it became clear.

Walker seemed to be trying to let me down gently. Whenever I texted him, no matter if I was just trying to check in on him or if I was hoping to offer a distraction for whatever he might have been dealing with, he always responded. But his responses were short and sweet and rarely invited additional conversation.

It hurt.

Unfortunately, there wasn't anything I could do about it. If he wasn't interested in maintaining any sort of friendship with me beyond what we had now, I wasn't going to force it. I knew he was still dealing with his mom's illness. My feelings about how communicative he'd been with me paled in comparison.

So, I was disappointed, but I wasn't going to do anything about it.

Well, other than feel my body become wrought with nerves in anticipation of seeing him, even if only briefly, for the first time in nearly two months.

I'd already had my dress and shoes picked out for the night and had already showered when I got home from my day out with my mom.

So, I made my way into my bathroom and immediately got started on my makeup. After I finished that, I styled my hair. I had a lot of hair, so that ate up most of my time. Ten minutes before I needed to leave, I was slipping my dress on.

I'd never really been one for wearing anything that was super revealing. If the top was more formfitting, I'd make sure the skirt was not. If the dress was short, I'd make sure the top had more coverage. I guess I liked the idea of leaving something to the imagination.

Tonight's blush-colored dress was a fit and flare style. The bodice fit snug to my body, with spaghetti straps and lace detailing on the bust. The skirt of the dress fit loose and flowy and had a small ruffle on the hem. I combined it with a pair of four-inch rose gold stilettos, a pendant necklace, and hoop earrings.

Once I'd gotten everything on, I stood in front of the mirror and checked myself out.

Would Walker like this?

I didn't like that I cared what he might think, but I couldn't seem to help it either. I felt like I'd been crushing on the guy for years, and he didn't seem to be the least bit affected by me.

Not when I touched his arm and not when I hugged him.

I wanted him to take one look at me today and maybe, just maybe, feel the tiniest bit of longing.

On that thought, I snatched up my phone, dropped it into my clutch, and grabbed my keys. A minute later, I was out the door and on my way to meet Beck.

When I pulled into the lot at the studio, I saw all the cars. I didn't know what everyone drove, but I knew how to count. There were enough cars there to account for each member of the band.

I reapplied my lip gloss before I got out of my car.

When I walked in, I heard several muted voices coming from down the hall. That was an indication that Beck had been right. They were finished, and it was likely they were just hanging around and talking to one another.

I made my way down the long corridor to the room I knew I'd find them in when I saw Beck peek his head out into the hall. He saw me, smiled, and stepped completely from the room just as I approached.

"Perfect timing," he said as I came to a stop in front of him. "Happy birthday, Sadie."

Beck gave me a hug and a kiss on the cheek.

"Thanks, Beck."

"Come on in," he urged, jerking his head to the room. "We just finished up."

I stepped inside, and the minute I did, all conversation ceased to exist. This was mostly because Holland charged toward me and bubbled, "Sadie! Happy birthday!"

"Thank you," I returned as she gave me a hug.

When she stepped back, she said, "I love your dress."

"Thanks. It was a little birthday present to myself," I told her.

"It's gorgeous."

Before I could respond to her, Cash invaded our space. My attention went to him. He reached an arm out and said, "Happy birthday, Sadie."

I grinned and thanked him.

That's when it started. A line formed behind Cash. As he stepped away, Roscoe stepped forward to offer birthday wishes before he stated, "If we had known sooner that it was your birthday tonight, we could have all planned to join you to celebrate."

"It's okay," I assured him.

"This is ours," Beck interrupted.

"What?" Killian asked.

"Sadie and I do this every year on her birthday," Beck explained. "I take her out for dinner to celebrate. Just the two of us."

"Okay. So, you could have still done that and we could have all gone out together later," Roscoe suggested.

"Sadie's twenty now," Beck informed him. "That doesn't exactly fit with your typical night out."

Holland took that opportunity to share, "Well, Sadie and I are going out dancing tonight. I'd say you could all join us, but I think we're going to keep this as a girls' night tonight. Maybe another time."

"Well, happy birthday, Sadie," Killian said as he gave me a hug. "Next year, we've got you."

I let out a laugh and replied, "Okay. That sounds like fun."

Just then, Walker stepped forward. For the first time in nearly two months, my eyes connected with his. There was something in them that I couldn't read, and before I had the chance to really memorize the look on his face, he reached out, gave me a one-armed hug, and said, "Happy birthday, Sadie."

This was so different.

So, so different.

He couldn't even bring himself to put both arms around me to hug me. I wanted to burst into tears.

"Thanks, Walker," I rasped.

Awkward.

Awkward and uncomfortable.

He knew it, too, because it was written all over his face.

I didn't understand how we'd gone from being what we were with each other to this. It was beyond upsetting.

"We should get going," Beck said, interrupting all of the thoughts I had about the state of things between Walker and me.

I tore my gaze from Walker, looked at Beck, and agreed, "Okay." Not wanting to be completely rude, I glanced back at the rest of the band and said, "It was wonderful seeing all of you."

They all replied in unison with similar sentiments, so it was hard to make out any individual one. My eyes slid to Holland. "I'll call you when I'm on my way back from dinner."

"Sounds great. See you later, babe," she replied.

Before I turned to walk away, my eyes shifted to Walker. Well, I'd gotten my wish. There was no denying it. The look on his face was filled with longing. When I was home, I thought that it would make me feel good to know that he felt that way.

I quickly realized that wasn't the case.

Because now, all I wanted to do was ask him how he could look at me like that when he'd been making it clear he didn't really want much of anything to do with me.

Instead of doing that, I sighed and turned toward Beck. I smiled at him so he wouldn't think anything was wrong and we walked out. But with each step we took down the hall to leave the studio, I felt my heart breaking for something I didn't understand.

"So, how'd it go today?"

"Really good. We completed a song, which was a huge relief."

I smiled at my brother as we noshed on some warm predinner bread. Ever since we were little, I'd always loved spaghetti. It was my favorite food, so every year on my birthday, Beck always brought me out to an Italian restaurant so I could order spaghetti.

As was customary in every Italian restaurant I'd been to, having bread before and during dinner was a staple.

"That's great news," I replied. "Have you guys been struggling lately?"

"We've had both good and bad days," Beck answered. "Some days, I'm impressed with how well we're doing and everything is coming together, and other days, I wonder how we ever managed to become a successful band because it's going so bad."

Shooting him a sympathetic look, I said, "Well, I think that's all normal. Hopefully you're having more good days than bad days."

Beck nodded. "We are. It just takes time. But we've been torn."

"Why is that?" I asked.

"Well, I'm sure you recall that Walker's mom has cancer," he started as I felt my body tense. After I gave him a nod, he continued, "We are sympathetic to that and want to make sure he has all the time he needs to be with her and cope with that, but on the other hand, he's determined to finish this album before she passes."

My heart broke for him.

I had wanted to be upset and hold a grudge that he'd seemed less than interested in me, but hearing this from Beck, I couldn't help but feel sorrow for what Walker was facing.

"How is she doing?" I questioned him, wanting to know all that I could without being obvious.

"I saw her a couple weeks ago, and…" Beck trailed off.

"And what?" I pressed.

Beck shook his head. "We need to finish this album soon because I don't think she's got a lot of time left."

"Oh, that's awful," I said. Then, because I wanted to make sure he was okay, I asked, "How's Walker handling it?"

My brother shrugged. "I wish I knew," he replied. My stomach sank before Beck added, "I mean, he comes to the studio and does his thing, but he's been incredibly quiet lately. I know it's weighing on his mind, and I can't imagine it's been easy for him at all. But he's tough because he keeps showing up."

It was at that moment I was grateful for bread. As my brother was speaking about Walker, I'd shoved a huge piece of that bread in my mouth. So, when he finished speaking and I didn't immediately respond, I was sure he assumed it was because my mouth was full. The truth was that my heart hurt so much, and I didn't think I could immediately reply without giving myself a minute to grasp what was happening.

When I finally swallowed my bite, I did my best to appear casual and said, "I hope he has someone to talk to if it's affecting him that much. It's got to be so horrible to go through that and not feel like you have a place to unload your emotions or have any sort of distraction. Though, I guess working on the album is providing him with some distraction."

Beck nodded. "Yeah. Walker's always been the quiet one of the bunch of us, but I've seen that side of him more now. He used to go out with us, and he hasn't been out even once since we returned from the tour earlier in the year. That said, we've all made it clear to him that we're there for him if he ever needs to talk. I think he's just trying to figure it out on his own right now."

This was strange to me.

Walker had made it clear to me on more than one occasion that he liked having the distraction from what was going on in his life. If he wasn't talking to anyone in the band about what was going on and they were his best friends, I worried that he might not be talking to anyone.

Of course, he had talked to me about it.

That's when it hit me that perhaps he had someone else he was sharing his feelings with, someone else he was getting distracted by.

No.

No way.

If that were the case, there was no way he would have looked at me the way he did at the studio.

He wasn't reaching out to me any longer for some other reason entirely. With no way to get any real answers, I knew I'd have to simply suck it up and hope he got through it all.

"I can't even imagine what he must be going through," I shared. "Putting myself in his shoes… if you were sick or Mom was sick like that, I don't think I'd survive it."

Beck reached across the table and gave my hand a squeeze. "We're good. Mom is fine, and I'm fine. Today is your birthday. We shouldn't be talking about something so upsetting and depressing."

"I don't mind," I assured him. "I think it's good to remind ourselves of how lucky we are to have one another."

"Yeah, I know. But I don't think that's something we'd ever forget anyway," he noted. "So, tell me what the plan is for tonight. You and Holland are going dancing. Do I need to make an appearance so nobody messes with you?"

I laughed and rolled my eyes. "No," I answered. "We're big girls who are completely capable of taking care of ourselves."

"I know that, but that doesn't mean I won't always worry about you," Beck said.

I cocked an eyebrow. "I always worry about you. Do you think you'd be cool with me raining on your parade when you go out looking for a night of fun?"

Beck's head snapped up. "A night of fun, Sadie? Please tell me I didn't just hear you say that," he begged.

"We're not discussing this," I told him. "But if you must know, the plan is only for Holland and me to go dancing and have a good time. That's it. I promise."

Beck and I were close, and he was super protective of me.

But he didn't need to be so crazy about it.

In fact, not that I *ever* had any intention of telling him this, but I hadn't exactly experienced his version of a night of fun.

Ever.

It wasn't that I'd never kissed a guy, but things never went beyond that.

And considering I'd had a crush on Walker for so long, I hadn't exactly been searching for more with anyone else.

"Alright. Fair enough," he returned just as our server walked up with our meals.

After he'd set them down and confirmed we didn't need anything else, Beck turned the conversation to me. Through piles of spaghetti, we talked about my upcoming final year of school and my goals for my career moving forward.

But if I was honest, I did it all while images of Walker's look of longing danced in my mind.

CHAPTER 7

Walker

I WAS A FOOL.

And I was beyond confused.

I'd made a lot of stupid mistakes in my life, but I always believed that was part of growing and learning. I tried my best now not to make stupid mistakes.

Yet, I had the feeling that if I didn't figure out how to fix what I'd done, I was going to regret this for the rest of my life.

Then again, it was possible that by fixing it the way that I wanted to, I'd end up regretting it anyway.

I'd just left the studio, and my mind was a mess.

Sadie.

It was her birthday, and I had no idea until Beck mentioned it sometime earlier in the afternoon. After she'd dropped everything she had going on to be there for me when I needed her, I felt awful about not even knowing it was her birthday.

Seeing her walk into the studio, seeing her in that dress, it was a wonder I didn't fall to my knees.

God, she was beautiful. And she was nothing but pure class. Sadie would have had every reason to be upset with me and not be cordial, but that wasn't who she was. The minute we locked eyes, I knew she felt the tension between us.

She seemed to be affected by me at least as much as I was affected by her.

There was so much I wanted to say, but it seemed all I could muster up was a halfhearted hug and a birthday wish that was just the same as everyone else's in the room. She deserved better from me, especially after everything she'd done for me.

I let her walk out of there without showing her precisely what I thought about her and what she meant to me.

So, yeah, I was a fool.

And being such, I needed help. I needed advice.

That's why I hopped in my car at the studio and decided to go to the one place I knew I could get that guidance.

In the end, it might not only help me, but it would also likely help her.

My mom.

It was hitting me then that as much as I sometimes needed the distraction from what was happening with my mom that perhaps she needed the same. Maybe talking to her about what I was currently struggling with that was unrelated to her illness would give her something else to focus on, too.

I pulled up outside my parents' house—the same house they'd lived in since we moved to the neighborhood where I met Cash, Beck, and Killian—and saw my dad outside on the lawn mower.

Over the last several months, I hadn't been able to really work out where things were with him. He continued doing the things he always did, and I guess I understood it. He still needed to go to work, someone still needed to take out the trash, and the grass still needed to be cut.

So, he did all the things he always did.

Whenever I stopped by, he generally kept himself busy. Unless, of course, we were having a meal together as a family.

I wasn't sure if he was simply trying to give me time alone with my mom, or if he was constantly aware of the fact that the love of his life was fading and he simply didn't know how to cope with it.

I waved at him as I walked through the open garage door and into the house.

"Hey, Mom," I greeted her when I came face-to-face with her in the kitchen.

"Walker," she replied, a bit of surprise in her tone. "I didn't know you were stopping over today."

Moving toward her, I kissed her cheek before I declared, "Impromptu visit. Plus, I wanted to get your advice."

The surprise had moved out of her voice and into her expression. Concern littered her tone when she asked, "My advice? Are you okay?"

I nodded. "Everything is fine," I assured her. "Do you want to go sit down first?"

"Asking me to sit doesn't indicate that everything is fine," my mom informed me.

I let out a laugh and promised, "I'm okay, Mom. I just want to talk to you about something."

She held my gaze for a few seconds and assessed me, clearly trying to confirm whether I was being truthful or not. "Alright, let's go sit," she agreed.

As she turned to walk into the next room, I watched her frail body move. She'd lost a lot of weight in the last few months, and it always hurt to see her wasting away. I tried to tamp down the sadness I felt over that and focus on what drove me here in the first place. Not only did I need that, but I had a feeling my mom needed it, too.

"So, what's going on?" she asked when we were both sitting down.

I hesitated a moment, suddenly realizing I hadn't come up

with a good way to share what I wanted to share. That's why I ended up blurting, "There's this girl—"

My mom audibly gasped as both her hands came up to cover her mouth in a prayer position. Tears instantly formed in her eyes.

"What?" I asked, feeling alarmed as my body grew tense. "What's wrong? Are you alright?"

She nodded slowly. "This is the best news," she rasped.

I relaxed slightly and came to the conclusion that she'd assumed I was officially dating someone. Holding my hand up, I urged, "Don't get ahead of yourself. I'm here because I don't know what to do about this girl I like."

My mom's head tipped to the side. Looking curiously at me, she asked, "What do you mean you don't know what to do? If you like a girl, you ask her to go on a date with you. And I mean that. I know how things are these days, especially in your profession. That might get you what you want in the short term, but it's not likely to work in the long run."

I shook my head and fought the grin threatening to spread across my face. This was why I was here right now. We'd always been close. My mom was never too embarrassed to talk to me about anything under the sun. I could talk to her about absolutely anything, and I knew she'd give me sound advice.

I hated to think that all she thought was that I was using my career to advance my sexual exploits. That said, I couldn't lie and say I hadn't taken advantage of the perks of the job on a few occasions. I just knew that, moving forward, I wasn't exactly excited about continuing with that lifestyle. Especially not if there was a chance I could have Sadie in my life.

"You're misunderstanding the situation," I finally shared.

"Oh," she replied. "Okay. I just… I got excited for a minute there. I'll be quiet. Tell me what's going on with this girl."

"She's incredible," I started. "She's beautiful, talented, and utterly selfless. I met her earlier this year, and I had no intention of pursuing anything with her even though I was attracted to her. But then I ran into her while I was out one afternoon, and something changed. We had lunch together, we talked for a while, and we exchanged numbers. But we didn't ever go out on a date, and I never called her. Or, at least, I didn't call her until one day about two months ago."

I paused a moment, recalling my reason for reaching out to Sadie. I didn't want to let my mom know just how much I was struggling with her being sick.

"I was having a bad day, and I just wanted to talk to her. But the minute she heard my voice, she ordered me to send her my address so she could come to me."

"Did you give it to her?" she asked.

I nodded.

"What happened when she got there?" my mom pressed.

"She took me miniature golfing," I shared.

Something softened in my mom's expression as a smile tugged at the corners of her mouth. "Did you have a good time?" she questioned me, her voice hoarse.

I wasn't quite sure why it seemed she was getting emotional in a good way, so I hesitated to respond. When I realized she wasn't going to let me not answer, I replied, "I had the best time."

A full-blown grin spread across her face, and tears were shining in her eyes. "So, what do you need my help with?" she asked.

"After that day, I stopped reaching out to her," I began. "She has contacted me a few times since then, but I've been very distant, trying my best not to get too deep into a conversation or any situation with her."

Confusion littered my mom's features. "Why would you do such a stupid thing like that?"

"Her name is Sadie."

"Okay? Is that a problem?"

"It is when her last name is Emerson," I answered.

My mom's lips parted in shock. "She's Beck's sister, isn't she?"

I nodded.

"I don't understand," she announced. "Why is this a problem?"

Her curiosity and concern was so genuine. It literally made no sense to her why me having a massive crush on my best friend's little sister would be a problem.

"Beck is very protective of Sadie," I explained.

"And he needs to protect her from you?" she asked, her brows shooting up.

"I don't think so, but I'm not sure he'll see it that way," I reasoned. "Beck took on that role of looking out for Sadie about two seconds after their dad walked out on them. I don't think it'll matter who it is. Plus, it's like you just said. There's a bit of a stigma surrounding rock stars. I'm not sure Beck will take kindly to thinking his sister is just another notch on my bedpost."

"Walker Rhodes, I do not need to even think about how many notches could be on your bedpost," my mom scolded me. "That said, if you like her, want to be with her, and don't want her to be some passing fling, why don't you just prove Beck wrong?"

She made it sound so easy.

I didn't think it was nearly as simple as that. There was no way I could walk up to Beck, tell him I wanted to date his sister, and then expect him to stand by and see how it all worked out. He'd lose his mind.

"How does she feel about this?" my mom wondered, interrupting my thoughts.

"I don't know."

"You don't know?" she repeated.

"Sadie has no idea how I feel," I confessed.

My mom stared at me in silence for several long seconds

before she asked, "What made you come here today to talk about this?"

I swallowed hard. "I saw her for the first time in nearly two months today," I admitted. "It's her birthday, she came to meet Beck at the studio, and I felt awful for not even knowing it was her birthday."

"Oh, Walker," my mom murmured.

"She's so beautiful, Mom," I shared. "And while I won't deny that she's physically gorgeous, that's not what I'm talking about. It's just her. Who she is… she's unlike any woman I've ever known."

Tipping her head to the side once again, my mom smiled at me. "You need to make sure you don't let her get away, Walker," she urged. "If you want my advice, that's the biggest part of it. *Do not* let this woman get away."

She sounded so sure of what she was saying, and she hadn't even met Sadie. Of course, I'd been sitting here communicating how incredible I thought she was, but I didn't expect my mom would make such a quick decision on someone like this.

"I can see you sitting there looking confused," she interrupted my thoughts once more. "Sadie dropped what she was doing because you needed her. That tells me everything I need to know about who this woman is, and I have to tell you that I think you'll be making a huge mistake if you don't figure out how to get past whatever your hang up is with Beck."

"You think I should tell Sadie how I feel?" I asked, still unsure if it was the right thing to do.

"Yes, because whether or not you believe it, she's probably feeling exactly the same way that you do," my mom declared. "If she was just trying to be a good friend, she would have talked with you on the phone. Instead, she came to you, and I think she did that because the feeling you're experiencing is mutual."

I had a slight inkling that she was right. The look in Sadie's eyes today told me that. The look on her face two months ago when she hugged me outside my house communicated that. The way she touched my arm in her car spoke volumes of her feelings.

Maybe I was reading too much into it, but I didn't think I could stomach the possibility that she wasn't into me the same way I was into her.

I began nodding my head, deciding that my mom was right. I couldn't let Sadie get away.

"So, talk to Sadie, and don't worry about Beck?" I asked.

She shook her head. "Talk to Sadie, see how she feels, and then if you two choose to give yourselves a shot, decide together how to approach Beck," she suggested.

"Right. That makes sense," I said.

And it seemed so obvious. But when it came to Sadie, it seemed I had trouble doing anything truly logical.

"Walker?" my mom called.

"Yeah?"

"If it's okay with you, I'd really love to meet her," she said softly. There was an edge of nervousness in her tone. I had a feeling it had to do with the fact that my mom wasn't entirely sure how much time she had left. If I happened to find someone who made me happy, it only made sense she'd want me to introduce her to that woman.

"Let me first make sure she doesn't hate me," I advised. "If we can get to a good place, I'd love for you to meet her."

Before my mom could respond, we heard the door open. A moment later, my dad was standing in front of us.

"What's going on?" he asked.

"Walker has met someone," my mom answered.

My dad directed his attention to me, and something strange washed over his face before he replied, "Really?"

"It's Beck Emerson's younger sister," my mom added.

My dad still hadn't taken his eyes off me. "Is that wise?"

"Of course, it is," my mom insisted.

CLOSER

For the first time since he entered the room, my dad focused his gaze on his wife, something moved through him, and he sighed, "Right. I'm going to grab a shower, and then we'll eat dinner. Walker, are you staying to eat with us?"

I wanted to reach out to Sadie right away, but I knew she was out for dinner with Beck. I didn't want to risk contacting her when she was with him, so there was no reason I couldn't stay with my parents for dinner.

"Sure, I'll stay," I responded.

My mom's face lit up, and my dad gave me a nod.

With that, he took off toward the bathroom to grab a shower. I sat there contemplating the best way to approach this situation with Sadie.

By the time I left my parents' place later that evening, it was safe to say I was going to have to wing it because I hadn't figured anything out.

CHAPTER 8

Sadie

I T HAPPENED AFTER DINNER WITH BECK.

It was after being out dancing with Holland to celebrate my birthday for a few hours.

And it wasn't until after I got home and looked at my phone
before I was ready to crawl into bed for the night.

There it was.

Something I'd longed to see for nearly two full months.

A text from Walker Rhodes. A text sent a few hours ago. A
text that was the beginning of a conversation initiated by him.

**Walker: Happy birthday, Sadie. I really hope you enjoyed
yourself today.**

I didn't know what to do.

Part of me wanted to immediately text him back and respond like everything was normal. But in doing that, I'd get my
hopes up. I'd start to wonder if perhaps seeing me again made
him rethink things.

The other part of me didn't want to say anything to him tonight. That part of me wanted to make him wait until sometime
tomorrow afternoon to receive a one-word response from me.

That was the part of me that didn't want to admit how much it hurt that the crush I had on him wasn't reciprocated.

But when it all boiled down to it and I took a moment to really think about it, I knew I wouldn't be able to follow through on the negative reaction. It just wasn't me, especially when I knew that he was also dealing with something that I couldn't begin to comprehend.

So, I took in a deep breath and tapped out a reply.

Me: Thank you, Walker. I had a wonderful birthday today.

It had been hours since he sent his original text. I didn't want to make assumptions about how he was spending his night, but it was late. I wasn't expecting a response to my reply tonight. On that thought, I set my phone on the nightstand, curled up under my covers, and reached out to turn off my light.

Just as I closed my eyes, my phone buzzed on the nightstand.

My eyes shot open in the dark, and for a moment, I remained still.

Was I imagining this?

I wasn't entirely sure I'd gotten over the fact that things had been strained for the last few weeks with Walker and that I'd wanted them to return to normal. So, at this point, it was completely possible that I'd imagined my phone buzzed with a response from him.

But because I was desperate to confirm my suspicions, I reached out for my phone and lifted it up.

Sure enough, there was a response from Walker there.

Walker: I'm happy to hear that. I know it's late, but I wanted to know if there was any chance we could get together tomorrow to talk.

Walker wanted to talk.

He wanted to *get together* and talk.

I didn't know what he'd say. I had no idea where this was

coming from. But what I did know was that I was entirely too curious not to agree to get together with him tomorrow.

And since I'd already made a decision not to play games, because that just wasn't who I was, I did not delay in communicating my response to Walker.

Me: I'm free tomorrow. Can you meet in the afternoon?

Walker: This is important, so I'll make any time that works for you work for me.

Me: Important?

Suffice it to say, I was starting to feel a bit nervous. Knowing he wanted to talk was one thing. Having him admit that this was important was something else altogether. I didn't think I could handle the anticipation, and I'd probably stay up all night worrying about it.

My phone buzzed in my hand.

Walker: I promise it's nothing bad. But it's not something I want to share via text message if that's okay.

Ignoring all my nerves, pretending I wasn't the least bit concerned, I tapped out a quick response.

Me: That's totally okay. Do you want to meet here at my apartment?

Walker: If you text me the address, I'll get there around one in the afternoon. Does that work?

I didn't think I could wait that long.

Me: Could you make it a half hour sooner?

Walker: Sure. I'll see you then. And thank you for agreeing.

Me: No problem. See you tomorrow.

With that, I sent him one additional text with my address. Then I put my phone back down on the nightstand and did my best to get some sleep.

I hadn't sat still all day long.

And for the last thirty minutes, I'd been pacing.

Walker was supposed to be arriving at any moment now, and it was as though I was losing my mind.

Question after question ran through my head. What was this about? What did he want?

He said that it wasn't anything bad, but gave no indication that it was good either. I mean, couldn't he have shared just a small clue of what it was about last night?

Was it because the meeting between us yesterday in the studio had been so awkward? Maybe he wanted to simply clear the air and make sure we didn't ever experience anything like that again.

It was crazy because I didn't even understand how or, more importantly, why we got to that point.

Things had gone from being effortlessly easy between us to uncomfortable and tense. And I couldn't pinpoint where it all went wrong.

As much as I wanted answers and believed I'd get them today, I was also dreading it. Walker's assurance that this wasn't going to be bad was doing nothing to help calm me down.

A knock came at the door, and I froze.

Whether I was ready for it or not, it seemed as though I no longer had any choice. It was about to happen, and I was just going to have to suck it up.

No matter how awkward.

After taking in two settling breaths, I moved to the door and opened it.

My eyes connected with Walker's and there was an immediate, unspoken exchange between us. The only problem was that while I was silently pleading with him not to let this get uncomfortable, I wasn't entirely sure he was trying to convey the same message to me. The problem was, I didn't exactly know what he was saying. Walker looked like he was the very definition of cool and composed.

"Hi," I rasped as I stepped back slightly to allow him to come inside.

"Hey," he returned as he stepped forward. His eyes roamed over my face, and I watched as something moved through them.

About to break from the pressure I felt being under his intense scrutiny, I started to walk away from the door and into the living room. When we made it there, I asked, "Can I get you anything? A drink or—"

"I'm okay, Sadie," he insisted, cutting me off. "I'm actually getting the distinct feeling I should have given you some indication last night what this was about."

"Why is that?" I questioned him.

He chuckled and replied, "You're a nervous wreck right now."

He was laughing. That was a good thing, wasn't it?

"Um, well, yeah," I confirmed as we both sat down on the couch. Walker was on one end; I was on the other. But where he kept his feet planted on the floor in front of the couch, I turned my body so my back was against the armrest and my knees were pulled up to my chest.

"I owe you an apology," he declared.

"I'm sorry?"

Shaking his head as the corners of his mouth twitched, Walker said, "No, I'm sorry."

"Why are you apologizing to me?" I asked.

This was a complete turn of events. I had no idea what I thought was going to happen here today, but this was definitely not it.

Walker let out a sigh. "I like you, Sadie," he started, and my body immediately tensed. "I've liked you since the day I met you. And after getting to know you a bit, especially after you showed up at my place about two months ago to offer me a distraction from my thoughts about my mom getting sicker, that attraction to you only grew deeper."

My lips parted.

Nope.

I didn't expect this at all.

And because I hadn't anticipated any of what he was saying, I couldn't seem to come up with a reply.

Luckily, I didn't need to because Walker added, "I've been purposely trying to distance myself from you ever since you left my place that day."

"Why?" I asked, feeling hurt slice through me. If he liked me, why wouldn't he have told me about it months ago?

Walker shot me an incredulous look. "Are you serious?" he countered.

My eyes widened and darted back and forth. Was it supposed to be obvious? "Um, yeah," I replied, drawing it out so it sounded like more of a question rather than an answer.

"Sadie, Beck will lose his mind," Walker shared.

Okay.

He had a point.

A valid one.

But I was inclined to believe that he hadn't recently spoken with Beck and gotten the all clear from him.

"So, what changed?" I asked.

Walker didn't hesitate to respond. "I saw you yesterday," he declared.

I cocked an eyebrow. "You saw me yesterday," I repeated.

He nodded. "Yes. I saw you and realized just how much I've missed you," he started. "I thought you looked beautiful, and I wanted nothing more than to drag you out of there. But I didn't because among other things, it was awkward between us. And it was awkward because I made it that way."

He wanted to drag me out of there.

I bit my lip, trying to figure out how to respond. It was

difficult, though. Because all I could think about was what might have happened if Walker had dragged me out of the studio. And I wondered if he still wanted to do that. A shiver ran through me at the thought.

"So, you like me," I said.

It wasn't a question, but Walker confirmed he did when he returned, "I do, Sadie. Very much."

I nodded slowly as I tried to digest the fact that the man I'd had a crush on for years had just admitted he liked me too.

After I licked my lips and belatedly noticed his eyes drop to my mouth, I asked, "What now?"

Once again, Walker did not hesitate. "That's entirely up to you," he claimed. "I don't know where you stand or how you feel, but I decided I didn't want to go another day without telling you where I stood. If you feel the same, I'd like to explore this between us. If the feeling isn't mutual, I understand. And if that's the case, I hope we can at least get back on track and remain friends."

I stared at him.

Unmoving.

Was this it? Was it really happening?

Walker wanted to explore this between us. I wanted to jump for joy, but I couldn't. My mind and my body were evidently too stunned to do much of anything.

After several long moments, moments where I started to see the tiniest bit of doubt and worry creeping into Walker's face, I spoke. My voice was hushed as I shared, "I've had a crush on you since I was fifteen."

Walker's head jerked back in surprise as he narrowed his eyes on me. "What?"

"For nearly five years now, I've been insanely attracted to you," I told him.

"Come here," he demanded.

I didn't move. Why did he want me there? Why did he sound so different?

His voice had dropped several octaves as he made his order. Hearing it did nothing to help my mind or my body regain any of the function that had already fled.

When I made no move to go there, Walker commanded, "Sadie, come here."

The way he said it, I couldn't not go.

I didn't know where it came from—perhaps it was from the look in his eyes, the sound of his voice, or the fact that I'd do anything to be closer to him—but I wasted no more time. I moved across the couch toward him.

The second I was within touching distance, Walker reached out and hauled me up against him. He drove one hand into my hair at the side of my head until his fingertips reached the back of my skull. With his face inches away from mine, his rough voice demanded, "Are we going to do this?"

I couldn't think.

His mouth was *this close* to mine. It was making it impossible to concentrate.

"Sadie." His voice was pleading with me. "Are we going to do this?"

"Yes," I whispered.

His fingers pressed into the back of my head as his arm around my waist got tighter. "You understand this could get sticky with your brother, right?" he pressed. The tone of his voice was bordering on the edge of something. Desperation, maybe?

I nodded.

"Kiss me," he demanded softly.

Kiss him.

Walker Rhodes wanted me to kiss him.

My eyes dropped to his gorgeous lips.

Oh God.

What was I going to do?

What if… what if I failed miserably at this?

My experience was limited. Very limited. I'd kissed a few guys before, but that was the extent of it. One thing about having an overprotective brother was that finding someone willing to take me on a date didn't happen very often. And when I realized that anyone who had been willing to take me only for one reason or that they just didn't measure up to be the kind of guy I thought I deserved, I quickly moved on.

So, kissing was the extent of my very limited experience.

What if Walker hated the way I kissed?

"Sadie," Walker called.

I lifted my gaze to his.

Once he had my attention, he urged, "Kiss me, sunshine."

At that, all my worries flew out the window. I leaned forward and brushed my lips against Walker's. Tingles shot through my body seconds before he claimed my mouth and kissed me back.

For the first few moments, I tried to take it all in. Walker's lips were soft and framed by his full beard. One of my hands reached up to the side of his face, some fingers landing on his bare cheeks and the others in the coarse hair.

Warmth and heat and desire flowed through my veins. My breasts grew heavy as I craved more of him.

The tip of Walker's tongue came out to touch my lips in a silent demand to gain access to my mouth. I willingly parted my lips and moaned the very second his tongue slid inside.

Walker's arm tightened around my waist, leaving no space between us. And yet, it still wasn't enough. I wanted more. Needed it.

I swung a leg out and over him. My thighs were straddling him, and beneath me I could feel the evidence of what our make-out session was doing to him.

He wasn't lying.

CLOSER

He liked me. Very much.

I didn't know if it was the right thing to do, but my body was demanding I do it. So, I rolled my hips over him.

Walker groaned as his hand on the arm that had been wrapped around my waist drifted down and over my ass. He squeezed me there, forcing a moan out from somewhere deep inside me.

It was incredible. He was magnificent. And he tasted amazing.

This was all better than I could have ever imagined it would be. Considering I'd done a lot of imagining for nearly five years, that was saying something.

Long before I wanted it to stop, Walker tugged gently on my hair and separated his mouth from mine. Seconds passed as we stared into each other's eyes, breathing heavily.

"We're doing this," Walker declared.

"Yeah," I agreed, knowing there was no way I was going to deny myself having more of what we just had.

"What are your plans for the rest of the day?" he asked.

"I didn't make any," I informed him.

Walker grinned at me, and I swear I felt the effects of that right between my legs. He tugged back on my hair, tilting my chin up to expose my throat, and leaned forward. Then he began to lick and kiss me along my neck and the front of my throat. It was all I could do not to squirm right off his lap.

"Walker," I breathed.

He stopped, pulled back, and looked up at me.

Worried that I'd done something wrong, I asked, "Is… is everything okay?"

He smiled again and nodded. "Yeah, I just didn't realize how much I'd like hearing you say my name like that."

"I've said your name before," I noted.

Walker chuckled. "Not when I've had my mouth on you,

not when you were sitting on my lap, and definitely not with your voice sounding like that," he returned.

"Oh."

For the next few seconds, Walker sat there looking at me. I remained silent because this was not something I could take the lead on. He had to be the one to do it.

Eventually, he made a move. It just wasn't the one I expected.

"Are you ready?" he asked.

"For what?" I replied, nervous that he was already ready for a whole lot more than kissing.

"We're celebrating your birthday today," he announced.

That surprised me.

"We are?" I asked.

"We are," he said, as he started to move. By some miracle, he stood from the couch while keeping me pressed close. After pressing a sweet kiss to my lips, he instructed, "Go get yourself ready, sunshine. I'm taking you out."

For the first time since he'd arrived, I did not hesitate. I pressed up on my toes, kissed the corner of his mouth, and turned to get myself ready.

The afternoon conversation with Walker hadn't gone anything like I had expected, but that didn't mean it was anything less than spectacular.

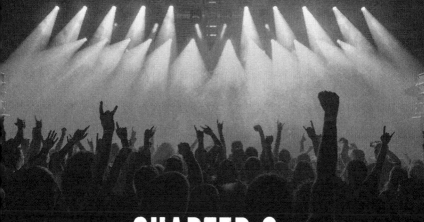

CHAPTER 9

Sadie

"**S**O, WHAT DO YOU THINK WE SHOULD DO?"

I posed the question to Walker, staring at him from across the table at the restaurant he'd brought me out to for lunch, still in a bit of disbelief that I was here with him like this.

It was official. We were exploring this.

And after all these years of me wanting something like this to be my reality, it was actually happening. It was a wonder I could contain my excitement.

We'd just given our drink order to our server, and I thought it was smart to dive right into the biggest issue Walker and I were facing.

"I hadn't really figured it all out yet," Walker replied. "I was thinking we'd have lunch and then you could tell me a bit more about what you like to do so we can come up with something fun to do after we eat."

I let out a laugh.

"What's so funny?" Walker asked, a glimmer in his eyes.

"I wasn't asking you what we should do after lunch," I answered.

"Oh. What were you talking about then?"

I sighed, hating that this even needed to be discussed. "Beck."

Walker lifted his chin in acknowledgment and sat back in his seat. "I wish I had a good solution there, Sadie, but I don't. I really don't know what to do about him. He's the whole reason I held myself back from asking you out on a date the first night I met you."

The reality of that smacked me in the face. Walker and I could have been dating for months now. There was so much I could have learned about him and experienced with him by now. I didn't get that chance because my brother was protective of me and Walker knew it.

"It shouldn't matter," I insisted. "But I know it will, and I hate that."

"What do you think we should do?" Walker asked.

Part of me wanted to throw my hands in the air and say that it didn't matter what Beck thought. I was a grown woman, Walker was a grown man, and we were both capable of making our own decisions. But there was a lot to consider here that went beyond just that.

This wasn't simply a situation where a guy's best friend starts dating his younger sister. This was about Beck stepping into a role that he felt he needed to step into after our father walked out on us when Beck was only six. Of course, I didn't think of Beck as being my dad or anything like that, but he certainly took his role as big brother much more seriously than I imagined he would have if our father had still been around and had not completely abandoned us.

Not only that, but Walker and Beck worked together. And their relationship in their work wasn't simply them being a couple of guys who worked in an office in their own cubicles doing their separate work-related tasks. Their jobs as members of a band required them to work together to create new music. And if something happened to jeopardize their relationship, it would not only affect them, it would also affect Holland, Killian, Cash, and Roscoe, too.

"This isn't just about us," I started. "We have to consider everyone who will be affected by this. Because while it'd be easy to assume that it would just be you, Beck, and me, it's the rest of the band, too."

Walker nodded. "You're absolutely right. So, do you think we should come up with a plan to talk to Beck about it right away, or do you think we should wait a while?"

I honestly wasn't sure what the best option was, so I shrugged and confessed, "I don't know. I mean, you guys are in the middle of recording a new album right now. I can't imagine this would help things."

"No, I can't say that it will either," Walker agreed. "But I don't know how much I like the idea of lying to Beck."

I felt the same. Beck and I were incredibly close, and lying to him would easily put a damper on our relationship with each other.

Our waiter returned with our drinks. Walker and I each gave him our lunch selections before he took off again. That's when I shared my own thoughts about hiding the truth from Beck that Walker and I had decided to explore the attraction we had to one another.

"And it's going to be awful having to sneak around," I added. "You know if the band gets any bigger, it'll become more and more difficult for you and I to do something simple like this without being caught. I can't imagine we're going to enjoy not being able to go out on a date every now and then."

Walker grunted as he set his drink back down on the table. "I want the band to be successful, but I have to think that you and I going out in public together if the band gets bigger is going to be harder whether we tell Beck what's going on or not. I've seen a little bit of that already while we were on tour."

While I was an outgoing and bubbly person around people I knew, the truth was that I was, generally speaking, a relatively private person. That was the reason why I'd started focusing my career efforts in the direction I had. I could do what I loved, have my clients, and keep a relatively low profile. But I hadn't really considered how ending up in a relationship with Walker could change that.

"So, we should tell him?" I asked, though I was still feeling hesitant about it. "That seems like the best option, right?"

Tipping his head to the side and eyeing me curiously, Walker countered, "Do you really want to do that? You seem unsure."

"Well," I began, drawing that single word out. "What if it's unnecessary?"

Walker's brows shot up. "Unnecessary?" he repeated, clearly confused with where I was going with this.

I couldn't say I blamed him. Who in their right mind would be thinking about something like this right off the bat? I didn't want to make it sound like I thought we were doomed from the start—heck, I'd wanted this for years—but what if physical attraction to someone wasn't enough? What if Walker and I spent more time with one another and realized we were better off as friends instead of lovers?

A shiver ran through me at the thought of being Walker's lover. I was getting way ahead of myself.

"You and I don't really know each other that well just yet," I declared. "What if we don't…"

I trailed off and looked down at the table because I didn't exactly like the idea of us not working out.

A moment later, Walker reached across the table and wrapped his hand around mine. He gave me a gentle squeeze, and once I returned my gaze to his, he said softly, "Let's take a step back for a minute. You're making a valid point. We just decided to pursue something with one another about five minutes ago. We don't have to figure this all out today."

I did my best to swallow past the lump that had formed in my throat. "So, you're saying that we shouldn't tell him?" I asked.

"I'm not saying that at all," he assured me. "I just think that you're not wrong when you acknowledge that we don't really know each other that well yet. Relationships are hard enough as it is. It might be smart for us to just keep this between us for right now."

It made the most sense, and I'd brought this point to the table, but I had to wonder if maybe Walker didn't think we'd stand the test of time. Or worse... what if he didn't *want* us to make it?

He was a rock star, after all.

It was no surprise that if and when My Violent Heart became a name in the homes of millions of people all over the world that Walker would have no shortage of women at his disposal.

"Sadie?" Walker called, interrupting my thoughts.

"Yeah?" I returned.

"I really want us to get to a place where it makes sense to tell everyone we love about what we've got between us," he shared. "Let's give ourselves the chance to get to that place without adding any unnecessary obstacles. This way, if we have some adverse reactions, we've got what it takes to come out the other side together."

That made a lot of sense. Not only that, it eased the concerns I had about whether Walker would want this to be some kind of long-term thing. I wasn't necessarily a jealous person by nature, but I wasn't interested in getting into a relationship with someone if that person had no intention of seeing it go somewhere serious.

It was nice to know that Walker wanted to see it get somewhere that we could weather a storm that might come in the form of an older, overprotective brother.

"Okay," I agreed. "I think that's a really great option. There's no sense in getting anyone else involved in what's happening until we're sure we're serious about one another."

Walker let out a soft laugh. "Make no mistake, Sadie," he started. "I am serious about you. This is exclusive for me, and I hope you're of the same mindset."

Did he think I was insinuating I'd be dating other people?

Smiling, I assured him, "I'm serious about you, Walker. And I'm totally cool with this being exclusive."

"Good."

Just then, our waiter returned with our meals. I'd ordered a quinoa salad that was loaded with cucumbers, tomatoes, carrots, bell peppers, and chick peas. Walker had gone for the classic burger and fries.

Once our waiter walked away, Walker asked, "Is this the norm for you?"

My ear dropped toward my shoulder as I shot Walker a questioning look. "Is what the norm?" I wondered.

"Last time we had lunch together you had a sandwich that was about a foot tall filled with vegetables," he reminded me. "Now, you're eating a... what is that supposed to be? A salad? There's no lettuce, but it's all vegetables."

I giggled. "It's a quinoa salad, and it's really good. You know it wouldn't kill you to eat some vegetables that aren't just fried potatoes, right?" I retorted, my gaze dropping to the pile of fries in front of him.

"Oh, I know that, but all I've seen you eat is vegetables like they're candy. I'm just curious if you ever indulge in other stuff," he said.

"You should have seen me last night," I noted.

"For your birthday? What did you do? Have an extra slice of cake?" he questioned me.

I shook my head. "I actually didn't have any cake," I said.

"But every year when Beck takes me out, we always go out to an Italian restaurant because my absolute favorite food is spaghetti."

Walker's brows shot up in surprise. "Spaghetti?"

I nodded. "Spaghetti. And it has to be actual spaghetti. Not fettuccini. Not rotini. Not penne. And not rigatoni. Just spaghetti."

"I never would have guessed that. You're full of surprises."

"How does my favorite food make me full of surprises?" I asked.

Shaking his head slowly with a grin on his face, Walker insisted, "It's not about the food."

"What's it about?"

He hesitated to respond, and I found myself growing tense at what he could possibly be referring to. A moment later, his voice went low, and he asked, "Have you really had a crush on me since you were fifteen?"

I bit my lip at his question. I wondered if he genuinely didn't believe me when I'd shared that information earlier this afternoon or if he simply wanted to hear me admit it again. But then I realized I didn't really care what the reason was, and I confirmed it for him again.

"Yes," I rasped.

His lips formed a smile.

"Do *not* rub this in," I warned him. "It won't bode well for you."

Walker set his burger down, lifted his arms in surrender, and insisted, "I'm not rubbing anything in. I just wanted to confirm I heard you correctly earlier."

I rolled my eyes at him. "You already knew exactly what you heard. You just wanted to hear it again."

Walker sighed. "Alright. It's probably not a good idea to start a relationship with a lie, so I'll admit it. I just wanted to hear you say it again."

Letting out a laugh, I said, "I appreciate the honesty."

"So, what's the plan?" he asked.

"The plan?" I repeated. "I thought we were going to give ourselves some time to get to know each other better before we came up with a plan."

It was Walker's turn to laugh. "It seems we're going to need to learn to communicate better with one another," he began. "I meant your plan for the next couple of weeks. Do you have anything going on with work?"

"Right now, I'm actually on vacation," I told him.

"You're self-employed," he declared.

I nodded. "Yes, I am. But my birthday was yesterday, and I'm about to start my final year of school after this week, so I decided to give myself this week off."

"Did you plan your whole week out already?" Walker asked.

I shook my head. "Nope."

"What are the chances I could spend some of that time with you?" he pressed.

"High," I confirmed without a moment of hesitation.

I didn't care if it made me seem desperate or overly excited. I wanted to spend time with Walker. It was my vacation time, and I had the right to choose however I wanted to spend it.

"Last year of school," he said.

"Yeah," I replied.

"Tell me about your classes you're taking this year," he urged. "Any more of those history of art classes?"

I started laughing, recalling how thoroughly uninteresting my class last semester had been and how Walker had come into that café while I was studying for my final exam in that class.

Once I pulled myself together, I looked at Walker with shining eyes and told him all about what I had to look forward to with my final year at school. He listened intently. And if he thought it was all boring and uninteresting, I never knew it.

Time flew by, and before I knew it we had both finished eating and Walker had paid the bill.

He stood, held his hand out to me, and said, "Let's go."

"Where are we going now?" I asked, placing my hand in his and standing.

"The grocery store," he answered.

Okay. I definitely hadn't been expecting that. What was he up to now?

"Why?" I wondered as Walker led me to the exit.

"We're going to the store so you can pick out your favorite cake mix," he explained. "Then, once I know we've got that, the frosting, all the necessary ingredients, *and* some candles, we're going to go back to either your place or mine so I can bake it for you."

He was going to bake me a birthday cake?

"And you say I'm full of surprises," I mumbled.

At that, Walker stopped just inside the door to the restaurant, looked at me, and smiled. Then he leaned toward me and kissed me on the lips before he finally pushed the door open and led us outside.

Thirty minutes later, we'd returned to my place with a box of strawberry cake mix and vanilla frosting. Walker also insisted on candles. Twenty of them, to be exact. And since he didn't want me to have to wait too long to have cake, Walker decided to make cupcakes.

After he sang to me, which made me wonder why he only ever played the drums, and made me blow out the candles, he lifted a frosted cupcake to my mouth and fed it to me. Then he kissed me where the frosting had gotten on my lip.

Every time he fed me another bite, frosting would end up on my lip. I started to think he was doing it on purpose because he refused to let me lick it off myself.

But if I was being totally honest, I didn't mind. It was the best birthday celebration I could have ever dreamed up.

CHAPTER 10

Sadie

THIS WAS IT.

It had been just over two weeks since Walker and I decided to stop hiding our attraction to one another and take a chance on each other.

And during all that time, I felt like I'd been living on cloud nine. Walker was, by and large, my first real boyfriend. I'd dated before, but nothing ever amounted to anything serious. Nothing ever clicked with anyone else.

For quite some time, I started to wonder if it wasn't simply the fact that I had an overprotective big brother that was the reason for my lack of a love life. I started to think that maybe it was me. Maybe I was being too picky or maybe there was something else that just wasn't right.

Now I knew it wasn't any of that.

Because it had finally clicked for me with Walker Rhodes.

It almost seemed impossible that I could already feel such emotion for a man I'd been officially dating for just over two weeks, but here I was. And I wasn't the least bit upset by it.

The truth was, in the time after we'd decided to take this step with each other, Walker and I had spent a lot of time together. While he still had to go into the studio to work, he made the effort to talk to me every day. We'd seen each other and spent time together all but one day while I was taking my vacation. He'd come to my place, I'd gone to his, and we'd even had a few days out having fun. We even had a miniature golf rematch in which I managed to redeem myself. Of course, now that we were tied, I'd demanded a tie breaker at some point in the future.

Overall, my week off turned out to be far more exciting and eventful than I had originally anticipated. It was the perfect end to my summer.

It was now Friday, and I was at the end of my first week back at school. Just because I was doing that didn't mean that Walker didn't come around. Sure, we didn't spend nearly as much time together, but I still saw him twice this week. I'd stopped by his place one day in between classes since he hadn't yet gone into the studio, and another day, we'd met each other out for lunch.

Mostly, we'd just enjoyed being with one another, doing it while being as discreet as possible, and I found myself falling into a much deeper place with Walker.

So, it was during that lunch earlier this week that I'd made my move. I hadn't made the decision lightly, nor had I done it on a whim. As time went on and I spent more and more time with Walker, it was unavoidable.

Two days ago, I sat across the table from Walker at lunch and asked, "Do you have plans for this weekend?"

"Nothing in particular," he answered. "Why? Did you want to do something?"

I nodded, but I did not share what it was that I wanted to do.

When I made no move to speak, Walker pressed, "What is it?"

It was harder than I thought it would be to tell Walker what I wanted. It wasn't that I was nervous about the actual thing I wanted so much as I was worried that perhaps Walker wouldn't want the same thing.

I mean, I didn't think that was possible. He gave me no reason to believe that would be the case. But it wasn't unlike me to sometimes worry about the worst-case scenario, so that's where my mind was.

"I—" I stopped to clear my throat. I took in a deep breath and rasped, "I wanted to see if maybe you'd like to spend the night with me on Friday."

If I had any doubt about whether Walker would catch on to the underlying meaning behind my request, I no longer did.

The moment I got the words out, Walker's eyes burned into mine. And though I thought I'd go up in flames from the intensity in them, I didn't dare look away from him.

He knew precisely what I wanted.

It had only been a matter of seconds, but it felt like hours before Walker responded. The anticipation had nearly killed me.

When the words left the tip of his tongue, they did so in the slowest, most seductive manner possible. There was no denying the intention in his tone when he replied, "I would absolutely love to spend the night with you on Friday."

Relief swept through me, and the rest of our lunch that day had been one filled with far more knowing glances than ever. It had gotten me excited about what was ahead.

And now I was practically crawling out of my skin with anticipation. It was Friday evening, and I'd gotten home from school several hours ago. I'd dumped my bag and books the minute I entered my apartment, and immediately went about preparing myself for my night with Walker.

I wanted it to be perfect. I'd showered, shaved, slathered on lotion, and made myself look like I cared without having to try too hard. There were no plans to leave my apartment, so I didn't want to overdo it. But since I still wanted to make sure

Walker found me enticing, I put on a T-shirt dress and made my hair look nice.

Now, I was here on the couch with Walker after we'd had dinner, and I didn't know what to do.

We had decided to watch a movie, but I'd genuinely believed that was simply going to be a cover for what we were really going to be doing.

Unfortunately, Walker wasn't making any effort to take things to the next level. He seemed to be entirely content to just sit on the couch and actually watch the movie with my body curled into his.

I'd gotten us this far. I'd given him the invitation to spend the night. He had to be the one to make the next move. I *could not* take the lead on this.

But with him being so close, smelling so good, and feeling so warm beside me, I started to squirm. I'd never wanted anything so badly in my life.

I started to worry that perhaps Walker didn't want this. Or, maybe he was one of those guys who thought things like I wanted right now should only happen in a bed. Believing he wanted to wait until after the movie was over, I figured my best bet was going to be to move to the opposite end of the couch.

As I started to move away, Walker's arm tightened around me.

"You okay?" he asked.

Shit. What was I supposed to say?

"Um, yeah. I... my arm. I mean, my leg was getting stiff," I lied.

Walker's brows knit together, and I had a feeling he knew I hadn't been truthful. But a moment later, he kicked off his sneakers, swung his legs up onto the couch, and suggested, "Let's stretch out then."

What?

Without waiting for me to respond, Walker reached out

for me as he shifted his body on the couch. He was on his side, his back up against the cushions, and he'd settled my body in front of his. Then, with my back flat on the seat of the couch, he draped his arm over my torso, his fingers resting gently on my outer ribs.

"Better?" he asked.

I looked up at him, searched his face, and rasped, "Yeah."

"Good," he replied before directing his attention to the television again.

For the next few minutes, I tried to focus on what was on the screen, but I couldn't concentrate on it.

Why wasn't Walker taking the bait? I was a willing participant. Wasn't that obvious? Didn't the fact that I asked him to spend the night here with me for the first time ever indicate that I didn't have any intentions of sleeping at all tonight?

The next thing I knew, I felt Walker's fingers at my ribs start to stroke back and forth.

That felt nice. I liked that a lot. My body immediately started to relax at the tender caresses as other parts of me buzzed to life at the sensation.

My nipples hardened, and I was certain I'd glance down to find the evidence of that showing beneath my dress. Attempting to do it casually and without Walker noticing, I shifted my gaze in that direction. But before I could confirm what I already knew was the case there, Walker called, "Sadie?"

I tipped my chin up to look at him. The moment our eyes locked, his hand left my ribs and slid up over my breast. I squeezed my legs together and balled my hands into fists. Walker cupped my breast and held it firmly in his hand. Before I could even begin to memorize how good that felt, his thumb swept over my nipple.

That was all it took for me to lose the battle to keep myself composed. My lips parted and a moan escaped.

I didn't have the chance to be mortified because Walker dropped his mouth to mine and kissed me.

Relief.

God, the relief I felt having him kiss me while he kept his hand on my breast was so immense.

For a while, he continued to alternate between gliding his thumb back and forth over my nipple and squeezing my breast while his mouth devoured mine.

But eventually, as his tongue plundered the warm recesses of my mouth, his hand began to drift down my body toward my hip. He made it there and gripped it tightly before moving on.

I couldn't stop pressing my legs together as desire pulsed in my veins.

I hadn't even started to get used to the feeling of any part of what was happening when I felt Walker's fingertips brush gently over the bare skin of my thigh.

I whimpered in his mouth. And while I couldn't be certain, I had to imagine it was a good thing that he groaned in response. Sadly, I had no idea what made that happen since my hands hadn't been in any naughty places. One was resting at the side of his neck while the other was wedged between our bodies. I was a bit out of sorts as I tried to focus on the pleasure I felt from all the wonderful things Walker was doing to me while trying to figure out what I could do for him.

I wanted to hear him groan like that again. I wanted him to feel even just a small fraction of what I was feeling at that moment.

Any thoughts I could conjure up about what I should be doing went out the window the second I felt my dress gliding up my legs.

This was happening.

It was actually happening.

I was excited, ready, and scared shitless all at the same time.

But this was Walker. I knew he knew what he was doing. He'd make this good, right?

He pushed my dress up to expose my panties, and when his fingertips were resting just above the lace edge of them, he pulled his mouth from mine. Walker stared down at me as he slipped his fingers beneath the lace and moved down to my vagina.

My legs were still pressed together, so he asked gently, "Can you spread your legs for me, baby?"

Walker Rhodes had just asked me to spread my legs. I was convinced I'd died and gone to heaven.

My insides were trembling with nerves, but I parted my legs.

Walker did not delay. He slipped his fingers between them and groaned again. "Fuck, Sadie, you're so wet."

I was.

And hearing him groan like that again seconds after telling me to spread my legs only served to make me wetter.

Of course, he also started to rub his fingers against me, so that was helping things a lot, too.

It was amazing. Better than anything I'd ever done to myself.

"Walker," I breathed.

The look in his eyes intensified and his fingers continued to assault my sensitive clit. I edged closer and closer to the point of no return, my breathing becoming more and more shallow, until suddenly, Walker was no longer rubbing against me. Two of his fingers dipped lower and pushed inside my body.

I cried out at the unexpected invasion, and Walker's body went completely solid.

"Are you okay?" he asked, his tone sounding horrified.

I was instantly mortified. My eyes widened, and I started to feel my nails dig into the skin of my palm in the hand that was wedged between my body and Walker's.

"Sadie, talk to me," he demanded.

"I'm… I'm okay," I told him. Physically speaking, I was fine now. Emotionally, I was feeling nothing but humiliation.

I wanted to run and hide and bury my face anywhere that Walker wouldn't see me. But I couldn't because something washed over his face.

"Are you… Sadie, is there something I should know?" he asked, his voice a deep rasp.

I was horrified, and now my breathing was shallow for a completely different reason. I was certain I'd burst into tears at any moment. Considering Walker's fingers were still inside me, I didn't think that was a wise move.

So, I whispered, "I might not have much experience."

"What exactly do you mean by that?" he pressed.

I swallowed hard and closed my eyes. When I opened them again, I confessed, "I might not have any."

"Shit," he hissed. "Sadie, baby, you can't be serious."

Oh God.

What was he thinking now? Was he angry? Was he… was he turned off by this news?

"I am," I rasped, looking away from him.

Walker pulled his fingers from my body and brought his hand to my hip. "Look at me, sunshine," he urged.

I didn't know if I could. I was too afraid of what I might see.

The pads of his fingers pressed in, a silent plea to honor his request. By some miracle, I brought my attention back to his face. I was surprised by what I saw.

Warmth filled his expression, and the corners of his eyes had crinkled in a way that felt like he was telling me everything was going to be okay. As much as I wanted to believe that, it wasn't until he spoke that I actually accepted it as the truth.

"This is beautiful," he told me. "Do not feel embarrassed by this at all."

"But now instead of doing all that stuff, we're doing this," I noted.

"Sadie, trust me when I tell you that we'll get to all that stuff," he replied. "This is something we should talk about first. It's important."

"It's been twenty years, Walker. I think I know that," I said.

He smiled and shook his head. "That's not what I mean. I'm saying that I want to make sure you're ready to take this step."

"What makes you think that I'm not?" I asked.

"It all makes sense now, but I was slightly concerned before," he started. "The other day you asked me to spend the night with you tonight. I did not miss what you were hinting at when you made that invite. But all night tonight, you've been on edge. Your body has been tense, and I started to think that maybe you were having second thoughts. I wasn't going to say anything because I'm just as happy to be here with you watching a movie as I would be doing other things that involve a lot less clothing."

I bit my lip nervously. Walker's eyes dropped to it briefly before he brought them back to mine and continued, "The minute you moved to this position and I started rubbing your side, I felt you relax. When I saw your nipples get hard with just that simple touch, I realized it might have just been anticipation that was making you so tense before. But now I know that it's probably some of that and a lot of nerves."

Wow.

He'd worked all of that out without me needing to say a single word.

The man was either a genius or completely in tune with my body.

"That about sums it all up," I murmured.

"Okay, and what I'm saying now is that I want you to be sure," he said.

"I liked what was happening before," I assured him.

He nodded. "Yeah, you did. Until I hurt you. I'm sorry for that. It obviously wasn't intentional because I didn't know, but that doesn't mean I didn't do it. We can slow things down, Sadie."

"But if I wanted to slow things down I wouldn't have spread my legs when you asked me to," I pointed out.

Walker groaned and squeezed my hip again. I wanted to ask him why he did that, but he spoke before I could.

"There's a lot we can do to have some fun," he shared. "We don't have to dive right in and go for it all at once."

Did he not want this?

"Walker?" I called after a brief pause.

"Yeah?"

"Do you want to have sex with me?"

His brows shot up. "Is that a serious question?"

I nodded.

Walker's hand left my hip, moved to my hand that had been wedged between us, and lifted it to the front of his jeans. I felt his erection through his pants. "What do you think?" he asked when my hand was there.

He was like that for me. It felt incredible. "I think it seems like you'd be interested in the idea," I answered.

"I am, but I'm also interested in making sure you're okay, too."

Okay. I was going to need him to take the lead on all of this, but maybe I needed to offer him the encouragement and reassurance that where we'd been headed was a place I wanted to be.

"Trust me, Walker. I want this, and I really want you to be the one to give it to me," I told him.

That seemed to be all the encouragement Walker needed because after he searched my face briefly, he replied, "Then that's what I'll do."

I smiled at him seconds before he dropped his mouth to mine and started kissing me again.

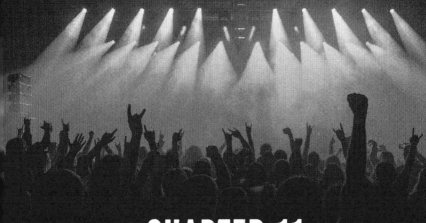

CHAPTER 11

Sadie

THE MOVIE BECAME A DISTANT MEMORY.

I hadn't been paying much, if any, attention to it to begin with, but now I knew that not even Walker was focused on it either.

It wasn't like he could be now that we were in my bed. I'd led Walker here just a few minutes ago, not long after he vowed to make tonight a special night for me, for the both of us. We had kissed for a few minutes on the couch, but ultimately decided to move things to the bedroom.

So, the movie was long forgotten.

And now I was on my back in my bed and Walker's body was half covering mine. Though I had no idea what was going to happen next or how it would all go, all the nerves I'd been feeling earlier in the day and even just a few minutes ago had vanished.

I was completely at ease and even a little excited about what was coming.

Walker had been right to stop us on the couch and talk about it. Because now I knew that he knew about my lack of experience. While I guessed that could have made me worried, surprisingly, it didn't.

I trusted him.

I trusted that Walker had every intention of taking care of me, and I didn't just mean that in the physical sense. Of course, I didn't doubt he'd be gentle and not physically harm me, but there was something else there. I believed Walker would make this a memorable experience, something I'd cherish for the rest of my life.

And I considered myself lucky for that very reason because I knew that a lot of women and girls didn't get that during their first experience with sex.

It was already going better than I could have imagined.

My body was relaxed, my nerves were gone, and Walker was making me feel incredible. He was no longer kissing my mouth, but that didn't mean he'd stopped kissing me altogether.

With one hand gently cupping the side of my face and one of his legs settled between my parted thighs, Walker ran his mouth along my jaw and down the side of my neck, peppering kisses over every inch. Each time his lips or his beard brushed along my rapidly heating skin, tingles shot through my body.

It felt so good, and I wondered how things could possibly get any better. But I didn't have to ponder that for too long because Walker lifted his torso from mine, brought his hands to the hem of my dress, and began sliding it up my body. I raised my hips to help him before I lifted my arms and shoulders so he could remove it completely.

Once it was gone, I kept myself still, remaining there in just a bra and pair of matching panties as Walker's heated and appreciative gaze traveled over my body.

"You're so beautiful," he said, his voice deep and husky.

There was no doubt he made me feel that way. God, the look in his eyes was undoing me.

Keeping his focus on me, Walker reached one hand behind his neck, grabbed a fistful of his shirt there, and tugged it over his head.

It was then I took the opportunity to allow my gaze to roam over his body. As his hands went to the fly of his jeans, I sat up in the bed. Looking at him was no longer enough; I wanted to touch him. I wanted to feel his skin beneath my fingertips.

Walker gave me some time to explore before he shifted and pushed his jeans down his legs. Then he was there in just his boxer briefs, and the reality of the situation began to hit me.

"Your body is incredible," I whispered, leaning forward slightly and gazing up at him. I kissed his abdomen, my hands going to his hips and drifting up his sides.

As my mouth roamed over Walker's abs, his hand came to the middle of my back. He unhooked my bra and brought his fingertips to my shoulders. After giving me another few seconds to kiss and touch him, he gently urged me back as he slid my bra straps down my arms.

Walker quickly tossed it aside and lowered his body over mine again. Wasting no time, he immediately captured one of my breasts in his mouth.

I whimpered as my back arched off the bed, never experiencing pleasure like that before, never knowing it was possible to feel pleasure like that.

A groan came from Walker, and I started to realize that every time I indicated how much I liked what he was doing, it turned him on even more.

It seemed crazy and impossible. Walker was getting more excited knowing that I was enjoying what he was doing to me.

His tongue licked and swirled around my nipple as I squirmed beneath him. The sensations were too much. I hadn't expected it would be anything like this.

"Walker," I panted, clamping my hand around the back of his head, holding him close to me.

He groaned again as he sucked my breast in deeper. I moaned louder.

When he moved to the opposite side, I felt his teeth bite

down gently before he used his tongue to soothe the hardened bud.

After he'd had his fill of my breasts, Walker kept his hands on them, allowing his thumbs to stroke back and forth over my nipples while his mouth claimed mine. His tongue plunged inside, our tongues tangling while desire built between us.

It seemed Walker couldn't get enough of me because no sooner had he devoured my mouth when he began leaving a trail of kisses down my body. Burying his face right between my legs, he inhaled the scent of me while his fingers curled around the lace edge of my panties at my hips. A moment later, he pulled his face back only so he could yank them down my legs.

Being completely naked was a bit unnerving, and unsurprisingly, Walker didn't miss it. He planted one palm on the mattress on the outside of my thigh while his other hand settled on my hip.

"Relax, baby," he urged gently, a rough edge to his voice.

He kept his eyes on mine until I relaxed. Then he allowed his hand to drift from my hip over toward my belly button and down between my legs. His gaze never drifted away from my face as his fingers began to rub and circle my clit.

I wanted more of that, more of what he'd started to give me when we were out on the couch, so I begged, "Walker, please."

"What do you want, Sadie?" he asked.

"More," I answered breathlessly.

Slowly, Walker took just one finger and slipped it inside me. "Are you okay?"

I nodded. "Yes."

And I was. Knowing what was coming, expecting it, and being ready, I was completely okay.

Half a second later, Walker pulled his finger back before pushing it in deep again. The pleasure, the sensation, was incredible. He began to work up to a steady rhythm, and I started to move my hips to match the movements of his fingers.

I was seeking.

Searching.

Desperate.

I'd given myself some self-induced orgasms, but the buildup to them had never been like this.

"Babe," I panted.

"Do you want more, baby?"

"Please."

Walker slowed his pace, waited for me to do the same, and carefully slid a second finger inside. This time, there was no pain.

"You good?" he asked.

"Yes."

He started off slow again, but we worked up to the same pace as before. Only this time, I knew it was going to happen. I knew it was going to happen because somewhere in the midst of it, Walker pressed his thumb to my clit and gave me the friction I so desperately needed.

My breaths came quicker, and when I was on the verge, one of my hands reached out to him. I curled my fingers around his wrist on the hand that was planted on the mattress.

"Babe," I called out a warning.

Then, without waiting for a response from him, I shattered. My body trembled as my eyes squeezed shut tight and indescribable sparks of pleasure shot through every fiber of my being. I held on tight, riding wave after delicious wave.

I finally came down, which took far longer than I had anticipated, and opened my eyes. Walker was looking at me like he wanted to eat me.

"You are gorgeous," he said.

"You're really good at that," I praised him.

"Sadie, that was nothing," he declared. "If you liked that, I'm inclined to believe you'll like my cock a whole lot more."

My eyes widened, and I licked my lips.

Walker chuckled and pulled his fingers from between my

legs. For several long moments, he looked down at me with such adoration.

I didn't know where my courage suddenly came from, but I asked, "Are you planning to prove that to me, or are you just going to talk about it?"

He cocked an eyebrow and muttered, "She doesn't like being kept waiting."

The next thing I knew, Walker was out of the bed. He reached for his jeans, yanked out his wallet, and pulled out a gold foil packet. Then, his boxer briefs were gone.

I sat up in the bed. My eyes dropped to his manhood, and my lips parted.

That was going inside me?

Sure, I'd felt how hard he'd been when he was pressed up against me, but I hadn't realized just how large he was. It had hurt the first time he put both of his fingers in me. And even though he had large hands, two of his fingers were nowhere near the same size as his penis.

I must have been wearing my thoughts on my face because Walker called, "Sadie?"

My lips still parted, I tipped my head up and looked at him.

"I promise I won't hurt you," he said.

I nodded my understanding slowly, but I wasn't entirely sure I believed him. I didn't think it was possible for me not to be injured, given his size.

Walker rolled on the condom and came back into the bed.

"Baby, do you still want to do this?" he asked. "I'm not going to do this if you're freaked out or having second thoughts."

I shook my head. I wanted this; I just didn't understand how it was going to happen.

"I do," I said softly. "But I'm a little nervous and a lot unsure."

"What are you nervous and unsure about?" he asked.

My eyes dropped to his penis briefly and back to his face.

"I… I'm not sure you're going to fit inside me," I worried. "And even if we could manage that, I'm not sure I know what I'm supposed to do."

"Sadie, I will not hurt you," he insisted in a voice not to be doubted. "I'll go slow and make sure you're okay every step of the way."

"Okay," I replied cautiously.

"As for what you should do, just enjoy it," he instructed. "There's no rule book. Do whatever comes naturally to you. You can kiss and touch. Move with me. And if you feel so inclined, you can moan all you want and say my name because I like it a whole lot when you do that."

I stared at him, digesting all of his words.

"What do you think?" he asked.

"I think I feel slightly more sure now, but I'm definitely still nervous," I confessed.

"Do you trust me, Sadie?"

I nodded.

"I promise I will not hurt you," he said. "But if you want to wait until you feel more ready, we can wait."

No.

No, I didn't want to wait.

I wanted this.

"You'll go slow?" I asked.

His features softened, and his voice dipped low. "I'll go slow."

I dipped my chin and lowered myself to my back again. Walker settled himself between my thighs, touched his fingers to my vagina, and teased me. While he did that, he lowered his mouth to my breast and sucked my nipple into his mouth. His tongue licked and swirled, and within seconds, the tension left my body.

In fact, Walker had done such a great job of relaxing me

that I actually started to feel the faint beginnings of another orgasm building.

But then Walker freed my breast from his mouth and his hand was suddenly no longer there playing between my legs. It was almost immediately replaced by the head of his penis.

Walker kept his eyes on me as he pushed inside just a little. He stopped, waited, and asked, "Are you good?"

I was. And seeing that he was doing exactly what he promised, I was even better than just good.

"Yes," I answered.

He pulled back and pushed forward again, stopping after he'd gone just a bit farther than he did the first time.

Once again, he paused and confirmed I was okay. He repeated the same thing again, going slightly deeper the third time.

And finally, on the fourth stroke, Walker was completely inside.

His hands framed my face as my emotions started to take over. "You fit," I rasped. "We fit."

He smiled at me and stroked his thumbs over my cheeks before he kissed me. "We fit, sunshine." Following a brief pause, he asked, "Are you good for me to move?"

I nodded. "Yeah," I replied.

With that, Walker moved. He pulled out slowly before pushing forward just as slowly. For the first few strokes, I simply allowed him to take the lead. I didn't want to focus on trying to do anything until I gave myself the chance to experience this while memorizing just how beautiful it felt to have Walker inside me like this.

But eventually, I couldn't hold myself back.

I did exactly what Walker had suggested I do.

I did what felt natural.

I kissed. I touched. I moved with him.

And I moaned.

I moaned a lot because it felt amazing. It wasn't just about having sex for the first time that was making it that way, either.

It was him. It was the way that he was gentle with me, the way he checked in with me, and the way he looked at me.

"Walker," I moaned.

That came out naturally, but it also served its purpose and caused him to groan.

I didn't expect it would happen, but with the combination of how wonderful this felt and all the touching Walker had done before we'd gotten to this point, I found myself on the verge of an orgasm.

"You feel beautiful, Sadie. You're so wet. So tight. Fuck, you're beautiful."

I loved that.

I loved hearing him talk to me like that.

A mess of tangled limbs, our bodies pressed close together, him talking like that, and Walker's cock thrusting effortlessly inside me, I knew I wasn't going to last much longer.

"Babe," I panted, my breathing quick and shallow.

He picked up his pace.

Oh God. That was really nice.

I didn't want to come now. I wanted him to keep doing that. But it felt too good and I couldn't hold back.

"Please don't stop, Walker," I begged, wanting it to go on forever.

He went faster. Harder.

A few strokes later, I was gone. Sparks of pleasure splintered through my body, and all I could manage to do was moan and hold on for how good Walker made me feel.

He was still going hard when I finally came down, and the minute I opened my eyes, I was mesmerized. For the first time, I took in the beauty, power, and strength of his body as it moved over mine. But I didn't have very long to do that. Because moments later, he surged forward three more times before he buried himself deep inside and found his own release. I was riveted to the sight of him like that.

The muscles flexing.

The jaw clenching.

The veins popping.

All of it was exquisite.

When it left him, Walker collapsed on top of me. He gave me his weight briefly, but ultimately rolled to his back, taking me with him.

With my body over his, I lifted my head from Walker's chest and looked up at his face.

"You were right," I declared.

"About what?" he wondered, his breathing still working to return to normal.

"I like your cock a whole lot more."

Walker's body vibrated with laughter beneath mine. I dropped my cheek back to his chest and smiled.

"You feel okay?" he asked after he pulled himself together. "Did I hurt you?"

"I'm good, Walker. Actually, I'm perfect," I responded.

His arms squeezed tight around me before he said, "Good. I'm going to go get rid of this condom. I'll be right back, okay?"

"Yeah."

With that, he rolled me to my back, kissed me on the cheek, and got himself out of the bed. I watched him as he walked away, thinking that I really liked the view of him from the back almost as much as I like him from the front.

I didn't know what to expect now that we'd done this. It wasn't like I had any past experience that I could recall, so I had no idea what to do. I sat up in the bed, pulled the sheet up to cover my chest, and began to fret.

My eyes darted around the room while I tried to come up with some plan as to what to do next. But before I could figure anything out, Walker entered the room again.

"Baby, why do you look so frazzled?" he asked as he came back toward the bed.

"Oh, um—"

"Lay back, sunshine," Walker urged quietly while pulling the sheet away from my body and cutting me off from having to respond.

I belatedly noticed he had a wet washcloth in his hand as I fell to my back in the bed. Keeping his eyes on mine, Walker put his free hand to my knee and said softly, "Spread your legs, Sadie."

Twice now, he'd asked me to do that.

I didn't hesitate. My knees dropped open, and I spread my legs. Barely a moment later, Walker brought the warm cloth to my body and held it there. Then he went about seeing to me before tossing the cloth aside and cuddling up next to me.

Part of me simply wanted to be in the moment, but the other part of me felt compelled to speak.

"Thank you," I whispered.

Walker's arm tightened around me. "You don't need to thank me," he assured me. "I should be thanking you." I didn't know how to respond to that, and luckily, I didn't have to try to figure it out because Walker added, "Giving me what you just gave me, trusting me with your body, and handing me something so precious… Sadie, I don't think you understand what it means to me."

Maybe I didn't know specifically what it meant to him. But I knew what it meant to me that I had it with him. If he felt even half of that, I figured that told me everything I needed to know. Even still, I wanted him to understand where I was coming from.

"You made it beautiful, Walker," I started. "And special. I didn't exactly know what to expect, but I know a lot of girls don't get what I just got out of their first experience. That's why I'm thanking you. Because you took the time to talk to me beforehand, you took care of me throughout, and you made it something I know I'll cherish for the rest of my life."

Walker's hand came up to the side of my face, his fingertips grazing my hair. "I'm glad I could give that to you, sunshine," he rasped. "It meant a lot to you. I get it, and I'm happy you got all that you did out of it. But I think it's only fair that you know that it feels like I've done nothing for you compared to the way you light up my world."

"Don't," I ordered.

"What?"

"Don't make me cry," I murmured.

He smiled at me. "Okay. How about you let me put my mouth between your legs instead? Do you think you'd be alright with that?" he asked.

My eyes widened in surprise as a shiver ran down my spine. He wanted to put his mouth between my legs.

"I… uh… I guess," I stammered.

"I promise it'll feel fantastic," he said.

Considering he came through on his last promise, I didn't have any reason to doubt him. So, I squeaked, "Okay."

He grinned at me. Then he stated, "If you don't like it, just say so. We'll stop and do something else. Okay?"

I nodded.

Barely a minute later, Walker had his mouth between my legs. He was crazy if he thought I was going to tell him to stop. His mouth was right up there with his cock, and if I didn't think it'd make me seem greedy, I'd have asked him to stay there all night long.

CHAPTER 12

Walker

"I'M READY."

The beautiful woman in my arms, the one I'd just made love to, lifted her head from my chest and looked at me.

Every time she did that, I felt something squeeze in my chest. It had been roughly four months since Sadie and I took that step and became an us. It had been the best decision of my life.

"Ready?" I repeated, not sure what she was referring to.

"Yes," she confirmed, nodding her head. "I've been thinking a lot over the last few weeks, and I don't want to do this again."

My body tensed. "Do what exactly?"

"Be apart on the holidays," she clarified. The tension quickly left my body as she continued, "I think, if you're ready, that I'd like to start talking about the two of us sharing the truth of our relationship with my mom and Beck."

"Really?" I asked.

There was a brief moment of silence before she said, "Walker, I don't want to ever go through the holidays again without having you with me."

I couldn't say I didn't see her point.

It was now New Year's Eve.

Sadie and I had opted for a quiet night in at my place because it was the first and only opportunity for us to spend an actual holiday together without anyone questioning why we weren't going to be around.

While my family knew about Sadie—I introduced her to my mom within the first month we were together—neither her mom nor her brother knew that I was in her life like this. So, when it came to celebrating Thanksgiving and Christmas, we didn't get to see each other until the evenings.

I appreciated every moment I had with her, but I'd have been lying if I said it didn't bother me that I had to wait all day to see her. So, if she was ready, I wasn't going to be the one to hold us back.

Unfortunately, I'd taken too long to consider all of this, so Sadie spoke again. "I mean, I understand if you're not ready for it just yet," she began. "I just wanted you to know that I'm ready. I'm tired of hiding it. I don't like that we have to look over our shoulders when we go somewhere, and I really just hate lying to my family."

"We can tell them," I assured her.

"Really? You're sure you're okay with it?" she asked.

My hand, which had been settled at the middle of her back, began drifting down toward her ass. Once there, it stopped moving, and I squeezed her. "Yes, sunshine, I'm okay with it. I was just thinking the same thing, too. I know you're starting your last semester shortly, so if you want to do this beforehand, I'm good with that. I don't know what the fallout is going to be from this, but I don't expect it's all going to be hearts and butterflies from Beck. If you'd rather not deal with his reaction and the stress it's going to put you under until after you're finished with school, I'm good with that, too. Either way, I think we're at a place where we're solid enough to get through whatever comes our way."

Sadie smiled at me, dropped her cheek back to my chest, and replied, "I'm glad you feel that way because I completely agree. These have been some of the best few months of my life. That's saying a whole lot considering I'm in school still."

"It's been the same for me. And I think that's saying something considering my mom is getting worse and worse with each week that passes and doesn't have much time left," I told her.

Sadie's fingers began to drift over the skin on my chest. "It breaks my heart to think that she might not be here this time next year," she said softly. "It hurts to even think about it."

"Yeah," I mumbled my agreement.

I knew Sadie was just trying to be positive by saying that my mom *might* not be here at this time next year. The truth was, my mom didn't have that much time left. She'd been deteriorating, particularly over the last few weeks.

My dad, Raid, and I all made the effort to make this holiday season a memorable one because there was that unspoken truth lingering among us. We all knew this was going to be our last holiday season with her.

Not wanting to kill the mood by thinking about my mom's impending death, I decided to turn the conversation back to what Sadie and I were originally discussing.

"So, what do you think? Do you want to talk to Beck and your mom sometime over the next week before you start school again, or do you want to wait until you're finished?" I asked.

"Neither," she answered.

"What?"

Sadie lifted her head again, looked at me, and explained, "I'd like to spend the next week enjoying the break I have before starting my last semester. If there's going to be a massive blowup about it, I'd rather wait until after I'm back in school. Beck might be less likely to push it."

"You sure that's what you want to do?" I asked.

"Yeah. I figure I'll need about a week or two to get a feel for my school schedule, but we can do it after that," she suggested.

At this point, it didn't matter to me when we did it. Sadie and I were solid, My Violent Heart had finished recording our newest album, and my free time was spent with either my mom and family or with Sadie. Since Sadie's schedule presented more challenges, and the reaction we'd receive would hit her the hardest, I thought it was best to allow her to decide what she could handle.

"You tell me when and where, and I'll be there with you," I told her.

"Okay. We'll have to discuss our strategy at some point," she noted as she began to squirm on top of me.

"Do you have any ideas yet?" I asked.

She nodded. "Yes, but I'm not interested in discussing them right now," she remarked. Her body shifted slightly on mine as she dropped her head down to press a kiss to my chest. Sadie didn't stop at a simple peck. She dragged her lips along my skin, her heated breath blazing a trail right toward my nipple. Then her tongue came out and licked me there.

My gaze followed her, and when she tipped her head back just enough to look up at me, she said, "I have other, more pressing, things to do right now."

I grinned at her. "Let's end this year with a bang, sunshine."

So, that's what we did.

I just hadn't realized it would be so soon afterward that things took a turn.

One week later

It came too soon.

We were all expecting it, we all knew it was coming, and somehow, I still wasn't prepared for it.

"I'm so proud of you."

Those words came from my mom. She was in bed, weak and fading. And yet, she was still the strongest woman I knew.

She fought hard, pushed through the pain, and gave us one last holiday season with her. I was the one who should have been saying those words to her.

"I feel the same about you," I told her.

Smiling at me, she said, "I never knew where you'd end up in life, but I'm so glad you've found what makes you happy."

"It's all thanks to you, you know?" I replied.

And that was the truth. I had no doubt that if it hadn't been for my mom being who she was that I might not have ever realized how much I loved music. I'd be forever grateful to her for giving me that.

"I simply gave you the tools, Walker," she started. "You did it all on your own. You forged your own path. And I couldn't be prouder of you for everything you've accomplished. I know it's only going to get better from here."

I had a feeling she was right. She'd heard the tracks from our newest album. Every member of My Violent Heart worked their ass off to make that happen and give that to my mom. She loved it, as I knew she would, and there was little doubt about how successful the album would be.

My emotions started to get the best of me, but there were things I needed to say to her. So, feeling devastated, I shared, "I wish you were going to be here to see it all."

"Walker Rhodes," she said softly with a smile on her face. "I will always be here to see it. I'm not going to miss a moment of it."

I blinked my eyes rapidly, trying to keep myself from completely breaking down. My mom reached her hand out, placed it on my heart, and said, "I'll follow you on your tours all over the world. Right here. I'm always going to be right here."

With that, I couldn't hold back any longer. I dropped my head forward into the bed and let all that I was feeling leak out of me.

For weeks, I'd managed to avoid having this happen because I was focused on the joy I was experiencing. Part of me felt guilty about that. I felt horrible for being happy when my mom was dying.

But I needed it.

I needed it more than I could ever explain.

Because this feeling—the helpless and hopeless feeling—was enough to pull me down into the darkest depths and swallow me whole.

The *only* thing that could pull me out of the turmoil, out of the emotional hell I was in, was Sadie. Somehow, she just knew what I needed and gave it to me. And she did it effortlessly.

When I needed to talk, she listened. If I needed a distraction, she provided it. In the rare case I needed space, she didn't begrudge me that either.

She was perfect, the most selfless and caring woman. I knew if it hadn't been for her, the last few weeks would have been especially difficult, more than they already were.

"Walker?" my mom called after some time passed.

I lifted my gaze to her, wiped away the evidence of my pain, and replied, "Yeah?"

"It's not just the music I'm proud of you for," she said.

Tipping my head to the side, I eyed her curiously.

She touched the side of my face and shared, "I'm proud of the man you've become in so many ways. The way you looked after your brother as kids always brought me such joy. But seeing the both of you as adults, knowing you're just as close now as you were then, is all I could have ever wanted as a mother to two boys."

She paused briefly, and I gave her the time to do that. A moment later, she continued, "On top of that, seeing you in a serious relationship has filled me up in a way I never would have imagined. As a mother, I've always worried about my boys and the woman who would come into each of their lives to take care of them. I couldn't have chosen anyone better than Sadie for you."

For the first time since I sat down beside my mom, I smiled. She hadn't hid the fact that she liked Sadie, but hearing her say she believed there was nobody better for me was really nice.

"I'm so glad you got to meet her," I said.

"Me too."

For several long seconds, neither of us said anything. We simply stared at one another, both of us wearing expressions that held a mix of emotions. Frustration and sadness for what we'd miss out on in the future. Relief and happiness for all the memories we had.

My mom eventually broke the silence, and she did it in a way I hadn't expected.

"I need to be selfish for a minute, Walker," she said.

"What do you mean?"

"There are a few things I need you to do for me," she replied.

I didn't hesitate to insist, "Anything you want. Anything, Mom."

The silence stretched between us again. "Grieve," she declared. "Grieve for me because I know you'll need to do that. But don't let it eat you alive. I want you to live your life. I want you to be happy. I want you to make music and tour. Keep me in your heart, and keep doing the one thing that I loved the most outside of your father, your brother, and you."

I nodded my understanding. I had no intention of giving up my music; it would be the only connection I had left to my mother. If anything, I had a feeling I'd lose myself in it even more than I already had.

"That's not it," my mom said.

"Okay. What else do you need me to do?"

She let out a deep sigh. "It might not need to be said, but I figure it's best to be sure," she started. "Raiden. Continue to look out for him. He's still searching for something. Be there for him, help him. I want him to feel as fulfilled as I know you already feel. A few more years, he'll figure it out, but I'll be happy to know you're helping to guide him where he needs to go."

"Of course, I will," I promised.

"And your father," she began again, her voice cracking. "I've already spoken to Raid about it. Dad's going to need the both of you. He's been trying to be strong for me, Walker. Just like you. But when I'm no longer here, he's going to crumble. Please don't let him lose sight of the man I fell in love with."

Emotions clogged my throat. Thinking back on the last few months, I realized she was right. My dad had been the picture-perfect image of strong and collected. The very idea that he was going to crumble just didn't seem possible. But my mom was his world, so it made perfect sense that he'd lose a bit of himself when she passed.

"We've got him," I promised her. "Raid and I will take care of him."

Tears filled her eyes. When she blinked, they rolled down her cheeks. "There's one more thing," she said.

"What?"

"Hold on to Sadie," she urged, her voice pleading with me. "No matter what happens, Walker, hold on to her. She loves you like I love your dad."

Something tightened in my chest.

My mom believed Sadie loved me. She'd only been around her a handful of times, and yet, she still managed to draw that conclusion. Part of me was surprised by her ability to do that at the same time I was trying to allow the actual words to penetrate.

Sadie loved me.

I tucked that piece of information somewhere deep inside so I could turn to it later and returned my focus to my mom.

"I don't know what life will throw at the two of you, but I know that she's got what it takes to get you through anything," she declared.

"It makes me happy to know you feel that way about her," I responded.

"Thank you for giving me the time you did with her. And now, you have it all. Those are my wishes for after I'm gone. Don't let anything come between you and Raid, and depend on each other to get through tough times. Look after your father, keep him on steady ground. Don't give up your music, and hold on to Sadie."

"Can I let you in on a little secret?" I asked her.

She nodded.

"Even without you asking all of this of me, I would have done all of that," I told her.

"I had a feeling that would be the case, but I had to say it to you anyway."

"What are we going to do without you?" I asked.

Smiling at me, tears shining in her eyes, she answered, "You'll grieve. Then, you'll pick yourselves up and be the men I know you are. Your father will be the man I married, and you and Raid will be the men I raised. You'll move on with your lives because that's what I want for you. You'll get married and start your own families. And every time you feel sad or lost or happy or excited, you'll remember that I'm there with you through all of it. Always."

I lifted her hand up, pressed a kiss to the back of it, and dropped my gaze down to the bed. I loved this woman for everything she gave me, everything she taught me, and all I wanted to do was continue to make her proud.

I was glad she had taken the opportunity to talk to me about what she wanted for me moving forward. I'd take her words and her guidance and use it for the rest of my life.

Sadly, I hated that it was only three days after she shared all of it that I needed to put it into practice.

She was gone. But like she said, she was always going to be there. I tried to hold on to that.

CHAPTER 13

Sadie
Two months later

WHEN THE KNOCK CAME AT MY DOOR, I TOOK IN A DEEP BREATH. I hoped this was the right thing to do.

Today was Walker's birthday. It was a Thursday, early evening, and I'd had school today. I was going to skip my classes so that I could spend the day with Walker, but he had planned to go to the studio.

He'd been doing that a lot over the last few weeks.

It broke my heart.

Walker playing music wasn't what broke my heart. What I was struggling with was the fact that I knew he was going to the studio to play that music simply because he missed his mom so much.

It was the only thing that seemed to help him.

I wished I knew what I could do to make things better because the first few weeks following her death had been tough for him. Heck, it had been tough for all of them. Walker, Raiden, and their father, Alan. I was sure I'd never seen three men who looked so strong physically weep and grieve for someone the way the three of them grieved for Lani.

I wanted to believe things were getting easier for Walker. It was hard to say. I just did what I'd always done before his mom passed and tried to give him whatever he needed when he needed it.

Walker was also very fortunate to have the love and support of the rest of the band. They stepped up to the plate to show him that no matter what he was going through, they'd all be there to have his back and see him through.

I was glad he had them, and I knew he was, too.

I'd been nervous about this day for a long time now, and I truly hoped I'd be able to give Walker a piece of his mom back.

So, I moved to the door, opened it, and saw him waiting there. I smiled and stepped back to allow him inside. Once I closed the door, I slid my arms around him and said, "Happy birthday."

Walker hugged me back. "Thanks, sunshine."

"How was it today?" I asked.

Nodding, he replied, "It was good."

That was the other thing. I'd regularly ask Walker about his time in the studio over the last several weeks, but I never really pried for more information than he was willing to share. Of course, this meant that I rarely knew exactly how it was going.

But it was okay. If this was what he needed to do to grieve and get through this, I wasn't going to push him.

"I hope you're hungry because I cooked," I declared.

Surprise washed over him at the same time I saw his nostrils flare. He could smell it. I had a feeling it was hitting him at that very moment.

"It smells..." He trailed off.

"What? What does it smell like?" I questioned him.

Sadness marred his expression as he shook his head. "Never mind."

"Does it smell like honey and garlic?" I asked as we began moving toward the kitchen.

"Sadie?" he called in a way that wasn't meant to get my attention but rather to discern whether I was telling him what he believed I was telling him.

We came to a stop in the kitchen, and I turned my body so I was facing him completely. Then I shared, "I have some surprises for you. The first is honey garlic steak bites."

Something moved through Walker's face, something profound. He remained quiet a long time, and I began to fret. What if this had been a bad idea?

I watched as Walker swallowed hard before he asked, "Did you make dessert?"

I nodded.

"Does it have anything to do with peanut butter?" he pressed.

I nodded again.

"How?"

His voice came out sounding strangled. This was doing a number on him.

"We should sit down and eat before it gets cold," I suggested. "I'll tell you then."

Walker accepted that. So, after I encouraged him to go sit at the table which already had napkins, forks, and drinks, I carried two plates over. Along with the steak bites, I'd made mashed potatoes from scratch and a batch of asparagus.

When I sat down with him, I urged, "Try it."

I waited, feeling anxious and hoping it measured up. Walker poked a piece of the steak with his fork, lifted it to his mouth, and ate it. I was on pins and needles as I watched him chew.

I couldn't take the suspense, so I decided to tell him how this all came to be.

"I visited her," I started. His eyes came to mine after he put another bite in his mouth, and he chewed slowly while he listened. "On my own. When you were at the studio recording and I had a break between classes, I would go and visit her."

My eyes focused on the change in Walker's face, but I couldn't quite read it. I had no idea what he was thinking. I didn't know if he was upset or if he liked it.

"Why did you do that?" he asked.

The tone of his voice didn't give me any indication what way this was leaning.

"I liked her, and I wanted her to have company to distract her from what she was facing," I started. "But I'd be lying to you if I told you that was the only reason."

I took in a deep breath, steeled my spine, and admitted, "I wanted to know how I could take care of you."

"What?" he replied, his voice just a touch over a whisper.

He still seemed so restrained, and I started getting the distinct feeling that he wasn't okay with any of this. Despite the fact that he'd continued to eat the food on his plate, the vibe just didn't feel good. I didn't think I was making it up in my head.

"Your mom and I talked about a lot of things, and she made it clear that she was most worried about you, Raiden, and your dad. I told her not to worry about you because I'd take care of you. She gave me a few pointers, I asked her about some specifics, and I promised her I'd never let you go through this alone. I assured her that I'd be here for you to lean on," I answered.

The muscle in Walker's jaw twitched after he swallowed his food and clenched his teeth together.

Oh God.

Was he angry?

Time to backtrack. Time to fix this.

"Walker, I… I never meant to hide this from you," I started to fret. "I just wanted to do something to reassure your mom while also preparing myself to help you through this. I like to think it helped her. She always seemed so happy, and I loved learning everything I did from her. I understand why you might be upset. Maybe there were things she told me that I should have learned from you. I'm sorry for that, but—"

"Sadie," Walker interrupted.

"Yes?"

He remained silent for a few moments. My insides had started to tremble with anticipation. This was it. I was sure this was going to be it. He was going to tell me he couldn't do this any longer.

"I love you," he finally declared.

I blinked my eyes in surprise. "I... you... what?" I stammered, certain I'd misheard him.

He shook his head with an expression of disbelief on it. "I love you," he repeated.

Nope.

I heard him perfectly fine. I was just too shocked at hearing him say those words.

Never.

Not once since we'd officially gotten together had Walker and I expressed our feelings to one another using those words. Admittedly, we'd taken time to get to know one another in the beginning, and then the holidays sort of took over. A lot of Walker's focus had been on his music and his mom. Seeing how much he loved her, how much he loved his music, and experiencing his kind heart, it was no surprise I had fallen in love with him.

But I was too much of a chicken to admit that to him first.

Still in shock, I asked, "You... you do?"

Walker nodded. "I've never known anyone like you," he began. "You're not just a beautiful woman with incredible talent for what you do. You're also the most selfless and compassionate woman I've ever met. You threw yourself into this situation with my mom and gave her something that I don't even think you realize."

"She did way more for me," I murmured.

The minute the words left my mouth, I felt Walker's fingers curl around my hand. He gave me a gentle squeeze and insisted, "I don't think you understand. She was worried. A few days before she passed, she started telling me all the things she needed me to promise her that I'd do. Now I realize that the reason she did that was because she knew I'd have you here to take care of me."

I felt a smile forming on my face. "She was a wonderful woman, Walker," I rasped.

"She loved you. She loved you for me," he shared. "And now I understand how it was possible for her to make that declaration."

I closed my eyes. It was so nice to hear that Walker's mom had communicated to him how much she liked me. Hearing it made me miss her a little more than I already did.

Opening my eyes, I stared at Walker and said, "I love you, too."

"Come here, sunshine."

I didn't hesitate. I got out of my seat and moved to him.

Walker pulled me into his lap, captured my mouth, and kissed me. It was heated and intense, and I loved every second of it.

"Thank you, Sadie," he said when he tore his mouth from mine. "Thank you for everything you've done for me. I hope you know how special you are to me."

I nodded. "I do."

"And thank you for keeping my birthday tradition alive by learning to make this meal," he added.

"You're welcome," I responded.

"There's one thing you got wrong, though," he noted.

I sat up a little straighter as I grew concerned. "What did I mess up?" I wondered.

"You added asparagus," he answered.

Biting my lip to stop myself from laughing, I confessed, "She told me you would give me a hard time if I added vege-tables. I told her I didn't care and that I was still going to make them. She liked that because she said there was no way you'd stop yourself from eating them if I made them for you."

Walker rolled his eyes. "She wasn't wrong."

I smiled, leaned forward, and kissed him. "Eat up, babe," I urged. "We have peanut butter bars for dessert. And I've got an evening of fun planned just for you after that."

"Fun?"

I nodded. "You'll get to kick back and relax while I do a lot of the work," I explained.

His eyes instantly heated. "If we're going to finish this meal, you need to go back to your chair now, Sadie," he ordered.

I wiggled my booty in his lap and kissed him once more before I moved back to my chair. Walker and I then finished our dinner. It was delicious, and I was glad he felt it lived up to the standard he'd come to expect from his mom. Dessert was just as yummy, but if I was completely honest, I liked what we had afterward so much more.

In the end, Walker's birthday had turned out to be a success. I was beyond relieved to know that I'd managed to make it special for him.

Two months later

It was supposed to be a happy occasion.

In a way, it was. I mean, I was officially graduating from college. So, the truth was that I did feel some joy. It was nice to know I was finally done with this chapter of my life.

But the bottom line was that no matter how wonderful the day was supposed to make me feel, I couldn't stop the sadness from creeping in.

I was seconds away from walking up on stage to receive my

diploma. My mom, Beck, and my grandma were all there to support me. I loved that I had them, and I never would have wanted them to miss this moment, especially Beck. He was the reason I even had this opportunity. Even Holland had come to see me graduate because she and I had grown incredibly close ever since we met each other at the beginning of the year last year.

I realized how lucky I was to have the love and support that I did when there were others graduating who didn't have anyone there.

But for me, there was someone missing.

Walker.

I wanted him here more than anything. Unfortunately, despite the conversation we'd had months ago about wanting to share the truth of our relationship with Beck, we never did. Everything happened with Walker's mom, and he'd been dealing with his grief over that ever since.

I couldn't bring myself to demand that he take on another thing that would be stressful for him. He deserved some understanding and compassion.

So, I did my best to give him that.

And since I could still see how much he struggled with the loss of his mom, I didn't bring up the topic of our relationship reveal again.

In keeping how much I wanted that to myself, it meant that I ended up not getting the chance to have him here for this. It meant that, even though I had already been on my career path for a while now, Walker was still missing out on such a big accomplishment.

It hurt my heart.

"Sadie Emerson."

My name was announced, and I climbed the stairs to go receive my diploma. I heard the cheers from the crowd and smiled. My people. Mom, Grandma, Beck, and Holland were all so proud of me.

I took my diploma, made it to the center of the stage at the outdoor ceremony, and looked toward my family. They were so excited, and I couldn't help smiling at them.

When I reached out to grab the rail to descend the stairs, my gaze shifted to the back of the crowd, and that's when I froze.

He was there.

Standing at the back, his arms crossed over his chest as he leaned up against a huge tree, wearing a proud smile was Walker.

My man.

My guy.

He didn't miss this.

Warmth spread through me, and I kept my eyes on him as I descended the stairs. As I walked back to my seat with tears threatening to fall, I felt my heart pounding in my chest. This man loved me.

He loved me and made sure he was here to witness this.

But the longer I sat there, the more that I started to think about everything. I should have just been grateful he came. That was all that should have mattered.

Unfortunately, my mind was running wild with a million thoughts and unanswered questions. If Walker knew how important it was for him to be here for this, why hadn't he just said something sooner about talking to my family? Did he no longer want to do that? Was he simply content to keep things as they were?

Maybe I was being unreasonable.

Before I'd gone up to receive my diploma, I was upset at the thought that Walker would miss this. And now that he was here, I was happy but still disappointed.

I wanted it all.

I wanted more.

And I wanted it from a man who was still dealing with such a tremendous loss.

Or, was that it?

Was it possible that this was how it would always be? Had I gone and fallen in love with a man who might not ever want to make our relationship public?

As I sat through the rest of the ceremony, I didn't come up with any more answers. In fact, by the time it was over, I found I had more questions.

The only thing I could do to pull it together before I met up with my family was tell myself that this was all part of the process. The struggles that Walker and I were facing would only make us stronger in the end.

He was here.

He came for me.

Nobody else should have mattered.

Sadly, I knew I was lying to myself.

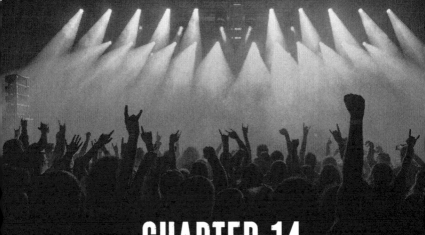

CHAPTER 14

Walker
Seven Years Later

"YOU SOUND MISERABLE."

"I'm fine."

Fine.

That was the code word for *not fine* when it came to women.

I knew this was particularly true for Sadie. The truth was that my woman was talkative and bubbly with me.

Always.

Unless things were just *fine.*

So, I knew something was wrong.

"Talk to me, sunshine," I urged quietly into the phone.

I was sitting in a chair in the lobby of a hotel in a small town in New Hampshire for the second time in a matter of weeks. My Violent Heart was in the middle of a tour, and we were currently on a break. But instead of taking our break at our next location, we ended up returning here.

Cash was on a mission to get a woman to show some interest in him. I had to admit that, after all these years, it was nice to see him put in so much effort with a woman. All the guys had grown accustomed to this life. I couldn't say I blamed them. If I hadn't had Sadie, I'm not sure I would have been much different.

But I had her.

And I loved her more than I ever thought was possible.

So, while I went on tour and partied with the band after shows, I never took things to the level they did. That didn't mean that I was never approached by women. I was. And while I was never downright rude to them, I made it clear I wasn't interested.

I was sure the rest of my bandmates wondered why I never took any of the women up on their offers since none of them knew that Sadie and I were together. But I didn't care if they thought it was strange.

Sadie was far too important to me, and there was no way I'd ever do anything to jeopardize what I had with her.

"Really, Walker," Sadie replied. "It's nothing."

"Sadie, do you honestly think that after all these years that I don't know when something is wrong?" I countered.

I shouldn't have been pushing this with her.

I had a feeling I knew what this was about. Sadie and I had been together for nearly eight years now, and nobody knew.

Well, nobody outside of the two of us, my brother, and my dad.

That was it.

I hadn't meant for it to go on this long. But to say that the last eight years had proven to be challenging for both of us would have been an understatement.

The start of our struggles began with losing my mom. For a long time, I really had a difficult time getting myself to a place where the pain wasn't so bad. There were days and moments that were better than others—most of those came about because of Sadie—but there were significantly more days that were far more challenging.

By the time I started to turn the corner with my own grief, I was able to see what was happening around me. My dad was spiraling. He seemed to be completely lost without my mom, and I felt guilty for not noticing how much he needed me sooner.

Of course, the more I came around, the better he became at hiding just how bad it was. In fact, it wasn't until Thanksgiving—our first one without my mom—that Raid and I realized the extent of our father's heartache.

He was drinking. Excessively.

Foolishly, Raid and I tried to monitor it on our own. But things were getting worse and worse. He wasn't even doing basic maintenance on the house, and we weren't convinced he was even showering regularly.

Mom was probably so upset and disappointed with me for not stepping in sooner. Over the years, my dad ended up in and out of rehab. He went to meetings. I paid for people to come and take care of the house because he couldn't bear the thought of leaving the home he shared with her. I did whatever I could to help him because I couldn't imagine being in his position.

Yes, she was my mother, but she was the love of his life.

For now, he was sober and doing well. But I knew his sobriety would be something he'd battle the rest of his life.

In the midst of all that, Sadie lost her grandmother and My Violent Heart released several more albums and went on a bunch of tours..

So, it was no surprise that before we knew it, so much time had passed and our relationship remained a secret.

Maybe it shouldn't have been a big deal. At this point, we'd been together all these years, we loved each other, and it wasn't as though we needed anyone's permission.

Even still, we hadn't made it happen. And I'd have been lying if I said that every time I considered the possibility of doing it that it didn't give me an excessive amount of anxiety.

Knowing all of this, convinced this was what Sadie's melancholy mood was all about, I still pressed her to open up and be honest with me.

"Okay, fine, something is wrong," she declared. "But it's really nothing new. It's not as though you haven't heard this from me before."

"Baby, I'm sorry," I lamented.

"I miss you, Walker," she said. "This is your longest tour, and I just hate being apart from you all the time."

"I know," I replied quietly. "I miss you, too. We'll be back in Pennsylvania in three weeks, though."

I barely got the words out, thinking I was sharing good news, when Sadie fired back, "Yeah, for a whopping five days. And I'm not going to get all five days with you."

"I'm going to give you every minute I can," I promised her. "You know that. But I've got to check in on my dad. And we do have a couple shows to play."

"Just let me do it," she begged.

"Do what?" I asked.

"When you guys are home in three weeks, I'll talk to Beck," she said. "I'll tell him the truth, and we can finally stop hiding."

"Sadie, you can't tell him that in the middle of the tour," I remarked. "He'll lose his mind, and everyone else is going to be affected. That's not fair to the rest of the band, the security, and everyone who is working with us."

"What about what's important to us?" she countered. "Do you know what it's like for me? I'm alone every night, wishing I was falling asleep in your arms. I hate being so far away from you."

I stood up from the couch and started pacing in the lobby. I hated this. Over the last couple of weeks, I'd noticed Sadie becoming more and more unhappy. We spoke to one another every day, but the separation was taking its toll.

"I miss you, too," I told her. "I hate not having you here with me. I hate that you're there while I'm going all over the country to play these shows only to sleep in a different hotel room every night. Most of all, I hate that you're feeling lonely. If I thought we could tell Beck and not have everyone else be affected by his reaction, I'd march myself up to his room right now. But I've got weeks of touring left, and I don't want to do anything that's going to cause tension for everyone else in the band."

"Maybe I should talk to him," she suggested. "We've always been close. Maybe he'll be reasonable."

"You know that's not going to happen," I replied.

She audibly sighed. "This is so frustrating."

I never should have let this go on for so long. Despite all that was happening around us, I should have found a way to do this years ago.

"Sadie?" I called.

"Yeah?" she murmured.

"I don't want to argue with you," I began. "I never want to argue with you, but I especially don't want to do it when I'm states away from you. I'll be home in three weeks. When I get back, I promise you we'll find some time to figure out how to handle this."

She sniffled, and my heart broke. This woman meant the world to me, and now she was upset. There was nothing I could do about it.

"Baby, please don't cry," I begged.

Following a brief hesitation, she insisted, "It's fine. I'm fine."

"I know you're not, and I'm so sorry about it," I apologized.

"It's been years. I can't do this much longer," she shared.

"I understand. We'll figure it out. I promise."

I don't know why I said that. I wasn't sure I knew what we were going to do because as much as I knew it needed to be done, I didn't think I could handle what the outcome was going to be.

I knew I'd need to make a decision. An impossible choice. Sadie or the band.

Sadie was my whole life. I couldn't be without her.

The band was my family. And being part of the band meant that I still had that connection to my mom.

If I had to choose between them, I knew which way it would go. I'd pick Sadie. And in doing that, I'd lose the band and my mom.

Don't give up your music, and hold on to Sadie.

One of my mom's final wishes for me. I didn't know how I was making a promise to Sadie that we'd figure it out when I had no clue how to fix this.

"Three weeks?" she asked.

"Three weeks," I said.

"Okay. I guess I'm going to get back to my painting now. Will you call me later?"

"You know I will."

The silence stretched between us. Sadie was the one to break it, though her voice was hushed.

"I love you, Walker," she said.

"I love you, Sadie. I'll call you tonight."

With that, we said goodbye and disconnected.

Then it was my turn to sigh.

"Sadie?"

I spun around at the mention of my girl's name and felt my heart start pounding in my chest. Holland was standing there.

I didn't know what to say, so I didn't say anything at all.

"Walker, did you just tell Sadie you love her?" Holland pressed.

"You can't say anything," I ordered. "Holland, please, you can't mention this to anyone. We're trying to figure this out right now."

Her eyes widened. "It's true?" she asked. "I was walking by and thought I misheard you. I honestly believed you were going to tell me I was hearing things."

I shook my head.

"Beck doesn't know, does he?" she questioned me.

"No. And I think you already know that if he does, he's not going to handle it well," I pointed out.

Shaking her head, she agreed, "No, he definitely won't. How long have you been dating each other?"

"Since the summer before my mom died," I answered honestly.

Holland's jaw dropped open at my declaration. "That's… that was like—"

"Eight years ago," I said, cutting her off.

"Holy crap," she marveled. "How have you kept it a secret this long?"

"It hasn't been easy, and it's only getting harder and harder now," I explained. "Sadie doesn't like being alone all the time when I'm on tour. With the work she does, she'd easily be able to come along with us. Unfortunately, I don't think that telling Beck in the middle of a tour is the way to go. But I know I need to figure this out because I can't keep doing this to Sadie."

There wasn't an ounce of hesitation when Holland responded, "I'll help you. Whatever I can do, I'll do. If we've got things going on at home that are band activities… like the pre-Thanksgiving party… I'll have her come there with me. This way, if Beck doesn't bring her along, at least she can be there without it seeming awkward."

I hadn't expected that, but I should have known that this was how Holland would react.

"I'd really appreciate that, Holls. And I know Sadie will, too. We could use an ally as we try to figure this out," I said.

"Anything I can do to help, Walker," she offered. "Do you think it'd be cool for me to call Sadie later and talk to her about it?"

I nodded. "Yeah, just check with me first," I said. "I want to make sure I let her know about it so she isn't blindsided by it."

Holland smiled. "I'm so happy for the both of you."

I returned the smile. "Thanks. You heading upstairs?"

"Yeah."

At that, Holland and I rode the elevator up to our floor. We got off the elevator and made our way to our separate rooms.

Since I didn't want to interrupt her while she was working, I sent a quick text off to Sadie letting her know that we had a temporary plan and that I'd explain it all later.

Ten minutes later, I went in search of the rest of the band. I decided to check in Cash's room first. He and Roscoe were sharing a suite during this trip.

"Hey, what's going on?" I asked after he'd opened the door.

"Nothing yet. Just hanging," he answered.

"How'd it go with Demi this afternoon?" I asked as I walked into the room.

"I've got a date with her tomorrow morning."

I was glad for that. The whole reason we came back here was so that he could make some progress in his pursuit of her. "Nice. Congratulations."

"Yeah, well, we'll have to see where it goes," Cash said. "In the meantime, the guys and I were just talking about you and Holland."

I grew tense and tried not to react. "What about us?"

"We were just thinking about going out tonight and wanted to see if you two were up to it," he replied.

"I'm down," I agreed with a bit of relief.

"Cool. Have you seen Holland?"

I shook my head and lied, "No."

Damn, I didn't like how easily I was able to lie to him. Why was I hiding the fact that I saw Holland just a few minutes ago anyway?

Just then, a knock came at the door. When Cash opened it, Holland asked, "Is everyone in here?"

"Yeah, come on in," he responded. "Where have you been?"

Holland's eyes slid to mine briefly before they returned to Cash. "Um, I was just hanging in my room," she lied.

Wow.

I didn't expect that.

I mean, I knew she said she'd be an ally, but that went beyond the lengths I thought she'd be willing to go. Maybe Holland would really be able to help facilitate more scenarios where I'd be able to have Sadie close when things were happening with the band.

"Well, we're going out tonight. You coming with us?" Cash asked.

She smiled and answered, "Of course."

A moment later, Holland and I had joined the rest of the band. Cash gave each of us a beer and all of the tension I had been feeling started to melt away.

But I did notice one thing that was a bit more difficult for me than it had been in recent years.

Beck.

I found it particularly difficult to even look at him. How was I supposed to look the man in the eyes? He was one of my best friends, and I'd been keeping this secret for years.

There was no doubt in my mind. Once he found out the truth, he might not ever speak to me again.

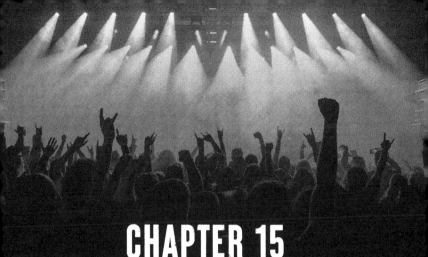

CHAPTER 15

Sadie
Three weeks later

MY PHONE RANG.

I already knew who it was because I had been expecting his call. It was Thursday afternoon, and Walker and the rest of the band were flying home today to play a couple shows and have a mini break in the middle of their tour. I would have Walker until Tuesday. And while I knew I wouldn't get all day every day with him, I would still have him every night.

That was a promise he'd made to me in the midst of our conversations over the last three weeks. He refused to allow me to sleep alone while he was home. I couldn't wait.

"Hey," I answered.

"Hey, sunshine. I just left the airport, and I'm in the car on the way back to my place. If you want to meet me, I should be there in about thirty minutes."

"Full disclosure?" I returned.

"Sure. What's up?" he asked.

"I kind of got antsy yesterday and was too excited about you coming home today," I started. "So, I hope you don't mind, but I came over to your place last night and slept in your bed."

A chuckle came through the line before he assured me, "I don't mind, baby."

I smiled and felt the anticipation creep up a couple notches. "I can't wait to see you," I told him, knowing what I had planned for when he got back.

"Me too. I'll be there soon."

"Okay. Love you."

"Love you, too."

Walker and I disconnected our call, and I spent the next twenty minutes pacing. I'd done all I could do to prepare, but I had to wait until the last minute for the final part of the surprise. Once I knew I could, I ran into the huge master bathroom and turned on the water in the bathtub.

Yes.

I was planning to be in the bath when Walker arrived.

I was cutting right to the chase. I didn't have any interest in talking about his flight, the tour, or when we were going to share the truth of our relationship with our family and friends.

It had been weeks of talking to him on the phone and seeing him through video chats. We'd done plenty of talking. I needed him.

We could talk later.

Once the tub was filled with warm water and bubbles, I turned off the water, noted the time, and realized Walker would be here at any minute. I left a trail of clothes on the floor from the front door to the bathroom.

A shirt. One sock. The second sock. A pair of shorts. My bra. And finally, my panties.

I thought it'd be nice to build a little excitement for him.

The moment I stepped into the tub and sat down, I heard the front door open.

He was home.

I remained still beneath the bubbles and listened. There was no way Walker didn't notice the trail of bread crumbs I left for him, so I had to believe he was taking his time because he wanted to tease me just the same as I was doing to him.

Finally, Walker's body filled the doorframe. It seemed I'd eventually get out of the tub and find that Walker's clothes would be dispersed throughout the house because by the time he entered the bathroom, he was only wearing his jeans.

His heated gaze locked on me, and he didn't make me wait.

Maybe it wasn't about me, though. Maybe he couldn't wait any longer. Either way, I didn't care.

Walker moved toward the bathtub, bent at his waist, and dropped his mouth to mine. Seconds after one of his hands disappeared beneath the bubbles and found my breasts, his lips touched mine and his tongue swept into my mouth.

I moaned, feeling nothing but sweet relief at having him back here with me. Walker's hand played at my breasts for a bit as he continued to kiss me, but eventually, his hand began to descend south.

When he was cupping me between the legs, he tore his mouth from mine and looked adoringly down at me.

"Missed you, Sadie," he rasped.

"Yeah," I agreed on a whisper. "I missed you, too."

He slipped a finger inside me and shot me a devious grin. As he began to stroke with his finger, my head dropped back against the edge of the bathtub. Walker didn't squander the opportunity to run his tongue along the front of my exposed throat.

His beard tickled, and despite the warm water, shivers ran through my body. It took almost no time at all for Walker to build me up. Using his free hand, he cupped the back of my head and looked into my eyes.

"Babe," I moaned. "Please don't stop."

"Never, baby," he promised.

Seconds passed and before I had the chance to prepare myself, it hit me. My orgasm tore through my body while Walker kept his eyes pinned on my face. He slowed the strokes of his finger as he helped me ride out the wave of pleasure until it left me.

When it did, he stood up, removed the remainder of his clothes, and stood in front of me with nothing but his hard cock.

I shifted up onto my knees, curled my fingers around him, and immediately took him into my mouth. One of his hands cupped me gently behind my head. I always loved feeling his hands on me, but it was the sound of the groan that came from him that did it for me.

To say I was enthusiastic about what I was doing to him, running my tongue along his length before parting my lips and taking him inside my mouth, would have been an understatement. It was as though I couldn't get enough of him. I wanted to stroke him with my hand, I wanted to lick his length, I wanted to take him deep into my mouth, and all I could do was alternate between the three as I occasionally looked up at him. Every time I did that, I was rewarded with an expression in his eyes that penetrated so deep, it was as though the man was seeing straight into my soul.

Walker allowed me some time to have my fun, but eventually pulled his hips back and freed himself from the confines of my mouth. He lifted one leg, stepped into the tub, and sat in the spot that I'd been in when he first walked in and found me here.

Then he urged me toward him, until my thighs were straddling his hips, and I was sinking down over his erection.

My head flew back, and I moaned again.

I was so glad for the fact that I decided years ago to get on birth control so Walker and I no longer needed to fuss with condoms. In moments like this, it would have killed the mood. I loved having him bare while he moved inside me.

No sooner was Walker inside me when any urge to go slow fled. Neither of us seemed content to take our time. This was about needing something we'd both been without for months.

It was about finding it, giving it, and getting it.

Water sloshed around us as I rode Walker hard. "God, I missed this," I panted.

Walker's fingertips pressed in deeper on my skin, one hand at my breast and the other at my hip. "Get what you need, Sadie," he urged. "Get what you need and take us there."

"It's never going to be enough," I gasped. "I'm always going to want more."

He brought both hands up and captured my face in them. Pulling me toward him, Walker rasped, "I love you so fucking much." Then, before I could respond, he claimed my mouth.

The more he kissed me, the faster I went. And even though he'd just given me an orgasm, I found myself teetering on the edge in no time at all.

"Walker," I breathed.

"Come with me, baby," he ordered.

That was all it took. My fingernails dug into the skin at Walker's shoulders as sparks flew. I couldn't catch my breath, and my heart felt like it was going to pound right out of my chest. I cried out, moaning through each wave of pleasure that rolled over me.

Walker's grip on my body tightened as he pressed his face into my chest and groaned through his release.

For a long time, we stayed like that, connected to one another and breathing heavy. Eventually, Walker was the one to break the silence.

"Best welcome home I've ever had," he declared.

I pulled my face back from his shoulder, looked at him, and smiled. "You liked it?" I asked.

"Loved it," he confirmed. "I walked in the front door, saw the trail of your clothes, and was hard just thinking about how I might find you."

I pressed a kiss to his lips and said, "My hips are starting to cramp."

"Okay. Let's get cleaned up and out of here. I just want to

get in bed and hold you for a few hours before I order us dinner," he replied.

That sounded marvelous.

So, I didn't delay in making all of that happen.

Hours later, after Walker and I decided to cuddle in his bed where we made out for a long time and did a lot of touching that resulted in a second but much slower round of lovemaking, he ordered dinner for us.

We were in the family room with the television on, although neither of us was paying any attention to it. Our focus was on the food and each other.

"So, it's time to talk," Walker said.

"Yeah," I agreed. "Do you have any thoughts?"

He let out a sarcastic laugh and answered, "I have a lot of thoughts, but I wouldn't exactly say that any of those thoughts leads me to a solution because so much of what I'm thinking is conflicting."

"How so?" I asked.

"I don't even know where to begin," he said. "Obviously, neither of us intended for things to play out like they have where we ended up keeping our relationship a secret for all these years. But we're here now, and I think it's just going to be a disaster when we finally do tell Beck."

"I get what you're saying, Walker, but we're grown adults," I argued. "Even if Beck gets upset, he can't tell either one of us what to do."

After swallowing a bite of his food and taking a sip of his drink, Walker replied, "No, he can't. But he can make life miserable for us. We've dealt with a lot over the years, so I'm not exactly thrilled about dealing with more. But that's not even the real issue I have."

"So, what is it?"

Long moments of silence stretched between us. Walker

simply stared at me. He didn't lift his fork to his mouth, he didn't take a sip of his drink, and he didn't speak. He just stared.

And that told me this wasn't going to be as easy as I thought it should be.

Finally, he explained, "I love you, and I will not live my life without you, Sadie. I won't do it. You remember how bad things got for my dad, right?"

I nodded.

"That wouldn't come close to showing anyone how I'd be if I didn't have you in my life," Walker went on.

"Okay, well, I think that's a good thing," I told him. "I feel the same about you."

"I know you do, but this isn't just about us," he noted. "I have to consider how us telling Beck is going to affect the band. We have to think about Cash, Holland, Killian, and Roscoe."

"It shouldn't affect them," I declared.

"Maybe not, but that doesn't mean it won't," he countered. "Baby, I'm stuck. Years ago, my mom told me some things before she died. Two of those things were that she never wanted me to walk away from my music and that she wanted me to hold on to you. Obviously, none of that has ever been difficult for me to do because I love you and I love my music. But what am I supposed to do when I get the distinct feeling that Beck is going to lose his mind and make life miserable? Do I have to make that choice?"

I stared at him, remaining silent. I hadn't realized how much he was struggling. This seemed like an easy fix to me. I loved my brother, and we'd always been close since we were kids, but this wasn't a situation I felt he had any right to make difficult for Walker or for me.

When I made no response to all that, Walker continued, "If it comes down to it, I'll walk away from the band. You're far more important to me. I hate that I won't have that connection with my mom any longer, and I hate that I'd be leaving people who have been like family to me for years. But I won't survive not having you."

"Walker…" I rasped.

"I'm just telling you the truth."

I sighed. "So, you don't want to tell anyone?" I asked. I tried not to sound angry because the truth was that I wasn't angry. I was, however, hurt and very concerned.

"You have to admit that life is freaking amazing for us when it's just the two of us," he reasoned.

"Of course, it is, but…" I trailed off.

"But what?" he pressed.

I shook my head. "I just really want us to figure this out because as good as it is between us, and it's really good, Walker, I simply hate this," I remarked. "I hate not being able to go on tour with you. I hate having to hide. I hate not being able to tell the people I love who are important to me that I'm madly in love with you."

Walker set his fork down, tipped his head to one side, and replied, "I hate all of that, too."

"So, we have no choice then?" I asked.

Disappointment washed over him. "I'm not saying that," he insisted. "But I don't know how to fix this without losing something important to me and possibly affecting the futures of the rest of my bandmates. I mean, they've all made enough money to be set for life, but that's not what this is about. Music isn't something that you just give up, Sadie. It's… it lives inside us. Even if I walked away from My Violent Heart today, I'd never stop playing."

God, I didn't want him walking away from his music. I knew how much it meant to him. I knew that because growing up, I saw what it meant to my brother. Not only that, but music was the one thing that allowed Walker to still feel connected to his mom.

There was no way I would ever expect him to give that up.

"Where does this leave us?" I questioned him.

"I wish I knew." He sighed and shook his head.

I didn't want to bring this up, but I knew I had to do it if I was going to get any answers about the one thing that I was struggling the most with.

"We were going to do it," I reminded him.

Confusion marred his features. "What?"

"Years ago," I clarified. "We were going to tell Beck about it years ago."

"Sadie, my mom died," he replied, his voice wounded.

I put my food down on the coffee table in front of us and moved closer to him. I placed one hand on his shoulder while I curled my fingers of the other hand around his bicep. "I know that," I assured him. "I know. And I'm not saying I don't understand why we didn't do it then. What I'm trying to figure out is why you were okay with telling Beck then. It just seems to me like you want to keep this a secret, and I can't figure out why that would be."

That wasn't entirely true. I had a million thoughts running through my mind about why that might be the case, but I didn't know if any of them were accurate. Not only that, but I didn't want to believe that the reasons I had in my head could be the reason that Walker no longer seemed interested in letting the world know we were together.

"Because of the lies," he returned without any hesitation.

My body tensed, and I blinked in surprise. "Lies?" I repeated.

Walker set his food down beside mine, turned toward me, and explained, "In the beginning, we kept quiet for a few months to get to know each other. I don't think anyone, not even Beck, could blame us for that. But things happened, times were challenging for us, and we never did it. Now, after eight years, it just feels like downright deceit. I can't imagine how I'd feel knowing Raid lied to me about something important for that many years."

He was right.

This was no longer about the fact that Walker was dating his best friend's younger sister. This was about Walker and me lying to everyone except for his dad and his brother. Obviously, Holland had only found out recently and had taken it well, but I couldn't imagine anybody else would, especially not Beck.

Even if he would have been upset about the relationship and would have gotten over it in the beginning, the simple fact remained that it had been years.

Years of lying.

Years of deceit.

Years of hiding.

Beck and I were thick as thieves. I should have told him a long time ago.

I didn't.

And now I was dealing with the consequences.

Sadly, those consequences had nothing to do with Beck's reaction, and everything to do with where I stood with Walker.

I had no idea how I could possibly tell him what was weighing on my mind now if we couldn't even figure out how to handle this.

Feeling frustrated and disappointed, I said, "So, you want to wait?"

Walker framed my face with his hands. "I don't want to ask you to do this because I know we've waited long enough as it is, but I really think we should wait until the tour is over. As much as I don't want there to be any fallout from this, I know there will be. Tension will be high, tempers might flare, and it's simply not fair to the rest of the band."

God, I hated this.

Even still, I agreed, "Okay. We can wait."

Walker's thumbs stroked back and forth over my cheeks. "I love you, Sadie," he said. "You know that, right?"

I nodded even as I felt my heart breaking.

"Do you love me?"

"I love you, Walker. I always have."

With that, Walker touched his mouth to mine and kissed me. Then we got back to our dinner and focused our attention on the television.

Or, I pretended to.

The truth was, I really wasn't hungry anymore.

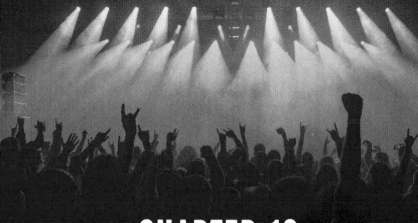

CHAPTER 16

Sadie

MY EYES FLUTTERED OPEN.

Judging by the way the room looked and the fact that I felt reasonably rested, I could only assume it was late.

It was Saturday morning, and I'd gone to bed late.

My Violent Heart played the first of two shows last night, so by the time Walker and I got back to his place, made love, and gotten to bed, it was sometime very early this morning.

I shifted in the bed, leaning my shoulder into Walker's chest. He loosened his hold slightly and scooted back to give me some space.

"Good morning, sunshine," he said after kissing me on the cheek.

"Good morning," I replied. "I think it's late."

Without any hesitation, Walker fell to his back, swung his arm out behind him, and reached for his phone on the night-stand beside the bed. "It's just after ten," he informed me.

"I have to get up and get moving," I told him. "Beck's picking me up this afternoon to take me for lunch."

Cuddling back into me, Walker's arm tightened around my waist again before he shared, "Yeah, I forgot to tell you about that last night. Beck was saying how he was taking you out today since we'll still be on tour for your birthday. He also mentioned that he was spending time with you today so he could cheer you up since you were so bummed about not being able to come to the show last night."

I groaned. "Great. That makes me feel like garbage," I muttered.

I felt so bad because telling Beck I couldn't go to the show last night was just another lie in a long list of lies. I had gone, but I'd done it in secret. I knew my brother. And if I had gone to the show last night, he would have made a big deal and wanted to show me a good time by taking me out afterward.

In any other situation—if this had been the last stop on the tour—I would have gone as his guest. The problem was that Beck, Walker, and the rest of the band were leaving again on Tuesday for another eleven or twelve weeks of touring. I wanted to gobble up as much time as I could with Walker before he left.

So, I told Beck I couldn't go with him because I was going to be spending the night with a friend I'd met back when I was still in college, a friend I hadn't seen in a long time. Technically, I guess it was the truth, but I knew that the way Beck took it was not the way that I meant it.

I had promised I would go tonight, though, so it wasn't only possible but extremely likely that Walker and I would have to see each other and pretend again.

Ugh. I hated it.

"Baby, don't do this to yourself," Walker pleaded with me.

"I feel awful for continuing to lie to him," I countered.

"You're doing it for me right now," he pointed out. "You're doing it to save the rest of the band from the stress and tension that's sure to result from Beck finding out."

I knew that. I understood that. I didn't want to create problems for Walker, Holland, Cash, Killian, or Roscoe. Heck, I didn't want to do anything to cause issues for Beck either. This was sure to cause issues.

But it still sucked.

I sighed. Time to change the subject.

"What are you going to do today?"

"I'm going to go visit my dad," Walker answered. "I want to check in and make sure he's doing okay. Every time I've talked to him, he seems to be in good spirits, all things considered. Even still, I want to spend some time with him. I'll probably take him out to lunch."

I nodded. "Okay."

Silence fell between us. Although I'd tried to change the subject, I felt so disheartened.

"Sadie?"

"Yeah?"

"Please look at me," Walker requested gently.

I rolled my head to the side and brought my gaze to him.

Walker took in the look on my face and said, "I hate seeing you like this."

"It is what it is," I replied. "It's just a few more weeks until the tour is over, right?"

Before he could respond, I pushed the blanket back and got out of the bed.

"Sadie," Walker called.

I didn't look back. I moved toward the bathroom while I, with a raised voice, returned, "It's fine, Walker. I need to get ready so I can leave."

He didn't say anything else. Or, at least, he didn't say anything to me. As I began closing the bathroom door, I heard him hiss, "Fuck."

When I emerged from the bathroom, I was surprised to find Walker was still in the bedroom. He was clearly waiting for me since he'd gotten out of the bed and gotten himself dressed.

Normally, he would have gone downstairs into the kitchen to start breakfast.

"Baby, you can't leave like this," he said as I moved toward the door.

I huffed and kept moving, knowing Walker was following behind me. "That's the thing, Walker. I actually *have* to leave like this because Beck is coming to pick me up at my place. He can't pick me up here, and since we're not telling him what's going on between us, I have to go now."

"You're going out for lunch. He isn't coming at ten thirty in the morning," Walker reasoned as we began descending the stairs.

"I need to shower, and I need to make sure I'm not in a bad mood when he gets there, or he's going to start asking questions," I replied.

When we made it to the bottom of the stairs, Walker asked, "So, I've put you in a bad mood, and you want me to be okay with you leaving here like this when I know that you're upset?"

"We don't have a choice right now," I told him as I bent down to put my shoes on. "I'm sorry, but we've said all there is to say about the situation. We decided two days ago that the best thing to do is to wait until the tour is over."

I stood up and focused my attention on him.

The expression on his face broke my heart. But there was a whole lot more happening inside my head that he didn't even know about that was also breaking my heart.

"If I thought there was another way, a better way, I'd do it in a heartbeat," he promised.

"I know."

There was that. Deep down, I believed that if Walker thought there was another way to handle this, he'd do it. Unfortunately, there was no other way for now, not as long as they were on tour.

"I have to go," I whispered when he made no reply.

"I love you," he said softly as he moved to put his arms around me.

"I love you, too."

I hugged him back, and worried as he was, he asked, "You're coming tonight, right?"

"Yes, I already worked it out with Holland."

If nothing else, Holland finding out that Walker and I were together was a good thing. I hadn't had much of a chance to talk to her about all of it yet, but she did step up to the plate immediately, demanding I come to the show tonight with her.

"You're still spending the night here with me, too, correct?"

I sighed at the same time my shoulders fell. "I am if you want me here," I answered.

"Baby?" he called, disbelief in his tone.

Tipping my head back, I looked up at him.

"You want to tell me why you think I wouldn't want you here?" he queried.

I held his gaze and considered how to best answer that question. Ultimately, I didn't come up with a reasonable response because this wasn't exactly a discussion I could have right now. "There's not enough time to do that," I confessed.

Walker clenched his jaw. He did that for a long time before he insisted, "I want you here tonight."

"Then I'll be here," I promised.

"We'll talk about this tonight," he demanded.

"Okay."

With that, Walker brought his hand up to the side of my face. His fingers drove back into my hair until his palm was cradling the back of my head.

A moment later, he was kissing me.

I found myself melting against him as I kissed him back.

I told myself it was a good thing. Because despite the foul mood I was in, I didn't want to leave with so much tension between us.

Walker was still the love of my life.

We just needed to get over this hurdle.

"I have been dying to talk to you for weeks."

I sat down and stared into the eyes of a woman who'd become one of my dearest friends. Of course, now I was beginning to question just how much I actually meant that considering I'd hidden the truth of my relationship with Walker from Holland all this time.

It was Saturday evening, I'd already gone out to lunch with Beck, and Holland and I were in her dressing room at the venue. The band was set to go on stage soon for their second performance during this stop on the tour.

"I'm really sorry for not telling you," I immediately apologized.

She shot me a look that indicated she thought I was crazy. "You don't need to apologize," she insisted. "I completely understand why you two have been keeping it quiet. I just don't know how you've done it for so long."

Shaking my head, I told her, "It hasn't been easy. I mean, in the beginning, we had our reasons. But then, Walker's mom and then his dad and then my Grandma. It's been one thing after another, and when we finally got through some of the really tough stuff, I think we both just wanted to enjoy being with each other and not have to worry about putting another difficult thing on our plate."

Holland eyed me as she fussed with her clothes, clearly wanting to make sure she looked perfect to go on stage. She didn't really need to work too hard to accomplish that because she was simply gorgeous.

"Why do I feel like there's a 'but' coming somewhere in the midst of all that?" she asked.

I sighed. "I'm just... I've reached a point where keeping the secret is really starting to bother me," I began. "I want it to be out in the open. We're missing out on so much because we've kept this quiet for so long."

"Well, it's not like Beck would have made it easy," she reasoned. "So, I get that part of it. Even now, I can't imagine it'll go over well with him. But you and Walker are grown adults. You need to do whatever is going to make you happy."

"That's just it, though. What if Walker is content to keep things just the way they are?" I questioned her.

Holland seemed surprised by my question. "Did he say that he was?" she asked.

I shook my head. "No. I mean, he said he'd risk telling Beck now if he wasn't worried about the rest of the band. He wants to wait until after the tour."

As Holland began getting her makeup set out in front of the mirror, she surmised, "Let me guess. You don't want to wait."

Shrugging, I replied, "It's not that I'm looking to cause a problem for everyone. It's just... this is getting more and more difficult. Beck took me out for lunch today to celebrate my birthday early. Not only do I have to pretend I know nothing about how the tour is going beyond whatever he tells me when we talk every week or what I tell him I get from you, but I also can't tell him about one of the most important things happening in my life."

"I'm sorry you're having such a hard time with this," she said.

"Do you think it's wrong?" I asked.

"Which part?" she countered.

I didn't even want to bring myself to say it. I never thought about myself as being this kind of person, but it was who I'd turned into over the years. And now that I'd been covering it

168

up for so long, it had all become like second nature to me. I no longer had to think about what I was going to say before I said it. That bothered me.

"Lying to everyone," I answered. "Holland, this isn't who I am. And yet, somehow, it's who I've become."

Holland sat down on the bench in front of the vanity and stared at me in silence for a long time. She'd always been friendly and open with me, which is why I grew nervous. I started to chew on the corner of my lip as I squirmed under the intense scrutiny of her gaze.

"I think we all do what we have to do to protect ourselves," she started, surprising me. "Sometimes, that might mean keeping big secrets from people who are the most important to us. It's not about how we feel about them. It's about how we feel about ourselves and what we need in those moments. You can't blame yourself for doing what you needed to do all these years. And if you and Walker are both content with where you are, there's no reason you should be worried about what you're doing to protect that space."

Hearing Holland's words was a relief. I liked knowing that she didn't seem the least bit bothered that the two of us had been friends only a few months longer than Walker and I had been officially dating.

Maybe that was the thing about having good friends. They gave you the space to be yourself and share what you needed or wanted whenever you were ready to do it.

It was at that moment I realized how lucky I was to have her.

"Thanks, Holland."

"You're welcome."

"I just wish I still felt content with where we are," I murmured.

"What do you mean?" she asked.

I took in a deep breath and blew it out slowly. "I'm trying to be patient, but I'm sick of hiding," I told her. "I love him more than I could ever tell you. I want to spend the rest of my life with him. And I know we've dealt with a lot over the years, but there's this one small part of me that is starting to wonder if he feels the same."

Holland's head jerked back. "Sadie, I never would have guessed it if I hadn't heard him speaking to you on the phone a few weeks ago," she started. "But now that I know that you two have been together for so long, everything makes sense. The way Walker is, especially when we're on tour, tells me that that man would sooner die than not have you in his life. He adores you."

I nodded my agreement and assured her, "I know that. I know how much he loves me. I'm just starting to wonder if he likes how it is right now with nobody knowing. And if that's the case, what does that say for our future?"

"But he didn't say that he wants to hide it forever, did he?" she asked.

Shaking my head, I answered, "No. But it's been eight years."

"I'm not sure I'm following you," she said.

"What man, after eight years of being with someone, doesn't want to make that official?" I asked.

Understanding dawned in her face. "You want to get married," she declared.

"Yes. And in all this time, he's never mentioned it. I worry that he doesn't feel the same. I mean, I know he adores me. But what if this is all I ever have with him?" I worried.

Holland sighed as she stood and moved to the couch where I was sitting. When she sat down beside me, she said, "You have to do what's best for you. Trust me when I tell you that you've got to make yourself happy. Sometimes, that means letting go of people who are important to you. I'm not saying that you should give up on Walker and move on. But I do think you should find a way to really talk to him about it. The man he is… Sadie, I don't think he'd ever want to risk losing you."

The mere thought of not being with Walker made my heart ache. I was physically ill at the mention of us not being together.

I knew I needed to talk to him, but I didn't exactly think I was prepared to give him some kind of ultimatum. At this point, I needed to give him the chance to prove that sharing the truth was important. All I had to do was get to the end of the tour. If things didn't change by then, I'd have to really think about what I wanted.

"This is so hard," I murmured.

"I'm on your side. I'll do whatever I can to support the both of you through this, and I won't make it obvious," she offered. "I can imagine how difficult it's been to hide the truth of your relationship for so long, and I would think that a night like tonight is going to be especially difficult. You're both here, and yet, you can't do the things that probably feel natural to you as a couple."

"That's exactly the truth. It's all the pretending that's really getting to me. So, thank you for being here, for listening, and for wanting to help us navigate through this. I'm happy that there's someone else I can finally talk to about this."

"So, nobody else knows at all?" she asked.

"Raid and Alan. That's it."

She smiled. "Well, you've got me now, so don't hesitate to ask for my help. It's what I do these days."

My brows pulled together. "What do you mean?" I asked.

Her smile turned into a full-blown grin. "Cash met a girl when we were back in New Hampshire. Maybe Walker told you about her?"

I nodded, recalling him telling me why they'd gone back to New Hampshire a few weeks ago. Cash had met a girl named Demi, and she was apparently not very interested in him.

"She's here."

"She's here?" I repeated.

"Well, she recently decided she no longer wanted to fight

her attraction to Cash. They've been talking on the phone for a couple weeks now. So, when she told me she wanted to surprise Cash here last night, I set everything up for her. I've been anxiously waiting for them to get here today because I can't wait to see what happened."

My eyes widened. I hadn't realized all of that was going on.

"I need this," I told her.

"What?"

"I need this distraction. When are they going to be here?" I asked.

She shrugged. "Let me go see if they're here yet."

With that, Holland stood and moved to the door. It was with near perfect timing because not much more than a minute later, she walked back into the room with Demi.

And I got a bit of the distraction I needed hearing her tell us all about her night with Cash. It was better to focus on that than the overwhelming sadness I felt that I'd need to be around Walker tonight and have to pretend that he wasn't the man who sent my heart racing with just a single look or one gentle touch.

CHAPTER 17

Walker

I T WAS A MESS.

All of it was one big mess.

Weeks ago, I had been looking forward to getting to the part of the tour that would put me back in Pennsylvania. I knew we'd have a bit of a break while we were there, which would give me time to be with Sadie.

This was the longest tour that My Violent Heart had ever done. So, while it was familiar territory in so many ways, it still somehow felt like we were exploring uncharted waters.

I loved touring.

There was nothing quite like having thousands of fans screaming because they were that excited about you doing what you loved to do. I got to live my dream. Night after night, I got to play the drums and make music with my best friends for people all over the world.

It was a bit surreal.

Even now, after all these years, I still felt the same amount of joy for what I was doing as I had when we played our first live show. The feeling I got from being out on stage never went away. It never even faded.

Most of all, I loved the fact that it kept me close to my mom. It was the one piece of her I had left.

That was one of the many reasons I had been struggling so much lately. It was one of the reasons I was stuck in this gigantic mess.

As much as I loved touring, my music, and the rest of the band, Sadie Emerson was my whole world.

There wasn't anything I wouldn't do for her. And yet, it felt like I'd done nothing to help the situation we were in when I was home.

It was now Monday, nearly a week after we left Pennsylvania to finish up the rest of the tour.

While we'd had several great moments together while I was home, for the first time, I didn't feel good about leaving.

Sadie had always been supportive of my career, the same as I'd been of hers. She'd never been jealous or catty, even though she knew the reputation some rock stars had. While I'd never given her any reason to doubt me—and I'd never even considered taking a groupie up on an offer for a night of fun—I loved that Sadie was confident in her knowledge of what she meant to me and had that level of trust in me.

But something changed.

I didn't understand where it was all coming from, and despite attempts to get her to talk, I hadn't had much success.

Following our last show in Pennsylvania last Saturday night, nobody immediately went home. We stayed out, and I had to pretend that Sadie was nothing more than a friendly acquaintance. But what made it so much worse was that we were already on shaky ground.

That wasn't to say that I thought there was an impending breakup or anything. It was just that there was tension between us now where none existed before. And by the time we'd gotten back to my place that night, Sadie wasn't interested in discussing it. It was late, we'd both had a long night, and we were tired.

So, we didn't talk about it then.

But when we woke the next morning and I brought it up, I was certain she'd fed me a line.

"Why did you think that I wouldn't want you here?" I asked her when we sat down to eat breakfast.

She shook her head. "I was having a bad day," she answered. "Plus, my birthday is next Monday, and I hate that you won't be here for it."

I could see why that might be upsetting, but I knew that wasn't what this was about. Even still, I wanted to ease her concerns.

"Well, you know we've got the cookout at Cash's place later today, but I'm planning to celebrate your birthday with you tomorrow. I know it's a week ahead of time, but I hope it feels just as special for you," I told her.

"I know. I appreciate that, and I'm sure it's going to be wonderful," she assured me, her voice slightly more upbeat than it had been the day before. "Like I said, I was just having a bad day. It's been hard not having you around this time. Maybe it's because this is a longer tour than you guys have ever done. It's all good now. We'll have a good time today, and I'm sure tomorrow is going to be spectacular."

"Sadie, I feel like you're trying to convince yourself of what you're saying instead of me," I noted.

Her shoulders fell. "Well, I mean, I'm not going to lie and say I'm not bummed that our situation is what it is right now and that we have to hide," she responded. "But I've had some time to think on it, and I know we've got a plan now. It's a few more weeks, and then we can finally make this a priority."

I frowned. "Sunshine, you've always been a priority to me," I said.

She tipped her head to the side, smiled at me, and

promised, "I know that. I just meant that we could finally deal with this situation that's sort of dragged on for far too long. That's all."

Something was gnawing at me, telling me that she wasn't being entirely truthful, but she seemed to be happy now.

When I took too much time assessing how to proceed, Sadie took the opportunity to speak again.

"And I just want to say that I'm really sorry about yesterday," she lamented. "I should have been feeling grateful for this time we have right now, but I let my emotions get the best of me. I didn't mean to put a damper on the day or on this part of the tour for you."

I reached my hand out, cupped the side of her face, and stroked my thumb over her cheek. "Baby, I don't want you to ever apologize for telling me how you feel," I said. "It is whatever it is. Don't keep that stuff inside, okay?"

Her eyes searched my face, and I thought she was going to tell me what was really bothering her, but she simply pushed her cheek into my hand and replied, "Okay."

With that, I let it go.

The next few days had gone alright. To anyone else, we might have seemed like we were completely fine. Sadie was doing a hell of a job of pretending she had nothing on her mind. But after eight years of being with her, I knew her better than that. The last thing I wanted was to force it out of her or bring it up and upset her, though. Especially when I knew I'd be leaving again.

And now that it was Monday morning, Sadie's birthday, and I'd been away from her for nearly a week now, I couldn't stop thinking about her.

She'd always been on my mind before, but it was different. My thoughts were generally always about all the good things, about all the things I loved about her. About the way she lit up my life when everything felt so dark and full of despair. She was the sunshine in my life.

But now she had that cloud hanging over her head, and I hated it. I hated seeing her so… gloomy. Normally, whenever I spoke to her on the phone or through a video chat, she was always so alive. Vibrant.

For the last week, she tried to appear the same, but I knew she wasn't. Behind the smiling face and cheerful voice was a downtrodden woman. I knew it, and I didn't know how to fix it.

And with today being Sadie's birthday, I certainly wasn't going to do anything to upset her. We didn't have a show until tomorrow night, so at the very least, I was planning to spend as much time as I could in my room talking to her.

Just as I was about to pick up the phone to call her, it started ringing. I looked at the display and saw my brother's name on it.

"Raid?" I answered.

"You're up?" he asked.

"I'm awake if that's what you're asking," I told him. "But I'm not out of bed. What's going on?"

"I'm coming to your room right now to help you," he said. "You've got to get your bags packed."

"What?" I asked.

"Just open the door. I'll be right there."

He disconnected the call, and I sat there staring at the phone for a moment. What the hell was going on?

My thoughts immediately went to my dad. Relapse, maybe?

By the time I flung the cover back and swung my legs out of the bed, there was a knock at the door. I snatched a pair of jeans off the chair and ran to the door. After confirming it was just Raid standing outside the door, I opened it and let him in.

As I pulled my jeans on, I demanded, "You need to talk to me now."

"You need to pack," he ordered, walking toward the bedroom where my suitcase was.

"What is going on?" I asked.

"I've already talked to Holland," he started. "She's letting Cash, Beck, Killian, and Roscoe know that Dad has an issue at home that requires your personal attention."

"Fuck," I hissed. "We just saw him. I took him out on Saturday afternoon, and I swear, he seemed like he was doing so well. The best he's been in years."

"Relax, Walker," Raid commanded. "Dad's fine. But that's not what everyone else thinks. I hadn't realized she knew, but Holland came to me and indicated that you told her about you and Sadie. She came up with a great idea, and I'm helping her pull it off."

I felt marginally better knowing that my dad was okay, but I was completely confused. "What?"

"You're going home today," Raid said. "I've already got a flight booked. You're spending Sadie's birthday where you belong. With her. You've got a flight leaving home tomorrow afternoon that'll get you to our next location."

The silence stretched between us as I stared at him in disbelief.

Sadie.

I was going home to spend her birthday with her.

Why hadn't I ever thought to come up with some story about needing to go home so I wouldn't have missed out on such a special day?

"Walker?"

I blinked my eyes and shook my head as though dismissing the thoughts. "Yeah?"

"We have to leave within the next fifteen minutes if we're going to get you to the airport on time," Raid shared.

Shit.

At that, I sprang into action and started shoving everything into my suitcase. I didn't care what it looked like. I was going to see my girl today.

"Does she know?" I asked after I'd gotten everything in my suitcase and was pulling a shirt over my head.

"No. We thought it would be best if you could go and surprise her," my brother answered.

This was going to be awesome. With how upset she'd been lately, I had no doubt this would cheer her up.

I reached out with one arm, wrapped it around Raid, and said, "Thanks, man. Thank you for doing this."

"I can't really take all the credit for it," he confessed. "Holland came up with the idea. I just handled the logistics."

Pulling back, I replied, "Well, either way, I'm grateful."

He nodded. "You ready?"

"Yeah."

With that, we took off, and Raid drove me to the airport.

Two hours and forty minutes after the plane took off, I had gone home, taken a shower, gotten my car, made a quick stop to pick up some flowers, and arrived at Sadie's place. I pulled up outside her townhouse and realized how much of a surprise this was going to be considering I had a key to her place and didn't even need to wait to go inside to see her. As soon as I'd gotten home earlier, I sent her a text and told her that I'd woken up late and would call her shortly. She replied and told me that she was just going to be painting, so I could call whenever I was ready.

Minutes later, I'd let myself inside, walked up the stairs, and made my way down to the bedroom Sadie had converted into a studio for her art.

She had My Violent Heart music blasting, something she often did when she worked.

The next thing I knew, I felt my heart pounding in my

chest. God, she was so beautiful. Wearing nothing but a pair of white cotton panties and a white camisole with all of her hair pulled up in a messy bun, Sadie herself was like a beautiful canvas.

Suddenly, I had an idea.

I backed out of the room slightly, slipped off my sneakers, tore my shirt over my head, and let my jeans fall to the floor.

I entered the room again and leaned against the doorframe. For a while, she continued to work on the canvas in front of her. I still hadn't quite figured out what she was doing when she bent down, picked up the can with the bright orange paint in it and hurled the paint at the canvas. She did it a second and third time before she turned to put the can down.

But before she could do that, she let out a startled cry.

"Walker," she gasped.

I didn't say anything. Our eyes were locked on one another as we both stood there wearing next to nothing.

When I smiled at her, Sadie's nipples hardened underneath her shirt. That was all it took. One look was all she needed, and she was turned on.

While she continued to stand there, motionless, I pushed off the doorframe and walked in her direction. Stopping in front of her, I reached my hand down into the bucket of paint. I lifted my fingers up to her collarbone and began painting her.

Sadie's chest rose and fell with her deep, slow breaths.

I dipped my whole hand into the paint can again, making sure my whole hand was coated, before bringing it to her breast. Keeping my eyes on her face, I watched her lips part while I squeezed her.

The next thing I knew, the paint can clattered to the floor. Sadie threw her arms over my shoulders and flattened her body against mine. I caught her around the waist before bending down and placing her on the floor on her back.

With her legs wrapped around my waist, Sadie pulled me down on top of her. I dropped my mouth to hers and began kissing her only seconds before I felt the wet fingers of one of her hands trailing down my spine. She had clearly dipped her hands into the paint and wanted to use me as her own personal canvas as well.

I didn't mind.

With my cock nestled firmly against her pussy, I tore my mouth from hers and pushed my palm into the floor beside her shoulder. Finding another open can of paint beside us, I reached my fingertips in, coated them in the pink paint, and pinched her nipple between my thumb and forefinger through her shirt.

Sadie's back arched off the floor as she let out a moan.

"You're so fucking beautiful, baby," I said, my voice deep and husky.

My other hand began sliding her shirt up her body to expose her gorgeous skin beneath. Pushing it up past her breasts, I wasted no time getting my mouth on her. I sucked her nipple in deep. Sadie moaned and rolled her hips.

Damn, she was sexy.

"Walker," she breathed.

I nibbled on her breast, made her squirm, and moved to the other side. She was seriously turned on, had made me the same, and all I wanted to do was prolong this.

We rolled once, and Sadie took her turn to cover my body in paint. She licked along my torso, her fingers traveling over every part her mouth touched. Sadie did all of that while grinding down on my dick, which felt about ready to explode.

I held out as long as I could, giving her the chance to cover my body with all the paint she wanted, but eventually flipped her to her back again. Covering my hands in electric blue paint, I started at her ankles and ran my hands up along the backs of her legs until I reached her knees. Once I was there, I brought my hands to the tops of her thighs and continued my ascent to her hips.

Seconds later, no longer able to hold myself back, I yanked her panties down her legs. Sadie gasped at the force of it, but I was on a mission.

I buried my face in her pussy. Licking, sucking, tasting. Devouring. Taking every last drop of her while she drove her hands into my hair and moaned.

"Please, babe," she begged.

I knew what she wanted. I'd give it to her. But first, I was giving her this. Not relenting, I went at her harder. Faster. My tongue went deeper.

And just as I had wanted, mere moments later, Sadie was holding me at the back of my head while she came apart. I continued to lick, devouring everything she had, until she made it to the end.

Giving her no time to recover, I managed to get my boxer briefs off in record time and drove inside.

"Walker," Sadie panted. "Fuck, I missed your cock."

"You like this, baby?" I grunted, driving in hard.

"I love it."

She loved it. I groaned and went deeper. Faster.

My hands came to her breasts and gripped them firmly as I continued to thrust my hips forward.

Every sound, breath, and whisper that came from Sadie was just one more thing that sent me higher and higher to the point of no return.

"Babe, I'm going to come," Sadie warned me.

I drove in quicker, wanting to see her come apart.

Several strokes later, Sadie moaned through her orgasm. Just as she was coming down from it, I found my release, burying my cock deep, and capturing her mouth in a brutal kiss.

When it left me, I collapsed on top of her briefly before rolling us. I was on my back, Sadie was on top of me, and we were both panting.

We stayed like that a long time until eventually, I broke the silence.

"Happy birthday, sunshine," I said, after we'd managed to catch our breath.

"How are you here?" Sadie asked.

"You ready for this?" I countered.

She lifted her head from my chest, looked down at me, and replied, "Yes."

"Holland and Raid planned it all out. I don't know all the details, but Raid told me it was Holland's idea. He just dealt with coming up with a story to tell everyone else and getting my flights sorted."

"Really?"

"Yeah."

"When do you leave?"

"Tomorrow afternoon."

She smiled.

And for the first time in more than a week, I felt that smile hit me somewhere deep. It wasn't a smile that was laced with hurt or sadness. Sadie was genuinely happy.

I owed my brother big time.

Him and Holland.

"What are we going to do?" she asked.

"I'll do whatever you want," I told her. "This was very last minute, so I didn't really have a chance to plan anything."

She thought about it for a moment before she said, "I think I just want to spend the whole day in with you. Watching movies, cuddling, and eating."

"If that's what you want, baby, that's what we'll do," I assured her.

"That's what I want."

"You want me to make you spaghetti later, or do you want it from somewhere special?" I asked.

"Surprise me," she said.

I gave her a gentle squeeze before I tipped my head back and to the side. "What exactly were you making there?"

"It was something special for myself," she explained. "Well, technically, I was going to give you the painting if you wanted it, but I'm practicing for something else."

My brows pulled together. "I don't understand."

"You see the spots where I covered the canvas?" she asked.

"Yeah."

"Well, once I remove that, you'll see it better. I'm working on a way to incorporate the two of us into a design."

She wanted to incorporate the two of us into a design?

"What do you mean?" I wondered.

"My art and your music," she clarified. "When this is complete, the drum sticks will look like they were formed by the paint splatter."

The paint splatter was her, the drum sticks were me.

"Alright, well, if you wanted to give me the painting, what are you practicing for?" I pressed.

She smiled before she shared, "My first tattoo." My arms tightened around her. That's when she added, "I want you inked on me, Walker."

It had been eight years. I knew there was nobody else for me. I'd known it from the beginning. And I knew Sadie felt the same about me. We were meant for each other.

But something about hearing her say she wanted me inked on her body, her beautiful body that had only ever been mine, made something profound move through me. Warmth flooded my veins as I felt an overwhelming need to prove to her how much she meant to me.

"Watching movies, cuddling, and eating has to wait, sunshine," I started as I began to lift myself off the floor while keeping a firm hold on her. "We need to wash off this paint so you can show me where on this gorgeous body you want to put us."

"Movies, cuddling, and food can wait," she breathed.

I got myself to standing, Sadie's legs wrapped around my waist, and I brought my mouth to hers. With my lips just brushing up against hers, I rasped, "Do you know how much I love you?"

"Show me," she begged.

I had every intention of doing that already. And since it was her birthday, I figured it was best not to delay.

So, I carried her to the bathroom so we could shower together. And then I showed her just how much I loved her.

And as the paint was washed from our bodies, I found that the worries we'd been feeling were washed away, too.

CHAPTER 18

Sadie
Two and a half months later

CONTENT.

That was the best word to describe how I felt at that moment. There were a bunch of other words I could have used to illustrate my feelings but content seemed to be about the best.

It was late Sunday morning, and I couldn't have imagined any better place to be than where I was right now—in Walker's bed, my body half on top of his with one of his arms wrapped around my back and his other hand covering mine.

We'd woken up a little bit ago. Or, I should say, Walker woke me up a little bit ago. He had his way with me, and now we were relishing in the bliss of morning sex.

I wasn't quite sure there was anything better than this.

Technically, that wasn't true.

What was better was knowing that I could have it every morning for the foreseeable future now because the tour was over. My Violent Heart played their final show on Friday evening in New Hampshire, and Walker came home to me yesterday.

We'd had a glorious reunion, not that I expected anything less.

In fact, as rough as things had been for me on an emotional level a couple months ago, I was now feeling pretty good. The remainder of the tour wasn't exactly easy, but with each week that passed, I found myself growing more and more excited about Walker's return. Because of that, so much of what was bringing me down started to dissipate.

And now that I was feeling so good, I wanted to communicate that to the man who'd put up with so much added stress during that time.

"This is the best," I declared, my voice sounding light and airy. And content.

"What is?"

I smiled. He knew what I was talking about. He simply wanted to hear me say it.

"Knowing that you're home, you're back, and we get to do this every day now," I answered.

"I can't say I disagree with that sentiment then," he said. "Without a doubt, this is the best. You know what I love about it?"

I lifted my cheek from his chest and asked, "What?"

"Knowing that you won't fall asleep alone at night," he shared.

My heart melted on the spot. Even after all these years, Walker was still just as romantic as ever. He knew what to say to make me feel good, and not once did he ever make me think he didn't mean precisely what he said.

One time.

One time I told him that I hated going to bed alone and wished I was falling asleep in his arms. It had stuck with him all this time. And now, he was in a place where he could fix what was causing me pain.

"Do you know how much I love you?" I asked.

His mouth formed a smile. "I think I have a pretty good idea."

"I don't want to get up," I told him.

"So, stay in bed," he suggested. "I can run downstairs, make breakfast, and bring it up."

"Mmm. As wonderful as that sounds, I need to get up and find my phone. I'm sure there's already a call from Beck. If I don't want him showing up at my place unannounced and not finding me there, I need to make sure I don't avoid his calls," I explained.

"I don't think Beck's going to call you," Walker said.

Narrowing my eyes on him, I argued, "But Beck calls me almost immediately every time he gets back from being on tour. I'm pretty sure there's already going to be a missed call from him."

Walker moved his head back and forth on the pillow indicating that I was wrong. "Beck might call you when he gets back from being on tour, Sadie, but the problem is that Beck didn't come home."

"What do you mean? Where is he?" I questioned him.

"He's still in New Hampshire."

Cocking an eyebrow, I pressed, "Why?"

"He met someone there back in the summer," Walker shared.

My eyes widened as my body tensed. "He did? Why didn't he tell me?" I asked.

Walker chuckled. "Probably because nothing came of it. He saw her on Friday night for the first time since we were there back in July."

Well, that made sense. While I initially felt a bit of shock that Beck hadn't told me about this woman, I started to think it might be a good thing because then he might understand why I'd kept my relationship with Walker a secret. Obviously, that wasn't the case here.

"So, I need to call him then," I decided.

"Why?"

"Because while I understand now why he's not home, the only reason that's the case is because you've told me," I noted. "If he's caught up in this woman now, he might not realize it right away, but he would eventually realize that I never reached out when I didn't hear from him."

"That makes sense."

Just then, my stomach growled.

"Hungry?" Walker asked.

I nodded.

"Do you want me to make you breakfast and bring it up, or do you want to come down with me?"

"I'll come down," I told him.

Ten minutes later, Walker and I had made it downstairs. He immediately got to work on breakfast while I went in search of my phone. I'd wait until after we ate to call Beck, but I wanted to make sure he hadn't reached out to me already.

Locating my phone, I found a text waiting for me. But it hadn't come from Beck. Holland had reached out.

Holland: Hey! I would have reached out sooner, but I figured you'd be busy reuniting with your man. I wanted to see if you're up for getting together sometime this coming week.

I smiled after I read her message. Long before she even knew about Walker and me, Holland had been such a great friend. Now that she was in on our secret, I realized just how good of a friend she actually was. I'd never forget what she helped to put together for my birthday this year.

As I moved back toward the kitchen to help Walker with breakfast, I tapped out a response.

Me: Yes, I was totally busy reuniting. But Walker's making me breakfast now. Anyway, I'm definitely up for getting together this week.

Holland: :sigh: I wish someone was making me breakfast.

Me: I don't know how it's possible that there's not.

Truer words have never been spoken. I couldn't imagine any man feeling anything less than lucky for the privilege of loving Holland. She was smart, funny, talented, and absolutely gorgeous.

Holland: Actually, I'd give up the breakfast if I could get the reunion. What I would give for that...

It dawned on me just how crazy this was. If anyone should have been able to land a guy, it was Holland. She was perfect, and it seemed completely impossible that she hadn't found someone who would have been entirely devoted to her.

Me: I'm sure he's out there.

Holland: Yeah, well, I won't hold my breath waiting. Anyway, do you have any days you can't do next week?

Me: I'll double-check that Walker doesn't have anything planned, but I should be good to do any day.

Holland: Okay. I'll let you go and enjoy your breakfast. Let me know on your schedule and we'll plan something.

Me: Sounds great.

Holland: Later. Tell Walker hello from me.

Me: I will.

I set my phone down on the counter and said, "Holland says hello."

"Yeah? What's going on with her?" he asked as he pushed the button for the toaster down. The bacon was already cooking, and he had already pulled out the eggs and cheese.

I grinned. Bacon, egg, and cheese on English muffins.

Yep.

Having Walker back made me feel very, very content.

Snapping myself out of it, I moved toward the refrigerator and said, "She wants to get together this week. Coffee or orange juice?"

"Juice," he replied. "When are you two going to be doing that?"

I swear, it was like the man knew what I wanted when I wanted it and always strived to make life easier for me by requesting the same thing. As I pulled out the juice, I shared, "We didn't nail anything down yet. I told her I wanted to ask you if you had anything planned before I committed to something with her."

"I don't have anything pressing planned," he started. "You schedule it whenever is good for the two of you, and I'll plan my stuff around it. I want to visit my dad at some point soon, but everything else can be done whenever. Right now, catching up on you is my priority."

I tipped my head to the side as I leaned up against the counter and looked at him curiously. "Catching up on me? What does that mean?" I asked.

He boxed me in, lowered his mouth to mine, and allowed his voice to drop a few octaves when he explained, "Catching up on kissing you, touching you, holding you, cuddling you, and my absolute favorite, fucking you."

My breath caught in my throat. He still could do this to me. He could turn me on with one look, one touch, or a handful of words.

"Catching up sounds like fun," I rasped. "Should I prepare for at least a week of that?"

"You have the time in your schedule?" he countered.

I licked my lips. "What do you think I did with all my time when you were away? I worked my butt off so I could focus all of my attention on you when you got home."

His lips twitched. "Looks like we'll be doing a lot of catching up then."

"Food first," I pleaded.

Walker chuckled, gave me a kiss on the lips, and moved back to the eggs. I poured the juice.

A few minutes later, we were eating.

And after that, I said, "I'm going to call Beck now. I'd rather get it out of the way now, so we can have the rest of the day to ourselves."

"Okay, sunshine. That works for me," he replied.

I picked up my phone, found Beck's number, and tapped on the screen. As the phone rang, I took in a deep breath and blew it out. I was going into this call having to remember that I didn't know he was still in New Hampshire.

Beck answered, "Hello?"

"Where are you?" I asked, an irritated edge to my tone.

I knew exactly how to make this convincing.

My brother sighed into the phone. "I'm still in New Hampshire," he told me.

"Why didn't you come home?" I asked. "Everyone else is back."

"How do you know that?" he countered.

Shit.

Shit, I totally slipped up.

Damn it. I needed to think quick.

Hoping I sounded casual, I answered, "Oh, well, I was out yesterday and saw Walker. He told me you guys played your last show in New Hampshire on Friday. Then I talked to Holland earlier this morning. We texted back and forth a few times, and we decided to get together this coming week. You always reach out to me when you get home, and since I hadn't heard from you, I thought you were blowing me off."

Technically, that was all the truth. I just hadn't said where exactly 'out' was and that I'd spent the night at Walker's place.

Beck immediately apologized, "I'm sorry, Sadie. I've been caught up in something here, and it completely slipped my mind."

God, he was apologizing for something he didn't need to apologize for. If he only knew how many times I'd lied to him.

"What's going on?" I asked, trying to keep the emotions out of my voice.

"I met someone," he declared.

"What?"

I did my best to sound shocked and surprised.

"Long story short," Beck started. "When we came here a couple months ago to play a few shows, I walked into the hotel we were going to be staying at and met this woman. Her name is Chasey. We talked for a few minutes that day, and I gave her my number. Unfortunately, she never called me. But with Cash meeting Demi and setting up one final performance for us at her cousin's bar here, I ended up running into the woman again on Friday night. I took her out to dinner yesterday."

"That's great news, Beck," I remarked. "How did it go?"

At least the faking part was over. For now anyway. Because I was genuinely interested in hearing how it went. Beck was, even if I had hidden something huge from him for years, so important to me. I would always worry about him.

"Well, I was about to head out to go to her place just as you called me," he shared.

Why wasn't she already with him at the hotel? Or, why hadn't he gone back to her place?

I hesitated a moment to consider why this would be the case. When I didn't come up with any explanations, I said, "Wait? Are you telling me you didn't bring her back to your hotel room last night?"

Beck laughed and confessed, "No, I didn't."

"Oh my God," I whispered as it hit me. "You like her."

"What?"

"You like her," I repeated. "You gave this woman your number, and she never called. But by some odd stroke of luck, you get this second chance, and she agrees to go to dinner with you. So, you don't come home to Pennsylvania, and instead, you extend your stay in New Hampshire. Presumably, dinner went well because you were just about to head to her place since she made you go back to the hotel after dinner."

"Where, in all of that, do you get some feeling that there's this profound thing happening?" he questioned me.

"You're putting in a lot of effort for this girl," I noted. "If you didn't like her, you wouldn't waste your time."

There was an extended pause before he admitted, "Okay, okay. I like her."

This was the best news ever. Walker had just returned to the living room to see me beaming, and I could tell that seeing that made him happy. He sat down beside me, pulled my feet into his lap, and started to massage them as I responded to Beck. "I knew it. So, tell me about Chasey," I demanded.

"We're just now getting to know each other, but she's a newly divorced single mom of the most adorable five-month-old little girl."

Okay, I hadn't been expecting that.

"How newly divorced?" I asked.

"I don't know the exact date, but when I met her about four months ago, she had just learned her husband was cheating on her," he shared.

This was new. Very, very new. As happy as I was about the prospect of Beck finding someone he liked, I had to be honest about it. It terrified me to think that he was jumping into something too soon with someone who might not be ready for it. "Oh, wow, Beck. Is she... are you sure she's ready to get involved with someone else this soon?"

"We're just getting to know one another right now," my brother assured me. "But I have every intention of taking this slow because I realize that whatever happens with her will also affect her daughter."

He was the best. And I hoped this worked out the way he wanted it to. I would have hated to see him end up hurt. "You're a good man, Beck. Just promise me you'll be careful," I pleaded.

"I promise I'll be careful," he said. "And when I get back, I'll reach out to you so we can hang."

"Alright. I'll let you go then. Talk to you later."

"Love you, Sadie."

"Love you, too. And good luck."

"Thanks."

With that, we disconnected the call and my eyes fell on Walker. He was still rubbing my feet, which felt amazing, and he had his gaze on me.

"This is *the best* thing that could have ever happened," I declared.

A crease formed between his brows. "What is?"

My eyes practically popped out of my head. How could he not know?

"Walker, Beck has found someone he's interested in," I noted. "If things go well between them, this might actually work in our favor."

A genuine look of surprise and curiosity washed over him. "In what way?"

Ugh. Men.

"Let's say Raid came and told you about a girl he was dating when you and I first got together," I began. "While I'm sure you'd have your thoughts about it, likely supportive, the majority of your focus would not be on his relationship. My thought is that you'd be focused on your relationship with me."

Understanding washed over him. "So, you think this is the perfect time to tell Beck about us because he'll be too busy putting all his time and effort into his new relationship?"

I nodded and clarified, "According to him, they aren't officially dating yet and are just getting to know one another. But I can tell he wants it to be serious. So, we'll give him some time to make that happen. Maybe waiting was the best thing we could have done."

He gave my foot one final squeeze. "I hope you're right."

Walker said it, and I knew he wholeheartedly felt that way.

But something about the sound of his voice just didn't sit right with me.

Instead of talking to him about it and leading us into another situation filled with tension, I decided to believe the best. I tossed my phone aside, cuddling up with Walker, and promised, "I am."

He didn't respond. But what he did do was immediately start catching up on cuddling with me.

CHAPTER 19

Sadie
Seven weeks later

THOUGHT THE TIMING WAS PERFECT.

In fact, I didn't think we could find ourselves in a more favorable position.

And yet, Walker didn't seem even remotely ready to make a move. He hadn't even brought it up when I'd shared the good news days ago.

We were now in the middle of the week between the Christmas and New Year holiday. There was a party planned for New Year's Eve at Beck's house, the house he was now going to share with his fiancée, Chasey.

Yes, fiancée.

On Christmas Eve, Beck had proposed to Chasey, and she accepted his proposal. So, my brother was engaged. He was on cloud nine, and I couldn't have been happier for him. I also believed it was the absolute best-case scenario for Walker and me to go to him and reveal the truth about our relationship.

Beck was no longer in the getting-to-know-you stage of his relationship with Chasey. They'd moved very quickly, and she and her daughter, Luna, were now living with him. With his focus and energy and attention on everything happening in his own life, I had believed that perhaps this would be the ideal time to break the news.

Walker wasn't even thinking about it.

I knew that because he hadn't mentioned it once since he finished the tour.

If I made mention of it first, he'd discuss it with me. But he hadn't gone out of his way to bring it up to me ever.

I didn't want to assume the worst, but it was kind of hard not to.

And now that we were two days away from the party at Beck's, I thought it would be nice to finally share the truth. Walker and I could get it out there, possibly spend the party being with each other, and start the new year off without any more secrets.

I just wasn't convinced I was going to get the reaction I was hoping for out of Walker.

Now that we'd just finished up dinner and were cuddling up on the couch to watch some television, I asked, "Can we talk?"

"Sure, sunshine. What do you want to talk about?"

"I want us to go to Beck's house tomorrow and tell him the truth," I said.

Walker's body instantly tensed up. "Are you... are you serious?" he stammered.

"Yes."

"Tomorrow?" he asked.

"Yes," I confirmed.

Caution washed over him. "I don't know if that's a good idea, Sadie," he warned.

"Why not?"

He hesitated to respond, but when I made it clear I wasn't going to speak until he gave me an answer, he explained, "Well, first, he's got Chasey and Luna living there with him. This will probably get uncomfortable. Do you really want them subjected to that?"

"That's the thing, Walker," I started. "While I don't want to put them in the middle of anything, Chasey is going to be my sister-in-law now. Luna is going to be my niece. They're in this family now, the same way I want *you* to be in this family. If Beck doesn't want things to get uncomfortable for them, he'll need to handle his reaction appropriately."

Walker shook his head. "I think that's a good idea in theory, but I'm not sure it's going to play out the way you want it to," he reasoned. "And what about New Year's Eve? Aren't you planning to be at Beck's for the party?"

"Yes, I am. I was hoping I could arrive and leave with you," I told him.

Surprise washed over him, and his brows shot up. "You think it's going to be that easy? Do you honestly believe that this is going to be as simple as showing up at Beck's house tomorrow and letting him know that we're together now? Do you think when he finds out that we're not only together but that we have been for eight years without ever once mentioning it that he won't feel the least bit betrayed and deceived?"

Walker wasn't wrong.

I knew Beck would feel that way. Deep down, I knew he didn't have a right to tell me who I could date, but he did have a right to be angry and upset that I lied to him.

So, no, I didn't think it was going to be as easy as Walker seemed to think I thought it would be.

"If we don't do this now, we're never going to do it," I rasped.

"Sadie, this is not the time to do it," Walker insisted. His words might have sounded like advice or a suggestion, but the tone of his voice made it clear he was begging me not to push to do this.

I couldn't understand why he was so against this.

And because I couldn't continue on with things the way they were, I knew I needed to give Walker the full truth of where things stood for me.

"Do you ever plan on telling him?" I asked as I stood from the couch.

"Of course," he answered, looking up at me. "I want to tell him, I know we need to, but I'm not exactly thrilled about doing it either."

He wasn't thrilled about it?

"Which part are you not thrilled about?" I demanded to know. "Is it the part where things might be tough for a little bit as we deal with some justifiable resentment from Beck for having lied for so many years? Or is it the part where the whole world knows we're together that you're not thrilled about?"

"What the hell is that supposed to mean?" he countered, now coming to his feet in front of me.

I stared at him, wishing the answer would be right there on his face for me. It wasn't.

"It means exactly what it means," I told him. "There always seems to be a reason for this to not happen. It's been one thing after another from the very beginning."

Shock and hurt washed over him. "My mom died," he rasped, his wounded tone clear as day.

I shut my mouth and pressed my lips together.

Walker stared at me in disbelief.

The silence stretched between us for so long, and I couldn't take it. "Walker, I wasn't—"

"You weren't what, Sadie?" he asked, cutting me off. He was clearly very angry now. "Twice now you've said something to me like that. My mom died, and I was trying to cope with the loss of her. If that wasn't enough, my dad became an alcoholic, your grandmother died, and I had five other people in the band whose futures I had to consider. Fuck, I realize this has gone on way too long, but without any notice you want to drag me to Beck's tomorrow to dump this on him?"

"It's been eight years," I reminded him. "Eight. Are we ever going to do it? Do you really even want to?"

"I can't believe you're asking me that," he shot back. "Sadie, I've been agonizing over this for months now. I want nothing more than to get this out in the open so we don't have to sneak around. Shit. I slipped up about a month ago at the studio when I asked Beck about how his trip to New Hampshire was when he hadn't told anyone about it. Luckily, he bought my lie when I said he'd mentioned something when we were all at Cash's house before the holiday. You don't think I want to be done with that shit? You think I want to continue hiding what I have with you every day and lying to people I love and care about?"

I shook my head back and forth in frustration. "I don't know, Walker," I said softly. "Maybe you want me to believe it's not how you feel, but I'm having a hard time."

His eyes widened in astonishment. "You're having a hard time?" he retorted. As he threw his hand out to the side, he asked, "Do you have any idea how difficult this is for me? Do you realize, and I mean do you truly understand, what doing this could mean for me? The odds are that I'm going to have to make a choice, Sadie. In making that choice, I might not ever make another album or do another tour. My career could be over. And I promised. I promised my mom I wouldn't ever give my music up and that I'd hold on to you. How do I do this knowing I'm going to have to make that decision?"

"The band isn't just Beck," I argued. "What about Cash, Holland, Killian, and Roscoe? Don't their opinions matter?"

He nodded. "They do," he confirmed, his voice slightly less angered. "But how successful do you think we'll be if there's enough tension between Beck and me? I'm not going to ruin everyone else's career just because… because—"

"Because what? Because you fell in love? Because you're

with someone that makes you happy? If that's what this really is Walker, there has to be a way to make it work that doesn't involve hiding," I told him.

His shoulders sagged and he looked simply defeated. "Sadie, I… I don't know how to fix this. I don't know how to make it so there isn't some awful outcome."

He didn't want it.

His words might have indicated that he'd choose me over his music. Personally, I didn't think he needed to make that choice. I didn't want this to have to be an either-or situation.

I paced back and forth for several moments, trying to figure out how to tell him where I was in this whole situation. Then, I realized it was just best to ask him. So, I stopped pacing and focused my attention on him again.

"Was this a mistake?" I rasped.

"What?"

"This," I said as I waved my hand between the two of us. "Was it a mistake? Did we do this all these years for nothing?"

His expression turned horrified. "Nothing?" he repeated.

I swallowed hard. This was it. I had to take a stand or I'd never get what I wanted in life. And I loved Walker. God, I loved him. But sometimes, love wasn't enough. I wanted everything, and I didn't think I should have to sacrifice what I wanted.

"Where are we going, Walker?" I wondered, my voice feeling very shaky.

"Baby, why do you sound like that?" he asked. The way he presented the question told me he knew exactly where this was heading.

My eyes searched his handsome face. My heart was breaking with every second that passed. "I want a future with you," I declared. My voice was now eerily calm.

"I want the same thing," he assured me.

Tears filled my eyes.

"I want more," I started. "I don't just want a future of hiding with you. I want to get married. I want to have babies one day. I want to celebrate holidays together with my family. I want to go on tour with you. And I can't do any of that. None of that will ever happen as long as we keep this secret."

"Sadie…" He trailed off.

"I can't do it any longer, Walker," I croaked. "I want to be closer to you. Every time I think we're nearly there, something else comes up and gets in the way. I can't do it anymore. And you shouldn't want to do it either."

I saw the muscle in his jaw working as he clenched his teeth together. "Let's just wait until after the New Year," he pleaded.

Shaking my head, I said, "I can't, Walker. There's always something else I have to wait for. And if I agree to wait until after the New Year, there will be another thing I come second to. So, I'm going."

"Going?"

I nodded. "I'm going home," I told him. "I'm leaving, and you need to think about what you want. I don't expect you to leave the band for me, Walker. But I deserve more than this. *You* deserve more than this. And if you don't want it, I'm not going to fight this battle on my own."

Walker seemed to be in a state of utter disbelief. "Sadie, I love you," he proclaimed.

"I love you, too."

"Don't leave here like this," he begged.

"I have to. Because every holiday we spend apart, every tour you'll go on down the road, every party we're at, my heart breaks that I can't do any of it as the woman in your life. I don't want to just be Beck's sister anymore. I want to be yours."

He moved toward me and his voice cracked when he declared, "Baby, you are mine."

I nodded in agreement. "Yeah. But I don't want to be yours in secret anymore."

Reaching a hand out to touch the side of my face, his eyes were pleading with mine. "Stay. Let's figure it out," he said.

"Will you go with me tomorrow to tell Beck the truth?" I asked.

He didn't respond.

"Will you take me to the New Year's Eve party with you?" I questioned him, offering another way to go about it.

He still didn't respond.

And his silence gave me my answer.

I lifted my hand to his at the side of my face. As I curled my fingers around it and squeezed, I said, "I love you. I love you so much that the very thought of walking out like this makes me feel sick. But I've made my decision, and now, you need to make yours. Please don't call me, Walker, until you're ready to make a commitment to me that doesn't involve keeping us tucked away from the people we love."

His fingers tightened around mine. "Sadie," he whispered.

The agony in his voice was going to make me change my mind. And I couldn't change my mind. We'd let this go on for long enough. It was well past the time to put it out there.

Pulling his hand from my face, I turned my head and kissed his palm. After lowering our connected hands, I stepped forward, touched my lips to his, and kissed him for what I hoped wouldn't be our last kiss.

His arms instantly came around me, and he held on tight. When I pulled my mouth from his, I said, "Please let me go."

"I can't."

"You have to," I told him. "If you aren't going to give me what I need in this relationship, you have to let me go."

His tortured eyes searched my face, and I was certain I was going to need to ask him to let me go again. But he eventually loosened his hold on me. Even though it was what I had asked him to do, there was a part of me that had been hoping he'd hold on and tell me to call Beck right then and there.

The disappointment could be felt throughout my entire body.

I looked away and started moving toward the door so I could get my shoes on. Without looking back, I could feel Walker following behind me.

He never said another word.

Even when he followed me out into the garage, where we parked my car as part of our plan to keep things hidden, he still didn't say anything.

I figured I'd be the one to break the silence. Standing beside my car, I looked up at him and said, "No matter what you decide, I will always love you."

He still said nothing.

But he didn't need to.

The pain and the anguish was swimming in the depths of his eyes. I knew he loved me. This was simply an impossible choice for him.

"Goodbye, Walker."

I reached out to open the door and felt his fingers curl around my bicep. Hope surged in me, but when I looked back at him, I knew he wasn't going to say what I wanted to hear.

In fact, he didn't say anything at all.

We stared at each other in silence for what felt like hours, but I knew it hadn't been more than a couple seconds. When I could no longer take it, I opened the door and got in the car. A moment later, I was backing out of the garage.

I gave him one last look, felt my heart shatter in my chest, and drove away.

I didn't look in the rearview mirror because I didn't think I could handle what I might see. If I had, I would have seen it when Walker completely lost his cool and trashed his garage.

CHAPTER 20

Sadie

I COULDN'T BELIEVE WHAT JUST HAPPENED.

It was New Year's Eve, and despite the fact that I was feeling miserable inside about the situation I was currently in, I still went to my brother's place for the New Year's Eve party.

I knew I'd see Walker there, but if I didn't show up, it would have set off alarm bells. I didn't need to deal with that on top of everything else I was dealing with.

So, I went.

But I didn't think it'd be as difficult as it had been. It's not like Walker and I hadn't been pretending to be nothing more than friendly acquaintances for years. It should have been a breeze.

Unfortunately, it was so much more difficult than I had anticipated.

Because what I hadn't prepared myself for was the fact that I was now worried about the future of my relationship with him.

When I arrived earlier in the evening, I was greeted by all the members of the band the same way they always greeted me. I knew I'd need to act like nothing was wrong when Walker stepped forward because if I didn't, Beck would have noticed and said something.

And when he put his arm around me, I wanted to burst into tears.

It had only been two days, and I already missed him terribly.

Obviously, I'd gone substantially longer than that without seeing Walker, but we hadn't ever had this hanging over us. For years, if he wasn't on tour, I fell asleep in his arms. And for the last two nights, that hadn't happened.

Feeling his arm around me, inhaling his scent, and hearing his voice was almost too much to take. "Hi, Sadie," he said softly.

"Walker," I rasped.

When he pulled back, his pained gaze lingered on my face before it dropped down my body to the dress I was wearing. The tension between us was so palpable, I didn't understand how nobody else could feel it.

Throughout the night, I did my best to stay distracted with everyone else, mingling with anyone who wasn't standing close to Walker. It was the only thing I could think of to help make it a little easier on myself.

But then I'd taken a seat at some point on the couch beside Demi. We'd been having a conversation when most of the other band members had sat down as well. That was when Demi ended up directing the conversation to Chasey to ask her about going on tour.

I knew there had been talks of another tour. It was something that had been a source of contention between Walker and me because I wanted to be there. Even if I wasn't at every show, I wanted to know that I could go to any show at any location whenever I wanted.

Of course, that didn't seem like it mattered any longer.

But the subject of the tour was when it all happened.

Everything imploded.

And now, I was sitting on the couch, still in shock. I hadn't been able to forget my brother's words to Walker.

You guys took a chance, kept it quiet, and it didn't work out. If she can move on from it, I know you can, too.

As soon as I heard those words, my body had gone on alert. It blew my mind that Beck knew about us all along, never said anything, and seemed to know that Walker and I were currently on the outs.

It hadn't been the reaction I expected.

Walker must have felt the same because he asked for Beck's clarification. I knew that neither of us had been prepared for Beck's response.

You and Holland.

Those words left me stunned.

Beck thought the man I'd been in love with for years was in a relationship with Holland. Why would he think that?

Even worse, it seemed Beck wasn't the only one.

Unfortunately, I didn't get an answer to that question because after Walker blew up on my brother, he had stormed off. Killian, and eventually Raid, followed behind him. I stayed right where I was even though everything inside me wanted to go to him.

"Holls?" Beck called gently.

She blinked away whatever thoughts were running through her mind and focused her attention on him.

"Yeah?" she rasped.

"I'm sorry," he apologized. "I was wrong. We all were."

She licked her lips, looked incredibly nervous, and insisted, "It's… it's okay. I just… I'm going to go use the restroom."

"Holland?" Cash called.

Her eyes slid to him.

"It was my fault," he admitted.

"What?"

"I got the thought in my head back when we were in New Hampshire months ago," he explained. "I'm sorry. I was wrong."

"Don't worry about it, Cash. It's totally okay," she assured him.

Her words were just what I'd expect her to say, but her voice indicated everything was not okay.

"Excuse me," Holland murmured as she got up and walked away.

Shit.

This was bad.

I'd been so focused on what was happening with Walker in this situation, it didn't even cross my mind what this meant for Holland. The whole band had been talking about her and Walker behind their backs, and they'd all assumed there was something going on between them. As much as I wanted to know why they would think that, I decided my best course of action was to be the friend Holland needed right now.

So, I got up, gave my brother an evil glare, and took off after my friend. I vaguely heard Demi saying something as I walked away, but I couldn't quite make out what it was.

I found Holland in the bathroom, and the minute I walked in, her horrified eyes came to mine.

"I have no idea what's going on," she panicked. "I can't imagine why they'd ever think there was something going on between Walker and me. I swear, Sadie. There's never been anything more than friendship between us."

"I believe you," I told her.

And I did. If there was one thing I could say about my relationship with Walker, it was that I wholeheartedly believed he loved me. He might have had reservations about sharing the truth of our relationship with others, but he'd never cheat on me.

Before she could respond, there was a knock on the door.

We hadn't even said anything when the door opened and Demi walked in.

"Are you okay?" she asked Holland.

Holland was visibly upset, but she nodded. "Yeah, I just don't understand where that all came from."

"Apparently, it was my man that put that idea in their heads," she said. "He said it happened in New Hampshire. I wonder what happened that would make him think that."

Holland looked at me, and I instantly figured it out. It had to have been when she first found out about us. Judging by the look on her face, she realized it, too.

She didn't get a chance to answer before there was another knock at the door. It cracked open and Chasey's voice asked, "Can I come in?"

"Yes."

Chasey's eyes immediately went to Holland. She looked a little unsure, but she pushed through the discomfort she was feeling and said, "Holland, Beck is so upset."

Tipping her head to the side, a sympathetic look washed over her. "I'm okay," she insisted.

"He really didn't think when he blurted all of that out," she declared. "Not only was it wrong for him to make assumptions about what was going on between you and Walker, but he also shouldn't have announced it in front of everyone."

"Is Walker okay?" Holland asked.

Chasey shrugged. "I don't know. He went outside, and Killian and Raid followed him. They haven't come back inside yet."

"He was so angry," Demi noted. "I've never seen him like that."

I did. Only once. And it happened just two days ago.

Of course, I didn't share that with them.

"Yeah," Holland murmured.

"I still don't understand why Beck, Cash, Killian, and Roscoe all thought there was something going on," Demi chimed in.

"Well, I just asked Beck why he brought it up now in front of everyone if he'd had this thought for months," Chasey said.

"What did he say?" I asked.

She looked from me, to Demi, and finally to Holland before she shared, "He said he hadn't intended to blurt it all out in front of everyone, but he didn't want Walker pulling back from something he loved doing simply because what he had with you didn't work out. I don't think he had any ill intentions."

I loved Chasey for my brother. She truly was concerned about him and how Holland was going to look at him now that he'd made such a gross error in judgment.

"But there's nothing going on between Walker and me," Holland assured her. "I hope Beck and the rest of the guys believe that."

"Was there?" she asked.

Holland shook her head.

I didn't know what came over me. Maybe it was because I felt like Holland was being subjected to all of this because of me. Maybe it was because my heart felt like it was in my throat. Or maybe it was something else entirely.

Regardless of the reason, I blurted, "It's me."

"You?" Demi asked. "What do you mean?"

My eyes moved through all three of them. Holland looked nervous while Chasey and Demi both looked curious and confused.

"I'm begging you to keep this private, but it's me," I started. "I'm the one that Walker's been dating."

Demi's jaw dropped open as Chasey's brows shot up in surprise. "Beck doesn't know this?" Chasey asked.

I shook my head. "No. And I really hope you'll keep this between us."

"Of course, but why haven't you told him?" she asked.

"Beck will probably lose his mind," I said. "And that'll be before he learns that I was with Walker for eight years."

Demi gasped.

"Eight years," Chasey whispered.

I nodded.

"Holland found out back when they were in New Hampshire, which is probably why Cash got the impression he did," I explained.

"Are you planning to tell Beck or anyone else?" Demi wondered.

Sadness washed over me. "I wanted to, but it doesn't really matter anymore," I said.

"Oh no," Holland murmured. "Please don't tell me something happened."

Tears filled my eyes. "Walker doesn't think this is the right time to tell Beck, and I can't keep hiding, so I told him that we can't be together until he's ready to make that commitment."

"What did he say?" Chasey asked.

"He begged me not to make that choice," I shared.

"When did this happen?" Demi asked.

"Two days ago."

Holland moved toward me and pulled me into a hug. "I'm so sorry, Sadie," she lamented. "I completely understand his need to feel like he has to keep this a secret, but I also completely understand your desire to have it all. It's not an easy place for either one of you to be."

Hugging her back, I cried, "I miss him so much already."

She held on to me for a long time before loosening her hold. When she took half a step back, she said, "Sadie, Walker is so in love with you. I can't begin to imagine why he'd ever let you go."

I shook my head and replied, "He didn't want to. But he wasn't prepared to share the truth of our relationship."

"Why doesn't he want to share it?" Demi chimed in.

"Because he believes he'll have to choose between his music and me," I answered.

"How so?" Chasey questioned me.

"Beck isn't going to make it easy," I told her. "He's always been very protective of me, so I knew from the beginning that this would be a tough battle. We were going to do it years ago, but with Walker's mom dying and everything else that followed, we didn't. And then it just never happened. But the bottom line is that Walker is concerned that there will be a lot of tension between Beck and him, and he's not willing to jeopardize everyone else's careers for this."

Holland sighed. "He's giving you up for all of us," she declared.

"Well, he didn't exactly make that decision either," I corrected her. "I made it for him because I couldn't continue to do this. Plus, he made a promise to his mom that he wouldn't give up his music and that he'd hold on to me."

"But he's letting you go," Demi reasoned.

Technically, he hadn't wanted to let me go. He merely wasn't willing to give me what I needed, and I couldn't accept that.

"I'd never make him give up his music," I said. "It's the only connection he has left to his mom."

"How can I help?" Chasey asked.

My eyes went to hers. There was so much worry and concern in her expression. All I could do is shake my head.

"I can talk to Beck," she offered.

"No!" I begged. "No, please don't. In fact, the best way to help me would be to say nothing to him about Walker and me. I don't want him to know. Not anymore, especially now that Walker and I are no longer together. Let them have peace between them."

"But what about you?" she asked.

I smiled, even though I didn't feel happy. "I'll be alright.

Eventually, I'll be okay. For now, I just want to figure out the best way to get out of here. I'm ready to go home."

"I'll take care of it," Holland announced. "After what just happened out there, I'm sure nobody will question me leaving. You can tell them you're coming home with me."

"I don't want to ruin your time here," I said.

"You're not. It's okay. I promise."

I looked to Demi and Chasey. "Are we good?" I asked.

"Totally," Demi answered as she gave me a hug. "If you need anything, grab my number from Holland."

"Thanks, Demi." When she stepped back, I looked at Chasey and confirmed, "You won't tell him, right?"

She seemed to be struggling with it, and while I loved that she probably didn't like the idea of hiding anything from Beck, I hoped she'd give me her word.

"I won't tell him," she finally said.

"Thank you."

With that, Holland and I came up with our plan to leave.

When we left the bathroom and returned to the room where everything had gone down, I was disappointed to see that Killian and Raid were both there but that Walker was not.

"Holls," Beck called as he moved toward us.

"Yeah?" she returned.

"I'm really, really sorry about what I said," he apologized.

She nodded. "I appreciate the apology. I'm alright, though. How's Walker?" she asked.

God, I loved her. I had a feeling she knew I would want to know that he was alright, even if I shouldn't have wanted to know.

"I honestly don't know," he answered. "Killian and Raid went out to talk to him. Killian came back in about five minutes before Raid did. They said he went home."

"Right. Well, I'm going to do the same," she said.

"So, you're not okay," he surmised.

She offered a sympathetic look. "I am, but it's been a night," she told him.

"Are we good?" he asked.

"We are," Holland assured him.

"I'd really like you to stay," Beck tried once more.

Holland offered a smile, stepped forward, and gave him a hug. "Thank you. But I'm going to go now."

"I'm going to leave with her," I chimed in.

"Really?" Beck asked.

He was definitely disappointed.

I nodded. "It's cool, Beck. I promise."

His eyes shifted between the two of us before he acquiesced, "Alright. Well, at least you're leaving together."

Technically, that was true. We were leaving his house together. We just weren't going to the same place when we left.

I gave him a hug and said, "Happy New Year, Beck. Give Luna a kiss from me in the morning."

"I will," he promised.

Holland and I said a quick round of goodbyes to everyone, and the remaining members of the band offered their apologies to Holland for their wrong assumptions.

A few minutes later, the two of us walked outside. And after we said goodbye to each other, I got in my car and drove home.

I'd have been lying if I said that I wasn't tempted to drive to Walker's place instead.

Sadly, that was no longer an option for me.

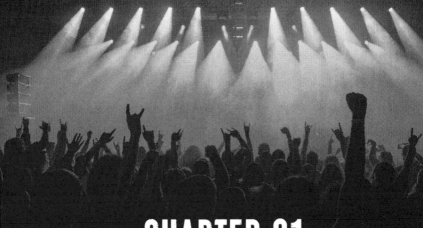

CHAPTER 21

Walker

I DIDN'T WANT TO BE HERE.

But I had no choice.

It was all I had left.

When I received a call from Cash last night asking me to meet at the studio with the band this morning, I had a feeling we weren't going to be meeting to work on new music.

This was about what happened nearly a week ago at Beck's place.

Unfortunately, as much as I wanted to forget that night—forget everything about that night—it didn't seem like that would be an option.

Before I even showed up at Beck's on New Year's Eve, I knew it was going to be a disaster. Although, my reasons for believing that would be the case had nothing to do with what actually went down with Beck and the rest of the band.

I had no idea they all thought Holland and I were dating in secret. Suffice it to say that it took me a long time to get over the fact that they had all clearly discussed this at some point behind my back.

But as bad as that was, it didn't compare to seeing her.

Sadie.

She was as beautiful as ever, and I didn't know how I held myself back from dragging her out of there.

Sadie looked absolutely stunning in the dress she was wearing. But it was the look on her face that had me feeling remorse. Showing up at her brother's house had been just as difficult for her as it was for me.

She was in a tremendous amount of pain, and it was all because of me. Because I couldn't be the man she needed me to be.

I want to get married. I want to have babies one day.

Fuck, I wanted to give her that. I wanted to give her the world.

And yet, I couldn't seem to bring myself to do what I continuously told myself I would do. I'd choose her. If it came down to it, I'd choose her over my career, over my love for the music and my commitment to the band.

Well, not anymore.

For more than a week, I'd suffered without her. And if the look on her face at that party was any indication of how she was doing, she was suffering all the same.

This was enough.

My plan was to get out of my car, go into the studio, deal with this meeting, and go to Sadie. Whatever she wanted to do, whenever she wanted to do it, it was happening.

I couldn't do this any longer. I wasn't willing to continue to do something that was going to risk my relationship with her. I couldn't lose her.

Because at the end of the day, she'd be the one standing by my side. When the rest of the band moved on and settled down, Sadie would be there with me.

And though my music would always be important to me, it would never make me feel the way she did.

Never.

On that thought, I got out of my car and walked into the studio.

Not surprisingly, everyone else had already arrived.

I walked down the hall and entered the room I knew I'd find everyone in. Sure enough, my suspicions were correct. This meeting had nothing to do with music.

Or, maybe it had everything to do with music.

Maybe they wanted to forget what happened the other night and get back to talking about touring.

It seemed like I wouldn't have to wait to find out because the moment I walked in, all their eyes came to me.

"Hey, Walker," Cash greeted me, sitting at one of the couches surrounding the coffee table. Killian was sitting on the opposite end of the same couch.

"What's up?" I returned as I moved to one of the oversized single leather chairs at one end of the table. Beck was sitting opposite me in the other chair while Holland and Roscoe occupied the other couch.

"Right. Well, now that everyone is here, we can get started," Cash began. "First things first, I owe a massive apology to both Holland and Walker. I clearly screwed up and thought I saw something that wasn't there. Not only that, but I went on to discuss my suspicions with the rest of the band and had them thinking the same thing. It was wrong, and I'm sorry."

Throughout his apology, my eyes went to Holland. She was looking at me, and I had to wonder if she knew where Sadie and I now stood. The two of them were close, so I could only assume so. The only person I'd shared the news with was Raid, and he let me know just how big of a mistake he thought I was making by allowing Sadie to walk away.

"You apologized to me the very same day, Cash," Holland replied. "You did it more than once, and I accept your apology."

He gave her a nod and shifted his attention to me. "Walker?"

"It's all good," I assured him.

"You sure about that?" he pressed.

I nodded. "I am."

And I was.

While I wasn't exactly thrilled that he'd come up with this idea and assumed it was the truth, he recognized his mistake and apologized. I wasn't going to hold a grudge.

"We're all sorry," Killian interjected. "Nobody wanted any of this to happen."

I realized that.

And yet, I wondered if they'd all feel the same if they knew the truth.

"It was my fault," Beck finally declared.

"Beck, I put the idea in your head," Cash reminded him.

Beck dipped his chin and confirmed, "Yes, you did. And not once did I tell you that you were wrong. We all thought it made sense. But I was the one who decided to just blurt it out in front of everyone a week ago."

I didn't really want to get into this any deeper.

"It's fine," I declared. "It's done and over."

"It's not fine," Beck insisted. "You and Holland are both a vital part of this band, and what I did was wrong. I'm grateful you're both sitting here and willing to have some grace to move on from it."

I nodded my understanding, realizing he was probably sitting on a lot of guilt that he'd assumed incorrectly about us. I recognized his need to ease that guilt and rectify the situation.

"It's cool. We can just let it go and move on."

"Walker?" Roscoe called.

I shifted my attention to him. "Yeah?" I replied.

"Do you mind me asking why you're against putting together another tour?" he asked.

"I'm not against it," I told him. "I just wanted to take some time off before we hopped right back into another one."

Killian joined the conversation at that point. "Are you feeling burned out?"

I shook my head. "No."

"So, you're not trying to cope from a breakup with Holland, you've always been all about the music, and you aren't burned out," Cash declared. "Why do you want a year off?"

My eyes left Cash and shifted to Holland. She was looking at me with nothing but nerves and worry and concern in her face.

I dropped my gaze to my feet, my elbows resting on my thighs, and let out a deep sigh as images of Sadie flashed in my mind. I did my best to push those thoughts of her to the back of my mind, lifted my head, and asked, "Can we just let this go?"

"Sure," Cash agreed. "But you know we're here if you need us."

I nodded.

That's when Beck cut in and said, "Walker, something isn't right."

"Let it go, Beck," I told him.

He shook his head. "No. You're a part of this band, and you're one of my best friends. I can't let this go."

"Beck, man, I'm telling you to drop it," I clipped, feeling myself growing more and more tense by the second.

"Something is wrong. You've been off lately," he noted.

"Do I do my job?" I countered as I shot up out of my seat.

"Yes," he answered, looking a bit concerned.

"Did I miss any time in the studio or rehearsals or shows while we were on tour or ever?" I pressed.

Shaking his head again, he said, "No."

"Alright, then. Let it go," I ordered. I looked at Cash and asked, "Was there anything else we needed to discuss this morning?"

A confused look washed over his face, and I thought he was going to push this, too. Instead, he replied, "No. I just wanted to try to clear the air so we could all move forward without this hanging over us."

I dipped my chin. "Good. The air is clear. I need to go."

I started to move toward the exit when Beck asked, "Is it something with your dad?"

My back to him, my body froze.

Before I could say anything, Roscoe urged, "Beck, I don't think you should push this now."

"Fuck that," Beck replied. "He's your best friend. You can see something is wrong. You're just going to pretend there isn't something that's eating him alive."

I closed my eyes.

Fuck.

My gut clenched thinking about Sadie and how much I missed her.

"Walker, is it something with Raid?" Beck pushed.

That was it.

I couldn't take it any longer.

At this point, he was going to continue to push it, and I figured I'd feel no worse off either way. So, I turned around, pinned my eyes on him, and announced, "It's Sadie."

He jerked his head back and responded, "What?"

"It's Sadie," I repeated. "You want to know what's wrong, Beck? Here it is. I've been in love with your sister for eight years."

The energy in the room shifted.

Beck's eyes widened in shock as he slowly stood from his seat. I didn't pull my attention away from him, and I still managed to notice Cash and Roscoe moving in closer to him. Killian shifted closer to me.

"I know you're not telling me what I think you're telling me," Beck declared.

"I'm telling you exactly what you think," I assured him. "Sadie and I have been together since the day after her twentieth birthday."

Curiosity quickly turned to anger. "You motherfucker," Beck seethed just seconds before he charged forward.

Killian put a hand to the center of my chest and pushed back as both Cash and Roscoe got a hold on Beck.

"Eight years," Beck shouted. "You're five years older than her. She was young, way too young, and you preyed on her."

"It was not like that," I countered.

"Fuck you. You've been fucking my sister for eight years, and you hid that shit because you knew it was exactly like that," he shot back, struggling against Cash and Roscoe.

I didn't respond because it wouldn't matter. He was pissed, and nothing I said was going to change his mind or calm him down.

"Beck, relax," Cash urged.

"No. Fuck no," Beck clipped. "He's been lying, hiding this shit for eight years. What the fuck else has he been lying to us about?"

"Beck, stop," Holland pleaded, jumping in for the first time since the conversation started.

His eyes went to her, and I knew he'd figured it out.

"Shit," he hissed. "You knew. You knew, and that's why you two were acting so strange. How many fucking lies were there?"

"You need to calm down, Beck," I finally ordered. "Do not take this out on Holland."

Pointing a finger at me, he demanded, "I don't have shit to say to you. I don't even want to look at you because I don't fucking trust you at all."

There it was.

The whole time I'd been concerned about sharing this with him, with all of them, that was precisely the reason why. If we'd told him in the beginning, he might not have liked it, but at least we wouldn't have been hiding anything.

This was now all about deceit. And I wasn't the least bit surprised Beck felt the way he did.

"Right," I muttered. "I expected this, so I'm going to go."

"Walker, wait," Killian urged.

I turned back, looked at him, allowed my eyes to scan through the rest of them, and said, "You need to do this without me here. I've lost somebody who meant everything to me, and I had no say in that. Sadie is my whole world, and I'm not going to lose her, too. If that means I no longer have this band, there's nothing I can do to change that. I love you all, and I'd hate for it to come down to that, but I'm not giving her up."

I barely caught a glimpse of Holland's smile before I registered the anger on Beck's face. Roscoe, Cash, and Killian seemed unable to react. It was a shock, no doubt, and they all probably felt like they were stuck between a rock and a hard place.

I moved toward the doorway, and when I got there, I stopped. Twisting my neck in their direction, I said, "If the only way for My Violent Heart to continue is without me in it, I'll back away gracefully."

"You're willing to give up your career?" Roscoe asked, a bit of disbelief present in his tone.

"I don't want to," I answered honestly. "But I'll do anything for Sadie."

With that, I walked out and down the hall to the exit with only one thing on my mind.

Go to my girl, and get her back.

Sadly, when I got to her place, she wasn't there. I pulled out my phone to call her, but her phone went right to voice mail.

I wasn't doing this over the phone, but I needed her to call me back. "I'm at your house, and I've made my decision, Sadie. We need to talk. Call me."

I was going to go home, cool down, and wait to hear from her.

I just didn't expect that I'd get home and find that Sadie had made another decision of her own.

Sitting on the island countertop in my kitchen was a note and the key to my house.

My gut clenched.

I lifted the piece of paper in my hand and read it.

Walker,

I didn't want to come by when you'd be here and make this any more difficult than it already is. I wanted to get my things and return your key to you. It's no longer mine. I've tried to hold out hope that you'd come back to me, but I've realized I'm torturing myself in believing that. Your silence tells me where this is headed, and I can't bear it any longer. It's only been a little over a week, and I'm dying inside without you.

The closer I am to you, the harder I have to work to stop myself from coming to see you. So, I'm leaving town for a while to try to mend my broken heart.

But before I leave I wanted to tell you that I'm sorry. I'm sorry I wanted to have it all. I thought I'd have it with you. And right now, the mere thought of having all of that with someone who isn't you hurts. But I deserve to have it, so I'm going to try to heal and find a way to get it.

I want to be happy, even if it means that I have to be that way without you. And I want you to be happy, even if it's not with me. Because you deserve it all, too.

No matter where this life takes us, I hope you know that I love you and that I always will. You'll have a huge piece of my heart forever. And I hope that in time we'll be able to see one another on the other side of this pain and remember just how beautiful it was when we were together.

I'll love you my whole life, Walker.

Yours,
Sadie

I read her note three times, and it didn't get any easier. Pain sliced through me with each word I read. How did I let this happen? The most important woman in my life had given up because I couldn't prove to her that she deserved to have the whole world, even when all that she wanted was me. Me without all the secrecy.

My heart was in my throat at the thought of the unnecessary pain I had put her in. She had sucked it up for years. She stood by my side through the worst moments of my life, seeing me through all of it.

And this was how I repaid her. By giving her nothing.

I called her again.

Voice mail.

Panic began to set in.

No way could I allow someone else to step in and give her what I wanted to give her. No way could I stand by and watch as she gave her heart to someone else. There was not a chance in hell that I'd ever find myself on the other side of this pain if she wasn't in my life the way she was always meant to be.

I picked up my phone again, tapped on the screen, and held it to my ear.

"Hey, Walker. What's up?"

"Raid, I need you, man. Sadie's gone."

"What? What do you mean she's gone?"

"Please. Can you just come to my place?" I begged.

"I'm already getting my sneakers on."

"Thanks."

Though I should have felt relieved that I had my brother there to help me, I didn't. If I couldn't figure out where Sadie went and do it quick, I could lose her forever.

CHAPTER 22

Walker

I PRESSED THE BASE OF MY PALMS INTO MY EYES AS I SAT ON THE couch in my family room. Raid was sitting in the chair diagonal from me. I'd just filled him in on what happened this morning at the studio.

"Okay, so Beck kept pushing you, you told him the truth, and then there was a bit of arguing back and forth," Raid recounted the story. "I don't understand how any of that translates into Sadie being gone."

I let out a deep sigh, lifted my gaze to him, and shared, "After I left the studio, I went to her place. She wasn't home, so I called and her phone went straight to voice mail. I thought that was strange because Sadie never turns off her phone. Anyway, I came back here, and that's when I found the key I'd given her to the house and a note."

Raid had winced when I mentioned she'd returned the key I'd given her.

"Ouch," he said. "It sounds like she's legitimately moving on. What did her note say?"

"In a nutshell, she's going away for a while to heal her

broken heart so she can move on and find happiness," I told him. "She wants to get married and have babies."

"And how do you feel about that?" he asked.

"Sick at the mere thought of anyone else touching her and giving any of that to her," I admitted.

Raid nodded his understanding, but I was sure he already knew that was how I felt. "So, what are you going to do about it?" he asked.

"I want to fix this, but I don't know where to find her," I said. "She's presumably turned off her phone, and she's not at home. I don't doubt she's going somewhere outside of Steel Ridge to heal and get past this."

Shaking his head, Raid asked, "How did things get here between the two of you?"

"My own stupidity," I answered.

"I mean, I just don't understand how everything was so good for so long, and suddenly, it's just a mess," he stated. "I feel for the both of you because I know how much you love her and how much she loves you."

"It's so fucked up, Raid. I never should have held back from telling Beck," I started. "The second he found out, he reacted exactly like I thought he would. I guess it was a good thing it happened at the studio with Cash, Roscoe, and Killian there because if it had just been Sadie and me telling him at his house, I have no doubt there would have been bloodshed. He's so pissed."

Disappointment washed over Raid's face. "It makes no sense to me why he'd react like that," my brother declared.

Now I was the one confused. "You don't?" I asked.

He shook his head again. "No. I get the whole big brother protector thing, but the truth is that you're not some asshole that's ever treated Sadie with anything less than love and respect. Why he wouldn't want someone like you for his sister is beyond me."

There was that.

I'd always liked to think about this situation going an entirely different way than what it did today. My hope had always been that Beck would have seen the way I carried myself for years and put all the pieces of the puzzle together. He'd then come to the conclusion that from the moment Sadie came into my life, I gave up the typical rock star life. I had my fun with it before she came along, but it didn't take me long to learn that that lifestyle was going to get really old really quickly.

Life with Sadie was never boring. Eight years with the same woman, and she could still make my heart pound in my chest. She still turned me on, made me laugh, and just felt good to be around.

Now I felt like a fool. Why had I let all these days go by without fixing this? Why didn't I just suck it up and give her the one thing she needed?

I couldn't change it now, but I was certainly going to try my best to fix it.

"I don't know what to do," I said.

"You have no idea where she went?" Raid asked.

"No. She didn't say, and we've been a lot of places over the years. It could be any number of them. Or, if she's trying to forget me, maybe she didn't go to any of them."

For several long moments, my brother and I sat there in silence. I continued to torture myself with a million questions about why I had been so stupid until Raid broke the silence.

"If you don't want to wait, you're going to have to call Royce," he said.

Royce was Killian's cousin. He was the owner of Harper Security Ops, a private investigation and security firm here in Steel Ridge.

That should have been my first thought, but I was clearly too distracted and distraught to think straight. If anyone could find Sadie, Royce and his team would be able to do that.

"That's a good idea," I praised him as I reached for my phone.

Before I could make the call, though, my doorbell rang.

My body instantly tensed as my eyes went to Raid's.

"Shit. That's got to be her," I said. "Maybe she got the message I left for her."

As quickly as I could, I moved to the front door and yanked it open. It was not Sadie.

Beck was standing there, still looking murderous.

"I want to talk to her."

"What?" I replied, mostly because I couldn't comprehend the fact that he was standing there speaking to me when he said all that he had to say at the studio.

"I want to talk to my sister," he demanded. "She's not home, and she's turned off her phone. So, if she wants to force me to come here just so I can speak with her, then that's what I'm going to do."

"Sadie's not here," I told him.

Beck shot me a look that told me he didn't believe me before he said, "I don't believe you. Then again, can you blame me?"

"Nope. But that doesn't change the fact that she's not here," I retorted.

"Well, then where is she?" he asked, sounding irritated more than anything else.

"If I knew, I wouldn't be here," I answered honestly.

For the first time since I opened my door to him, Beck dropped the pissed-off routine and looked genuinely concerned. "What does that mean?"

"It means I went to her place after I left the studio, and she wasn't there. So, I came home and found the key I'd given to her for my place on my kitchen counter along with a note from her," I shared.

Beck narrowed his eyes. "Why do I feel like I'm missing something?"

I had two options right now. Open my door and let him come inside, or be an asshole like he deserved and tell him to take a hike. As much as I wanted to be an asshole, I stepped back and opened the door a little wider.

"Do you want to come in?" I asked.

He hesitated briefly but eventually stepped forward and came inside. I led him into the family room where he saw my brother.

"Raid," he greeted him with an upward jerk of his chin.

"Beck," Raid returned.

Beck shifted his focus to me again and asked, "So, where is Sadie?"

"I don't know."

His brows shot up, silently questioning me.

"She left me a note telling me that she needed to go away for a while to mend her broken heart," I told him.

"What did you do to her?" he accused.

"I worried too much about you and the rest of the band," I answered. "Sadie walked away from me two days before the party at your place on New Year's Eve. She basically gave me an ultimatum. Either we arrived together or she was walking away."

Beck tipped his head to the side. "And after eight years, you let her walk away?" he pressed.

"I didn't think telling you about us right before the holiday was a smart idea, but Sadie didn't agree because we've had our fair share of reasons not to already," I began. "She was sick of waiting."

"You didn't want to tell me?"

"I didn't want what happened today to happen," I said. "But obviously that was my mistake because I have no idea where she is right now."

Shaking his head with a look of disgust on it, he clipped, "I still can't fucking believe this shit. All these years and neither one of you said a damn thing."

"I'm not doing this with you right now, Beck," I told him.

"Seems like that's the way it is with you, Walker," he shot back.

At that point, Raid stepped in and said, "Alright, that's enough, Beck. I get that you're pissed, and despite the fact that I think it's ludicrous, I guess I can understand it. That said, right now, the priority needs to be on finding Sadie."

"You think it's ludicrous that I'm pissed about being lied to for eight years?" Beck countered. "Maybe you feel that way because you've clearly known about this for a while. My sister lied to me, Raid."

"And, I've got to say, I love you like a brother, Beck, but it seems like Sadie might have had a valid reason to hide this from you," Raid noted.

Beck stood there staring at my brother for several long seconds. Something moved through his face—I wasn't sure what it was—before he brought his angry gaze to me and asked, "If you hear from her, can you please ask her to call me?"

I dipped my chin. "I'd appreciate the same in return."

"Yeah," Beck muttered before he moved back toward the front door.

I followed behind him and saw him out.

While it hadn't gone well, it was safe to say that it could have been far worse.

After Beck left, I immediately moved to my phone and made the call that would hopefully lead me to Sadie.

"Harper Security Ops."

"Can I speak to Royce, please?" I asked.

"Who's calling?"

"Walker Rhodes."

"Just a moment," the receptionist replied.

I was put on a brief hold before I heard, "Hey, Walker. What's going on?"

"Hey, Royce. I need you to track someone down for me," I said.

"Sure. Do we have any information on this someone?" he wondered.

"I know everything about her," I informed him.

Then, I spent the next few minutes telling him everything he needed to know about Sadie so we'd have the best possible chance to locate her.

"I think that should do it," he said. "I'll get one of my guys on this immediately. Depending on how far she's going and how she's traveling, this could be quick or it could take some time. Let's hope she stops for gas along the way or checks into a hotel soon using her credit card. If she does that, we'll be able to find her."

"Whatever it costs, however many men you need to put on it, please do it," I pleaded with him. "I need to get to her as soon as humanly possible."

"We'll find her," he promised.

"Thanks, Royce."

"No problem, Walker. Take it easy."

At that, we disconnected. I looked at my brother and felt nothing but hopelessness and despair.

I was confident in the ability of Royce and his crew, but I wasn't sure I was going to be able to relax until I not only knew where Sadie was but also got to see her with my own eyes again.

Raid spent the next few hours at my place as we waited for any news from Royce, one of his guys, or Sadie.

Nothing came.

"You should go," I said to Raid later that evening.

"I can stay," he replied.

"I know. I appreciate it, but I'm not sure we're going to hear anything tonight," I explained. "I'll call you if I get any news."

"Are you sure?" he asked.

I nodded. "I'm positive. Thanks for being here today, Raid."

"You're welcome. Anytime, Walker. You know that."

I did. And I appreciated that I'd had him. In a situation like this, normally it was Sadie that I found myself relying on. But since she was the reason for my worry and despair, I liked knowing Raid would step up to the plate and give me the support I needed. I would have done the same for him in a heartbeat.

Raid and I said goodbye, and once he left, I tried calling Sadie again. As had been the case all throughout the day whenever I tried, her phone went right to voice mail. I ended the call without leaving a message, dropped my head back, and looked up at the ceiling with a sigh.

The thought of Sadie being alone and upset somewhere tonight made me feel sick. All I could do was hope that the team at Harper Security could locate her quickly and that I'd be able to go to her and fix what I broke.

Throughout the rest of the night, I tried calling her phone a few times. Even though I knew deep down she wasn't going to answer, there was a small part of me hoping for a miracle.

By the time I got into bed that night, I had gotten myself so worked up that I barely managed to get any sleep.

And when I dragged myself out of bed the next morning, I tried calling Sadie again. Her phone was still off.

Deciding the best thing to do was to take a shower and try to wake myself up a bit, I did that. When it wasn't enough, I made myself some coffee.

Two hours later, just before eleven o'clock, my phone rang.

"Royce," I greeted him.

"We found her."

"Where is she?" I asked.

"It looks like Sadie used her credit card to check into a cabin resort about three hours northwest of us," he shared.

I was already moving to my bedroom to grab the bag that I'd packed up last night after Raid left. I figured it was best to be prepared to leave the moment they called me.

"Can you send over an exact address to me?" I asked.

"It's already on the way."

It's already on the way.

Three hours. I was just three hours away from her.

"Appreciate your help, Royce."

"No problem, man. Good luck."

"Thanks."

I disconnected the call, grabbed my bag, and was out the door within minutes. Once I got on the road, I called Raid to let him know what was happening. What I didn't do was call Beck. I needed to go and sort this out with Sadie before he got involved.

Just a few more hours.

All I could do was hope I wasn't too late.

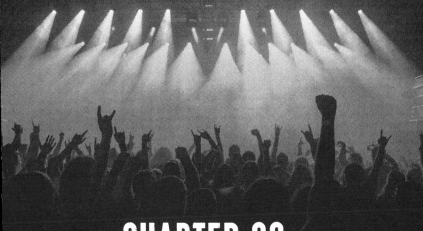

CHAPTER 23

Sadie

DISTANCE WASN'T MAKING THIS ANY EASIER.

I'd been at this cabin in the mountains for nearly twenty-four hours now, and I wasn't feeling any better about the end of my relationship with Walker.

Then again, I was probably being slightly unreasonable in my expectations that I'd be magically healed simply because I put some physical space between me and the man I'd loved for eight years, longer if I included the years I crushed on him.

As unreasonable as my expectations might have been, I really needed some kind of progress. Even just a shred of it. Because to continue to live day in and day out with the level of devastation I felt right now was torture.

In my defense, the cabin was the perfect escape from my problems in theory. The peace and serenity lingered in the air in a way that only made me believe that coming here was exactly what I needed.

I'd spent the better part of my evening yesterday painting. The scenery around the cabins provided the perfect landscape backdrop for a gorgeous painting. But even with the beauty that surrounded me, my heart was aching in a way I wasn't sure I'd ever be able to recover.

Walker had become so much a part of me. Even when he was on tour and I missed him terribly, I still knew that he was going to be coming home to me. Now, I had to learn to live with the fact that Walker would never come home to me again.

I wasn't sure I could do it.

I'd finished eating a late lunch about a half hour ago, which was a chore in itself considering I didn't have much of an appetite, and I decided to bundle up in several layers, grab the oversized blanket, and come sit out on the deck. I thought it would help me with trying to clear my head so I could figure out how I was going to live my life without Walker in it.

Unfortunately, the longer I sat here the more I started to think that perhaps I'd made a huge mistake in breaking things off with him. Because if it wasn't for this one thing that had pulled us apart, Walker and I wouldn't have had any problems. We were perfect for each other in every way, and rarely did we ever argue.

But as much as I felt some regret about the decision I'd made to end things, I was also very aware of the fact that it was necessary. No matter how painful this was now, I had no choice but to walk away. Because as perfect as Walker and I were together, we were only ever perfect in secret.

I wanted it to be out in the open. I wanted to tell the world how much I loved him. I wanted to marry him and have babies. I wanted a life with my husband that didn't involve hiding. I wanted to celebrate together all of the things that came our way. I wanted to be with him through good and bad times in the way a lover would be there for her partner without a care for who was watching.

Sadly, with Walker's unwillingness to share the truth about our relationship with my family and our friends, I knew

I'd never have any of that. And that wasn't fair to either one of us because I knew I'd start to resent him. I didn't want that.

I took in a deep breath. There was no doubt my nose and cheeks had turned bright red in the forty-five minutes I'd been sitting here. It was the middle of January in the northeast. The temperature was frigid, but I was secretly hoping it would somehow numb the pain in my heart.

Tears filled my eyes as I thought back over the last week or so.

Not once in all of that time, other than New Year's Eve at Beck's, did I see Walker. Not once did he call me. Not once did he do anything to indicate to me that he even cared that we were in this position.

As a single tear started to roll down my cheek, I saw movement out of the corner of my eye. I turned my head in that direction and felt my breath seize in my lungs.

The most beautiful man I'd ever seen was standing there looking at me with heartbreak written all over his face.

Walker.

I didn't know how he was there. I didn't know why he was there.

But in that moment, all I could do was burst into tears at the sight of him.

No sooner had I buried my face in my hands when I felt Walker's strong arms lifting me up and cradling me against his chest.

"Baby, you're frozen," he murmured as he began moving.

A moment later, I was inside the cabin and Walker was gently setting me down on the couch. Without another word, he moved to the opposite side of the room and began working to get a fire going in the fireplace. That was when my body began to tremble. I hadn't realized just how cold I was until that moment.

I remained silent as I shivered and kept my eyes focused

on Walker. Through the tears, there was still no missing the fact that he was breathtaking, confident, and strong.

It was no wonder I had fallen in love with him all those years ago.

Once the fire was crackling and warming the cabin, Walker shrugged off his jacket and moved back toward me. He lifted me in his arms again, sat on the couch, and settled me in his lap.

My mind had a million thoughts running through it, and at least a dozen questions I wanted to ask.

I started with the one at the forefront of my mind. "What are you doing here?" I rasped.

"Coming to get you," he answered, stroking his hands up and down my arms as my body continued to shake.

"Walker, I can't—"

"You're not leaving me, Sadie," he deadpanned, cutting me off.

I swallowed hard. I didn't want to leave him, but this was never going to work between us. I wanted far more than he was willing and able to give.

"It's not enough," I told him, my voice just a touch over a whisper. "What we had before, the way it was for so long, it's not enough for me."

"I know."

I sighed and closed my eyes. "Why did you come here? How did you even find me?"

"I called Harper Security and talked to Royce," Walker began. "He and his team found you. They called me this morning, told me where I could find you, and I left my place immediately."

Walker offered no additional explanation. He completely avoided answering the most pressing question.

I needed an answer.

"Why, Walker? Why would you come here and make this harder?"

"Because I'm not letting you go, Sadie," he said. "I can't do it."

"But I can't do this like this any longer," I argued.

As he reached a hand up to the side of my face and gently brushed a lock of hair away, he whispered, "You don't have to."

Was he saying what I thought he was saying?

"Are you... will you... can we tell my family?" I stammered.

"I already told Beck," he shared.

My whole body tensed in his lap.

Before I could respond, Walker added, "The whole band knows now."

I stared at him in disbelief, my eyes feeling like they were going to fall out of my head. "What? When did you do this?" I asked.

For several long moments, Walker didn't answer. He allowed his eyes to search my face for quite some time before he replied, "Yesterday morning when you were at my house leaving me a note and a key."

My lips parted at the same time a lump formed in my throat. While I was leaving Walker a note and a key, he was telling Beck about us. Until he mentioned it, I'd managed to find a way to forget about the key.

God, it had been one of the hardest things I'd ever done.

"I'm giving you your key back, Sadie," he informed me. "And you're coming home with me."

After eight long years, this felt like a dream come true. I was overwhelmed with emotions. Relief. Joy. Shock.

I felt it all.

And because I was so focused on trying to memorize

this moment and the way it made me feel, I didn't respond to Walker.

But that didn't seem to matter because he continued, "Nobody else, sunshine. Nobody else is going to give you what I should have given you years ago. I'm sorry that I didn't and allowed us to get to this place."

"Walker…" I trailed off.

"I love you, Sadie," he proclaimed. "I can't do what you said in your letter. I can't be happy without you, and I don't want you being happy with someone who isn't me. I want to give you the world, baby."

I couldn't find my voice, but I had something better to give him instead of a verbal response. Pulling my hand free from the warm confines of the blanket, I touched my fingertips to Walker's lips. They traced along his bottom lip until I leaned closer and replaced them with my mouth.

Walker's arms tightened around me as we both moaned. There was a strong sense of relief in having him like this again, and I was convinced he felt the same about me.

I parted my lips, and as his tongue swept into my mouth, I found I was no longer trembling from the cold. My body grew heated as desire flooded my veins. It took almost no time for me to start tearing the blanket away. Walker was just as frustrated by it, grabbed ahold of one section, and yanked it out from underneath me.

Then I was on top, straddling him, with my mouth still connected to his.

It felt like I was being driven by desperation and lust.

Wanting.

Needing.

Demanding to be closer. To have all of him I could get.

Walker started lifting the first of my many layers over my head while I tugged at his shirt. His was gone in a flash, and as much as I wanted to touch and kiss and taste his skin again, I decided he deserved to have the same.

It was a matter of seconds before all my shirts and my bra were off. Walker surged up, flipped me to my back and came over me. The next thing I knew, his hands were at my pants, yanking them down my legs. The moment they were gone, he pulled off my panties.

But when he put his hands to the fly of his jeans, preparing to remove them, he suddenly stopped and stared at me.

Something moved through his face that I couldn't quite read, and it alarmed me.

"Walker?" I called.

His hands gripped the waistband of his pants tighter as his eyes came to mine. The look in them was dark and intense. It was fascinating, even if I was unsure what it meant.

"I was with you," he rasped.

"What?"

Suddenly, Walker loosened his hold on his jeans and allowed his hands to reached for my bare thighs. One hand stayed planted there while the other began to drift up toward my hip. His hand stopped moving, several of his fingers beginning to curl around into the flesh of my outer hip, but his thumb reached out and caressed the skin just above the crease where my thigh met my hip.

That's when it hit me.

He was seeing it for the first time.

Two days after the New Year's Eve party at Beck's place, I did something I'd been meaning to do for a long time.

I'd gotten my tattoo. The one that was Walker and me. The one that took the things we loved and put them into one. Paint splatter that formed an outline of drum sticks in the middle.

Walker leaned forward, inspected it, touched his lips to it, and looked back at me. "When did you do this?" he asked.

"Two days after I saw you at Beck's on New Year's Eve," I whispered.

"So, you walked away from me and still put me on your beautiful body?" he pressed.

I nodded. "You were always going to be in my heart, Walker," I began. "But I needed to be able to look in the mirror every day and see that you were still with me somehow."

His thumb stroked over the tattoo again. "Sadie," he croaked. "Fuck, baby, there's nobody like you."

It was sweet and tender, but a moment later, his pants were gone, and he had one hand on my hip as he guided his erection to my vagina. He pushed inside, and I let out a moan. Walker cradled my hips in his hands, and despite the pleasure I felt between my legs, it was nothing compared to the adoring look in his eyes or the fact that I was acutely aware of his thumb on our tattoo.

That meant everything to him.

I reached for him, but instead of Walker lowering his torso to mine, he lifted my back from the couch. With my chest pressed against his and his mouth on mine, he sat back and allowed me to ride him. Several times, his eyes drifted to that tattoo.

Knowing how much he was affected by it, wanting to give him more of it, I moved my hips quicker over top of him.

And within minutes I'd built us both up to the edge of that cliff. When he knew it was about to hit, Walker's torso surged forward again, his mouth captured mine, and his hand gripped me firmly at the base of my skull.

We moaned through our orgasms, each of us swallowing down the sounds of the other. It was beautiful, intense, and unbelievably good.

For a long time afterward, neither of us said anything. Not only were we both working to bring our breathing back to normal, but if Walker was feeling anything like I was, he was simply content to soak up the feeling of being as wrapped up in me as I was in him.

"Love you, Sadie," he said, the first one to break the silence.

"I love you, Walker."

At that, he stood and carried me to the bathroom, where we both cleaned up.

A few minutes later, we were back on the couch and cuddling. Now that the reunion was over, we had to talk. I just wasn't sure how to bring it all up.

Luckily, I didn't have to fret over it for too long.

"He was pissed," Walker said, and I knew right away that he was referring to Beck.

"How did it happen?"

For the next several minutes, Walker explained how Cash had called a meeting at the studio and vehemently apologized for his role in what happened at Beck's the week before. Walker also explained how my brother acknowledged that something was on Walker's mind and refused to just let it go as he was asked. Feeling content there in his arms, I listened while Walker shared how he eventually shared the truth with Beck about our relationship. He went on to describe Beck's adverse, albeit expected, reaction to the news.

"So, he's pissed," I declared when Walker finished.

"To say the least," he confirmed. "But oddly enough, he did show up at my house later in the afternoon looking for you. Of course, at that point, I'd gotten your note and your key and was already distraught enough. Luckily, Raid was there and helped to defuse the situation."

This wasn't going to be good.

While I was glad that the truth was finally out, I hated that Walker felt forced to share it on his own. More than that,

I hated hearing that Beck didn't seem to be interested in accepting the relationship at all.

"Based on his reaction, do you think he's going to come around eventually?" I asked.

"I don't know," he replied. "But the band knows where I stand."

"How did they react? What do you mean?" I questioned him.

Walker's arm tightened around me. "Holland seemed a bit relieved and a lot ecstatic," he began. "I'm guessing she knows that we were going through a bit of a rough patch. Cash, Killian, and Roscoe didn't really say much. I think they're partly in shock but mostly feeling stuck."

"So, what's going to happen?" I wondered.

There was a long stretch of silence, and I grew even more worried than I already was about the whole situation. "I wish I knew the answer to that, sunshine, but I don't," he confessed. "There's not much I can do at this point. I told them they need to decide what they want moving forward and that I won't fight them on anything if they decide My Violent Heart is better off without me."

My body tensed. "Walker, you can't give it up," I told him.

"It might come down to that, Sadie," he noted. "But if it does, I'm okay with my decision. I'll hate not having them or everything that comes along with being part of that band, but I'd hate it more to have that and not have you. I'm not giving you up."

"They can't take this away from you," I insisted.

"I don't think they would necessarily take it away from me. I just think there's a strong possibility that they aren't going to know how to handle the tension."

I sighed.

This was wrong in so many ways. Walker and I were in love. That shouldn't have had any effect on his career.

In that moment, having him there with me, being in his arms again, and knowing we didn't have to hide any longer, I should have felt overwhelming joy.

I didn't.

Because now that I'd gotten exactly what I wanted, Walker stood to lose one of the most important things in his life.

I knew it wasn't going to be easy, but at that realization, I decided it was my turn. Walker had stood up and shared the truth of us on his own so he could try to fix what was happening between us.

Now, it was my turn to try to do the same for him and fix what was happening with the band.

CHAPTER 24

Sadie

THIS MOMENT HAD BEEN A LONG TIME COMING.

Considering how long it had taken to get here, I should have felt prepared. Ready.

Instead, I felt completely unnerved. Because while I didn't have a single doubt about my relationship with Walker, especially now that the truth was out, I was worried about what the truth might mean for the future of my relationship with my brother.

Beck and I had always been close. The thought that this might ruin what we had was beyond upsetting. It was downright frightening.

But I had to do it. I had to face this. And I had to be prepared for whatever outcome was ahead. In the same breath, I planned to make sure he knew precisely how I felt and what I hoped to see happen moving forward.

Walker and I were back in Steel Ridge. The two of us had decided to take advantage of one night in the cabin with each other.

Before we left the cabin this morning, I called my brother and told him that I was heading home and that I wanted to meet with him. To say that his tone when I spoke to him still held an edge of bitterness would have been an understatement. For that reason, and given that I was concerned about his unpredictability with regard to this situation, I figured it was best to meet in a public place.

While I knew that my brother would never do anything to physically harm me, I just didn't know if I could trust he wouldn't go after Walker. He'd already done it once before, and if he didn't like what we had to say, I didn't want to take any chances.

Walker was coming because, well, this pertained to both of us. Not only that, but Beck was also going to have to get used to seeing us together. For the first time in all the years that we'd been together, we officially separated for just over a week. It was the worst week of my life, and I was never going to go back.

"Are you ready?" Walker asked as we sat in the car outside the café.

"As ready as I'm ever going to be," I replied.

Walker reached for my hand, gave it a squeeze, and promised, "It's going to be okay. No matter what happens, we have each other. That's never changing, okay?"

I nodded.

He lifted the back of my hand to his mouth, kissed it, and said, "I'll come around and open your door."

"Okay."

A few minutes later, we walked hand in hand into the café. Almost instantly, my eyes landed on Beck. He dropped his gaze to my hand that was linked with Walker's and narrowed his eyes.

Yep.

This wasn't going to be easy at all.

We moved forward and came to a stop beside the table. Beck held his hand out, directing us to the empty seats at the table.

For the first few seconds after Walker and I sat, nobody said anything. There was a lot of nervous tension coming from me.

I couldn't quite work out what it was that was coming from my brother, though.

Luckily, I didn't have to spend too long trying to figure it out because he finally spoke.

"Eight years, Sadie?" he asked. The disbelief evident in his tone indicated he hadn't even come close to coming to grips with this.

I nodded and whispered, "Yes."

Disappointment washed over his face as he shook his head. "My best friend and my sister," he scoffed. "I can't even wrap my head around all the lies you've told me over all these years. Do I even want to know?"

"I'm sorry, Beck," I apologized.

"Sorry?" he repeated. "For what part, Sadie?"

God, he was so upset. I wanted to be sensitive to that and own up to my part in all of this, but I needed to be completely honest now about all of it.

"I'm sorry for hiding it for so long," I clarified. "It was never our intention to let so much time pass."

Beck lifted his chin in understanding as he sat back in his chair. He pinned his eyes on Walker and asked, "So, what about you? Do you feel any remorse that you went after my younger sister?"

Before Walker could respond, I jumped in. "It wasn't like you're making it out to be, Beck," I began. "It just started off as us being friends. We enjoyed being around each other."

"He took advantage of the situation," Beck insisted. "You were so young."

"I never took advantage of her," Walker argued. "And I've never treated her with anything less than the respect she deserved."

"It's the truth," I told him. "And you might not want to hear this, but I've had a crush on Walker since I was fifteen. He was my every dream come true."

My brother shook his head again, obviously still struggling with all of this.

"Beck, please," I pleaded. "I'm really sorry for hiding this for so long."

He assessed me a moment, and I could see he was contemplating saying something but held himself back.

"What?" I asked. "I can see you want to say something."

Beck hesitated before he finally said, "I just... I don't know if I can trust either of you again. Eight years. Eight whole years of sneaking around and lying. And even if I can get past this with you, I'm not sure I can ever look at Walker the same again."

No.

No way was he going to do this.

"So, what are you going to do?" I asked.

"What do you mean?"

"Well, you're either going to try to understand and forgive and move on, or you're not going to do that," I told him. "You have a choice to make."

Beck cocked an eyebrow. "It took years for you to share all of this with me, and you think I have to make a decision in a matter of minutes? I only found out two days ago when I practically forced this out of Walker."

I could understand that.

I mean, only to a certain degree, though.

"I'm happy, Beck," I reasoned. "That is all that should matter. I get that the hiding and secrecy is upsetting. I totally understand that. But if your issue is with regard to Walker and me actually being together, you really shouldn't be upset about it."

"I'm sorry, Sadie, but I am," he replied. "I know that's not what you want to hear, but that's how I feel. I'm having a difficult enough time sitting here at this table with him."

At that, I knew I needed to address the biggest issue. "So, what's going to happen with My Violent Heart?" I questioned him. "You can't sit here with Walker without feeling disgusted, so I'm curious how you're going to make music with him."

Beck's eyes left mine, shifted to Walker, and stayed there. When he brought them back to me, he shared, "Walker said he was prepared to leave the band."

My lips parted in shock.

I expected Beck to be upset. I was willing to accept needing to work to earn his trust back. But I really did not think he'd ever push the issue of Walker leaving the band. It angered me.

"I'm not going back," I said, my voice low and foreboding.

At my tone, I saw Beck grow alarmed as I felt Walker tense beside me.

"What?" Beck asked.

"I'm *not* going back," I repeated. "I will not go back to seeing Walker in the pain he was in when he lost his mom. I'll never forget what her death did to him, but I was comforted by the fact that he had something left that kept him connected to her."

"Sadie—" Walker said.

I twisted my neck and looked at him. "No," I declared. "He's going to hear this. He needs to hear this."

Walker held my gaze for a moment before he nodded, silently agreeing to give me what I needed in that moment.

Returning my attention to Beck, I said, "You want to be upset that we hid this from you, we'll take that. You want to be upset that in hiding this, we lied about things only to cover the truth about our relationship, we'll take that, too. But that's *all* we take."

I paused a moment, steeled my spine, and continued, "Walker will take nothing else. And if you can't figure out a way to get past Walker and me being together and you even attempt to make him take anything else, I'll never forget that, Beck. Because if you force this, even if he offered to walk away without a fight, you'll be taking away his music and the rest of the band from him. He'll do it because he loves me that much.

And you should be happy about that. You should be grateful that there's a man in my life who loves me so much he's willing to give it all up for me."

Something washed over Beck's face, but I didn't give him a chance to respond. He needed to know how deep this went for me.

"You want time to figure this out, take your time," I began again. "But there's one thing you should know. If you dare to push this to a point that Walker leaves the band, essentially forcing him to give up the last connection he has to his mom, I will *never* forgive you for that. Never, Beck."

With that, I stood.

Though he was much slower to do it, Walker stood beside me.

As I was about to walk away, he reached for my wrist and stopped me.

I looked back at him, but he wasn't looking at me. He was looking at Beck.

"Don't make her have to choose between us," Walker advised. "She doesn't deserve that. A couple months in she wanted to tell you. My mom got worse and died a week later. I was in no place to tell you then. When I finally thought I'd gotten through the worst of it, shit happened with my dad. Sadie sacrificed having what she wanted, what she desperately needed, for me. I'm begging you, Beck, don't make her choose between us because I won't give her up. I'm going to marry Sadie. With or without you, I'm going to do that. I'm going to give her that, and I'm going to give her babies. I hate to think what it would do to her if you weren't there for any of that. So, I'll say it again, don't make her choose."

I was so stunned by his words. I hadn't expected any of that. Not a single word. It was no surprise, then, that Walker had to put a hand to the small of my back to urge me out.

I started to move, stopped, and looked back at my brother.

"I love you," I rasped. "I don't know what I'd do if you weren't in my life."

At that, knowing I'd completely break down if I didn't get out of there, I continued to move in the direction Walker had urged me in only seconds before.

And when we got to the car and I was safe inside, only then did I burst into tears.

Two days later

I'd been agonizing and in a constant state of worry ever since Walker and I walked out of the café, leaving Beck behind.

I hated that things had gotten to the point that they did, but there was no way I could sit by and just allow the worst to happen.

Or, what I had assumed would be the worst. I guess it was possible that things could get even worse than they already were. I could lose my brother *and* Walker could walk away from the band.

It seemed I was finally going to get an answer.

Because about thirty minutes ago, Beck called and wanted to meet. I was at Walker's place, told him so, and he said he'd be willing to meet here if that was okay with Walker and me.

It was.

So, he was coming.

And I'd just watched him pull into the driveway, so my nerves were now completely on edge.

"Relax, baby," Walker urged, coming up behind me and sliding his arms around me.

"What if this is it?" I worried.

"Making yourself sick about it won't change that," he

answered. "But I want to believe this isn't going to be bad. Let's not assume the worst. We've done that for long enough."

He wasn't wrong about that, but it was still so much easier said than done to relax.

A knock came at the door.

Walker kissed my cheek and said, "Wait here. I'll get it."

I waited in the family room, but I didn't do it with any reasonable amount of ease. It felt like an eternity as I waited for Walker to return with Beck. If it weren't for the fact that I didn't hear any shouting or grunts or anything breaking, I might have assumed they'd gotten into a physical altercation.

Luckily, they eventually entered the room, and I stood there motionless and silent.

Walker made his way back over to my side, and the moment he was there, Beck said, "I owe you both an apology."

My eyes widened.

Beck registered that look and lamented, "I'm sorry. The last few days have been eye-opening, to say the least. I've done a lot of thinking since we met two days ago, and I've done a lot of talking. To Chasey. To Cash. To Killian and Roscoe. To Holland."

"And?" I asked nervously.

"And they made me see a lot of things I couldn't see when this all hit me days ago," he replied. "Even when I came here the day I found out, Raid said something that stuck with me. You both might have wanted to tell me the truth, but you had a good reason to hide it from me."

Shaking my head, I insisted, "I wanted to tell you in the beginning. I really did. But—"

"I know," he assured me, holding his hand up to stop me from fretting. "I don't know how the two of you pulled it off, I can't imagine how difficult it must have been, and I'm sorry you felt you had to hide it at all. We're here now, and all we can do is decide how to move forward."

He paused a moment, allowing his gaze to shift between

the both of us. I could tell he had more he wanted to say, so I remained silent while scooting myself closer to Walker. Beck eventually settled his attention on Walker, and I braced myself.

"I talked to the rest of the band," he declared.

I could feel Walker's body tense beside mine. "And?"

"And aside from the fact that we all believe My Violent Heart would cease to exist without you as a part of it, they got me to see some other things. Looking back over all the years, you never took advantage of the situation. None of us knew you were with Sadie. You could have had a different woman every night we were on tour, and we never would have thought twice about it. You never did that. *Never.* You remained faithful to her, giving her something she deserves. In recognizing that fact, I drew another conclusion."

"What is that?" Walker asked.

"Of all the guys in the band, there is no one better for her than you," he said. "I mean, I'm not sure I would have been able to sleep at night if she ended up with Killian or, dare I say, Roscoe."

Walker chuckled, which I took as a good sign.

Beck looked at me and continued, "I want you to be happy, Sadie. If you're happy with Walker, I'm not going to stand in your way, and I'm definitely not going to not have you in my life. I love you, and it'd kill me to know I've done something you can't ever forgive me for. Walker said he wants to give you babies. I'm not missing out on meeting my niece or nephew. And when Chasey and I give Luna some siblings, I want you to be there."

Tears filled my eyes. Unable to hold myself back, I propelled my body forward and threw my arms over Beck's shoulders. He hugged me back, his arms tight around me.

"I love you," I cried. "I'm so sorry."

"I love you, too," he returned. "And I'm sorry for how I handled this."

After a few seconds passed, we loosened our hold on one another, and I stepped back. Beck took a step toward Walker and said, "I'm sorry for how I reacted at the studio."

"It's cool, Beck," Walker assured him. "I expected as much."

"That doesn't make it right."

Shaking his head, Walker said, "No, it doesn't. But I'm kind of glad it happened."

"What?"

Walker smiled. "Eight years, man. I'd hate to think we were worried about telling you the truth for absolutely no reason at all."

Oh God.

I hadn't even thought about that.

How horrible would it have been if we told Beck the truth and he was completely fine with it? We would have spent all that time hiding, sneaking, and lying all for nothing.

Beck was amused by this and laughed. Then, he and Walker had a look of appreciation pass between the two of them.

I wanted to keep the good vibe going, so I asked, "Do you want to stay and have lunch with us?"

Beck shook his head. "No, I need to get home to my girls. But we can all plan to get together one day next week if you want."

I grinned. "I want."

Beck smiled back at me.

All the tension and worry was gone. For all of us. It felt really good, like I could finally breathe again.

A few minutes later, Walker and I had said goodbye to Beck. Standing there inside the front door, I felt the joy and relief radiating off of my man. He might have been playing it cool for my sake, but this had affected him more than he admitted.

"No more hiding," I whispered, wrapping my arms around his waist and leaning into him.

"No more hiding," he replied.

"When's the next one?" I asked.

"The next what?"

Smiling, I answered, "The next tour. I want to go with you."

Something moved through Walker's face. I had a feeling it just hit him that we wouldn't need to be separated throughout another tour.

"Well, considering I no longer have a reason to take a full year off and everyone else was on board, I'm guessing it might be sooner rather than later," he said.

"I can't wait."

"Yeah. Me too. Let's just hope all the drama with the band is done for now."

"Three down, three to go. There's still plenty of opportunity for more drama," I noted.

He thought on this a moment before he decided, "You know what? I've got you, so whatever happens, happens. I'll do what I can to support them, the same as they did for me from the beginning."

"They're your family," I remarked. "That's how it works."

Walker tightened his arms around me. "Love you, sunshine."

I pressed my cheek to his chest, squeezed him back, and said, "I love you, too."

We stayed like that a little longer before Walker asked, "Are you hungry?"

"Yeah."

"Come on," he urged. "Let's get ready. I'm taking you out. I want to see what it's like to be close to you without having to hide it."

That sounded incredible.

So, I pressed up on my toes and kissed him before I got myself ready.

EPILOGUE

Walker
Two Years Later

IT SEEMED IMPOSSIBLE.

How did my life get better?

I was sitting on the couch a few feet back from the scene in front of me while holding my seven-month-old niece, Rosie, in my arms. Sadie was holding our oldest niece in her arms. My wife and I had become very close with Beck's daughters.

Yes.

My wife.

Finally. After all these years, Sadie was my wife. It wasn't until I was able to call her that for the first time that I realized just how much I needed it. How much we both needed it.

Not long after the truth of our relationship came out, Sadie and I talked about getting married. I proposed within a month because I wanted her to know that I was serious about our future, about giving her what she'd so desperately wanted and was prevented from having for years. No sooner had I given her that ring when Sadie asked some questions of her own.

"How soon are you ready to get married?" she asked the day after I'd proposed.

"Baby, this is all your decision," I told her. "I love you. I want to be married. If you want to go to the courthouse right now, I'd do it. But if you want to plan a huge wedding complete with all the trimmings, I'll give you that, too."

She thought on that for all of ten seconds before she asked, "Can we do something smaller?"

"We can do whatever you want," I assured her.

Smiling at me, she shared, "I just want the people who are important to us to be there. The two of us, your dad, Raid, my mom, Beck, Chasey, Luna, and the rest of the band. And if there's anyone else you want, that's totally fine with me. I don't need something big and extravagant, but I do want all the people we love to be there."

I touched my mouth to hers and replied, "As long as you're there along with our families and the band, I'll be happy."

Two months later, Sadie and I got married in a small ceremony. It was a perfect day.

Then again, I shouldn't have been surprised. Every day with Sadie was perfect. Even now, when we spent the day with Luna and Rosie, spoiling them rotten so their parents could have a full day to themselves, it was perfect. Sadie spent the day doing arts and crafts with Luna, most of them involving lots of paint and tons of mess.

But it didn't matter.

Because Luna was happy, and Sadie was happy.

And that's all that mattered to me.

We'd just gotten a call from Beck about ten minutes ago letting us know that he and Chasey were on their way to pick up the girls. We expected them at any minute.

So, unsurprisingly, Sadie and Luna were soaking up every last ounce of affection they could get from one another.

Just then, the doorbell rang.

"I've got it," I said, standing up from the couch to move to the front door.

A moment later, Beck and Chasey were standing there looking completely refreshed. I didn't know how they spent their day together, but I had a feeling that if I were in their shoes raising two little girls, I'd have spent a good chunk of my time reconnecting physically with Sadie.

"How were they?" Chasey asked.

"Perfect little angels," I answered, stepping back to allow them to come inside.

Narrowing his eyes on me, Beck questioned me, "Why do I feel like that's not the whole truth?"

As we all moved to the family room, I let out a laugh and said, "Because if what happened here today happened at your place, you'd feel differently. But since Sadie loves the mess of paint all over herself and Luna, things were perfect. They both even got Rosie in on the fun for a bit."

"Daddy!" Luna bubbled as soon as she saw him enter the room.

She got up and ran toward Beck. To this day, it still blew my mind how easily Beck stepped into the role of being a father. He was incredibly good at it, too, because Luna and Rosie both adored him.

Crouching down, Beck braced himself for impact. "Hi, princess," he said. "Did you have fun with Aunt Sadie and Uncle Walker."

"Yes, we made so many projects," Luna told him.

"Thank you, again, for watching them for us today," Chasey chimed in.

"You're welcome," Sadie replied. "Did you two have a good time?"

"We did," Chasey answered. "We really needed this time today."

Sadie smiled and said, "I'm glad. And you know how much we love the girls, so we're happy to do it any time you need us."

"We appreciate that," Beck said. "But we should really give you two a break and get them home now."

Over the next few minutes, we all worked to gather up the girls' things. We'd all said a round of goodbyes before they left.

And the moment they started to make their way down the driveway, I closed the door and leaned my back against it.

Sadie was standing there staring at me with a strange look on her face. After ten years together, I would have thought I knew what every look meant.

I did not know what this look meant.

"Baby?" I called. My body was tense and on edge. "Is something wrong?"

She stared at me for a long time without responding. I was growing more and more concerned. And just when I was going to say something again, she reached her hand out to me and said, "I want to show you something."

Though I didn't hesitate to take her hand, I still felt particularly cautious. Something wasn't right.

"Are you okay?" I asked her.

She didn't respond, which only served to make me even more worried.

When we finally made it to Sadie's studio—an addition I had added to the house almost immediately after everyone knew we were together—she finally spoke.

"Luna and I had a lot of fun painting in here earlier today," she said. "On top of all the things she showed you earlier, we worked on one more surprise."

"What is it?" I asked.

Sadie opened the door and led me inside. Then she shifted to the side, out of my line of vision, and allowed me to take in the sight before me.

Propped up on an easel in the middle of the room was a

brand-new painting. I moved closer to inspect it. And the minute I was close enough to see all the details, my body froze as my breath caught in my lungs.

"What do you think?" Sadie asked.

I had to force my eyes away from the canvas to look at my wife's beautiful face. Tears were brimming in her eyes.

"No joke?" I whispered.

She shook her head.

I returned my eyes to the painting. It was the most accurate painting of my drum set I'd ever seen. Except there was one thing different about it. Instead of the My Violent Heart logo being on the front of the bass drum, there was something else.

A pair of baby feet. Beside them were five words. *Rock star buddy coming soon.*

"You're pregnant," I rasped.

"I'm pregnant," Sadie returned quietly.

I turned, wrapped my arms around Sadie, lifted her off the ground, and buried my face in her neck. My emotions were getting the best of me.

We made a baby.

"I love you," I told her.

She squeezed me tight and replied, "I love you, too."

Pulling my face from her neck, I looked up and asked, "When did you find out?"

"I took the test this morning before Luna and Rosie got here," she answered.

Feeling nothing but overwhelming joy, I smiled and declared, "We're going to be parents."

Sadie nodded. "You're going to be a daddy."

Daddy.

The word sounded so surreal.

I had just been thinking when my nieces were here that my life couldn't possibly get any better. But now, now I no longer had any reason to believe that was the case. So long as I had

Sadie in my life, I knew anything was possible. And there was no doubt in my mind that we had yet to experience the best this life had to offer us.

"You're going to be a mom," I noted, my voice still husky.

"I can't wait," she returned.

"Do you feel okay?" I asked.

"Mostly," she answered. "Just a little tired. And my boobs hurt really bad."

I cocked an eyebrow. "I can fix that," I told her.

"You can?"

Nodding as I turned and moved out of the studio to head to our bedroom, I explained, "I'll kiss them and make them feel better."

"They're super tender," she informed me.

"I'll be gentle," I promised.

Sadie's fingers moved delicately through my hair at the back of my head as I lowered her to the bed. "I remember the first time you said those words to me," she said.

I did, too.

"Ten years ago," I declared.

"Best ten years of my life," she announced.

Smiling against her lips, I remarked, "And it's only going to get better from here."

I didn't give Sadie a chance to respond. I captured her mouth with mine. Then I did as I promised and was gentle with her as we celebrated our little miracle.

Eight months later, Sadie and I welcomed our baby girl, Lani Rhodes.

I couldn't wait to teach my little rock star daughter everything her grandma—and namesake—had taught me about music.

Preview of

UNDERNEATH IT ALL

Rock Stars & Romance Book 4: Holland & Raiden

PROLOGUE

Holland

WAS THIS REAL?

That was the thought at the forefront of my mind as I stood on the stage and stared out into the crowd.

Thousands of screaming fans packed into an arena, and they were there to see me. Well, sort of. They were there to see My Violent Heart, the band I was a member of. The band with five other members, who graciously and encouragingly accepted me as one of their own from the moment they met me.

Was this real?

We'd just ended the first show of our newest tour, and for some reason, I stood there a bit longer than normal, just taking it all in.

A big part of me was beyond proud of myself. I'd done it. I'd made my dream come true—my dream to play sold-out shows for crowds all over the world. Even if I still held a lot of deep-seated regret for choices I made long ago, I couldn't help feeling a bit of pride for how far I'd made it.

Coming from such a dark place so many years ago, I only ever dreamed of this. I never believed I'd have it.

None of it.

Not the fans. Not the fame. Not the money.

Most importantly, not the band.

My family—Cash, Beck, Walker, Killian, and Roscoe.

They meant everything to me, and I knew I'd have them in my life until the day I died. They were men who were like the big brothers I never had. They were a group of guys who were already successful without me, and yet, when I came along, they opened their arms wide and accepted me without a second thought.

To this very day, none of them knew what they'd done for me. They had no idea that they saved me from my heartache and from my past.

In the beginning, I pretended. Eventually, the happy persona became my reality. I owed the band everything.

Of course, I knew that I was talented. I didn't become a member of the band for no reason at all. I could sing, and I could write music. I gave the band a different sound, a unique vibe. And the fans gobbled it up.

So, I certainly played my role in my success. It was just that, without them, I knew I wouldn't have been where I was now.

I wouldn't have been right here, standing on the stage, feeling nothing but overwhelming joy that this was where my life had finally taken me.

After everything.

All of it.

I was here.

And it was all better than I could have imagined it would be. There was only one thing that would have made it better. But since that would never happen, I knew this was the best it would ever be.

I was completely content with that knowledge.

After taking in a deep breath, I allowed my eyes to roam through the crowd and smiled. Once I locked up the feeling it gave me safely in my heart, I turned and walked off stage with the rest of my band.

It was time for us to do our thing and make the nights for a few of our fans who'd purchased backstage passes. We didn't offer them at every show on a tour, but we did for this one. It was the first one back after a few months off, so we wanted to start things on the right foot.

Several minutes after the fans started being let into the room backstage, things took a turn. Only, I was the single person in the room aware of it.

I'd looked up and saw him.

It had been years. I hadn't seen him in years, and at the very first sight of a man I thought I'd never see again, all I wanted to do was run and hide.

I didn't do that, though.

Instead, I froze. I froze and stared across the room, feeling sick.

He was standing in front of Walker, talking casually to him. To anyone else, he looked just like any normal fan having an interaction with a member of their favorite band.

But it wasn't that. I knew it wasn't.

Not after all this time.

"Holls?"

I jumped at the sound of Killian's voice.

"Are you okay?" he asked when I brought my gaze to him.

Blinking away the thoughts and feelings that had been running through me only seconds ago, I rasped, "Yeah. Yeah. I just… I need to grab a drink of water. I think the first day back on tour did a number on my throat."

Killian assessed me, and I had a feeling he thought I was lying. I didn't care. That was nothing compared to everything else they didn't know.

I turned and walked away in the direction of the drinks that had been stocked in the room.

Calm down and think, Holland.

Think? I had no idea what I was going to do. I just knew I needed to be away from the group. Because if and when he approached me, I didn't want to risk having any of my bandmates hearing anything.

I opened a bottle of water, brought it to my lips, and took a sip. After tightening the cap back on the bottle, I turned around and was face to face with him.

Inches away from a man I never wanted to see again.

He smiled at me. But it wasn't a genuine smile filled with happiness at seeing me doing so well after all these years.

Nope.

This was a smile that indicated he was happy to have me right where he wanted me. Feeling trapped with nowhere to go.

"Nick," I whispered.

"Hello, Holland," he returned, his voice sounding devious.

"What are you doing here?" I asked quietly.

He reached for my wrist, lifted my hand, and placed a piece of paper in the palm of it. "Call me, sweet cheeks. We need to talk."

No way. No way was I going to call him.

Of course, I wasn't going to tell him that. If he was going to walk out of here and these few words be the extent of our exchange, I refused to do anything to prolong it. He could walk out, and I'd be on to the next city tomorrow.

Apparently, even after years of practicing, I couldn't seem to hide my thoughts. Nick knew immediately what was going through my mind.

"I'm going to give you the benefit of the doubt, Holland," he started again. "I won't do this here. But I promise you don't want to ignore me. Give me a call tomorrow. If I don't hear from you, you won't like what happens."

"Please go," I begged, my voice still hushed.

Nick smiled at me again. He liked that he was making me

uncomfortable. "You better call," he warned before he turned his body to move away. Just when I thought he was going to walk away, he stopped, looked back, and allowed his eyes to drift down over my body. "It was nice seeing you again. You look good."

I swallowed hard, trying to stop myself from throwing up.

A moment later, Nick was gone.

I lifted the water to my mouth again and took another sip. Then I slid the piece of paper into my pocket and returned to the action.

Nick might not have stuck around, but the menacing tone of his voice rang in my head for the rest of the night.

OTHER BOOKS BY
A.K. EVANS

Archer Tactical

Line of Fire

Collateral Damage

Silent Target

Rock Stars & Romance

Fragile

Wish

Closer

Underneath It All

Terrible Lie

Complication

Road Trip Romance

Tip the Scales

Play the Part

One Wrong Turn

Just a Fling

Meant to Be

Take the Plunge

Miss the Shot

In the Cards

Only in Dreams

Break the Ice

ABOUT
A.K. EVANS

A.K. Evans is a contemporary romance author of over twenty published novels. While she enjoys writing a good romantic suspense novel, Andrea's favorite books to write have been her extreme sports romances. That might have something to do with the fact that she, along with her husband and two sons, can't get enough of extreme sports.

Before becoming a writer, Andrea did a brief stint in the insurance and financial services industry and managed her husband's performance automotive business. That love of extreme sports? She used to drive race cars!

When Andrea isn't writing, she can be found homeschooling her two sons, doing yoga, snowboarding, reading, or traveling with her family. She and her husband are currently taking road trips throughout the country to visit all 50 states with their boys.

For new release updates, sign up for the A.K. Evans newsletter: http://eepurl.com/dmeo6z

Be sure to follow Andrea on all social media platforms, too.

Facebook
www.facebook.com/authorAKEvans

Facebook Reader Group
http://bit.ly/2ys50mU

Instagram
www.instagram.com/authorakevans

Goodreads Author Page
www.goodreads.com/user/show/64525877-a-k-evans

Bookbub
www.bookbub.com/authors/a-k-evans

Twitter
twitter.com/AuthorAKEvans

Made in the USA
Columbia, SC
28 May 2022